DIRECT ACTION

LANCE BLACK

Legal Notices

WARNING – PARTS OF THIS BOOK ARE OF A SEXUAL AND/OR VIOLENT NATURE – IF YOU THINK YOU MIGHT BE OFFENDED BY SUCH CONTENT, PLEASE DO NOT READ THIS BOOK. BY READING BEYOND THIS POINT YOU CONFIRM YOU ARE AN ADULT WHO IS NOT EASILY OFFENDED.

All events in this book are entirely fictional.

First published on the 1st May 2006

ISBN 978-0-9555450-0-9

First published in 2006

PUBLISHING NOIR 2007

Dedication

This book is dedicated to people everywhere who believe in living peacefully with respect for the property, liberty and privacy of others.

'Tread lightly and make little impression'

Thanks to:

MK, DS, IS, GT, BB, LT, MCJ, MH, T and B.

AVDI, VIDE, TACE

HEAR, SEE,
BE SILENT

SCIENTIA
POTESTAS EST

KNOWLEDGE
IS POWER

Pitfodels

Crash!

The sound of glass shattering always causes heart-stopping panic.

"Ha, ha, ha, bugger it! Get me some fresh champagne goblets. Your finest Edinburgh crystal, not this cheap shite; and be quick about it or I'll sue this place for serving champagne in dangerous, sub-standard conduits. And get me a dozen bottles of *Cristal*, properly chilled. Take away this muck, it's warm and corked!" barked the voice of authority. A roar of laugher ensued as fifty overfed, overdressed men and women smiled warmly at the rowdy orator.

Jimmy Turnbull was drunk, but totally in command of everyone around him. Toasting his son with various business associates and courtiers, he'd just shattered four glasses with a single, overly-boisterous 'clink'. Jimmy was unrepentant; he could buy the restaurant; he could buy the hotel. Hell, he could buy the whole town. But why bother; he practically owned it anyway.

Jimmy's son, Bobby, was embarrassed by his famous father's uncouth, loutish antics. This was supposed to be *his* night, not just another oil industry piss-up. It was also not behaviour appropriate to the *Marcliffe at Pitfodels* Hotel, near Cults, Aberdeen's only true five-star luxury hotel.

A silver trolley, laden with a dozen aluminum ice-buckets containing the exclusive *Cristal* champagne, favourite tipple of hip-hop stars, rappers and the rich and famous, was wheeled-in across the *Carrick Hunting Tartan* carpet. Jimmy waited impatiently as fifty glasses were carefully filled.

"Ok. First things first!" Jimmy motioned to the maître d', "Another dozen bottles as fast as you like – these are empty now!"

The host vanished, keen to ensure the millionaire's every whim was instantly satisfied - more roars of laughter.

"Second. This is a toast to my son, Bobby. Bobby lad, stand up. Take a bow!"

Bobby stood up and nodded modestly.

"Ladies and Gentlemen, the next Formula One World Champion…...Bobby Turnbull!" Jimmy enthused bombastically.

Glasses were raised.

"Bobby Turnbull!" The assembled company shouted.

"And now a joke!" Laughter from everyone.

"Knock, knock!" Jimmy's favourite joke.

"Who's there?" yelled fifty guests

"Interrupting sheep!" Jimmy grinned.

Fifty highly intoxicated diners attempted a reply,

"Interrupting shee…….."

"BAAAAAAAA!" Jimmy 'interrupted' the chorus of 'interrupting sheep who?'

The whole place erupted; uncontrolled hysterical laughter; several guests fell off their seats, rolling with mirth on the deep-pile carpet styled after Robert the Bruce's family plaid. Jimmy could do this. He had the knack of enrapturing and captivating. One to one or one to fifty; Jimmy could charm, seduce, motivate, terrify or amuse effortlessly. It was just one secret of his phenomenal success.

Jimmy's son, the future would-be world champion, turned to his gorgeous young companion playing down his millionaire benefactor's high jinks and kissed her softly on the cheek.

Bobby Turnbull loved two things. He loved his fiancée and he loved driving fast. His successful father had secured a place for him as a driver in a Formula One team. There were several reasons for Bobby's good fortune: firstly, his father had a 25% share in the team; secondly, Bobby was phenomenally quick, and thirdly, at the tender age of 19 he weighed just 68 kilos: rich, fast and light - the perfect combination for Formula One. He was touted as a future champion.

Tonight, Bobby was attending the dinner arranged by his father for wealthy oilmen to raise money for the F1 team. High profile advertising was being offered in return for substantial investments.

Jimmy Turnbull was hell-bent on becoming Scotland's first billionaire and he was going to make bloody sure Bobby was world champion within three years. The dinner went well. Ten million was pledged in return for advertising space on the two racing cars competing in all 18 televised starts across the globe.

"That's just £60k a pop for global exposure!" Jimmy told the assembled millionaires like the super-salesmen he indubitably was.

As the champagne flowed and the stories of North Sea Oil fortunes became increasingly exaggerated, Bobby made a discreet exit. He was an athlete, not a boozer and schmoozer. He left with his fiancée, Debby Glennie; her father Des owned the largest offshore supply-boat company operating in the North Sea. Des was sitting next to Jimmy. He was smashed and laughing maniacally.

Des was listed as the 20th richest man in Scotland in the Sunday Times rich list. Jimmy was 2nd and closing fast on that top spot.

The young couple drove to the *International Casino* on Market Street, at the far end of the city's Union Street.

Bobby was flying to Spain the next day to practise and test modifications made to the F1 cars; his mind was on overdrive: setting up fast corners, hitting the brakes at the last second, flicking through the gears; squeezing every last rev out of the 2.5 litre V8 engine - he ignored his partying contemporaries, recollecting how he had spun the car on his last run by pushing too hard. The full bite of the 800 horses had punished him for lack of respect. The car had ended up going backwards at 120 mph - *'Never again'*.

At three in the morning, Debs was finally willing to leave the casino. She was happily drunk from pink champagne and colourful cocktails. Bobby was stone-cold sober, his father's words indelibly etched on his mind:

'Drinking is for losers – time enough for champagne on the winner's podium'

Bobby was driving a new Honda Civic Type R with numerous modifications. A road-going rally car, it roared and snarled as he carefully negotiated the ultra low-profile tyres on magnesium alloys away from the pavement. A plethora of Aberdeen's infamous, hated boy-racers charged up behind him as they spotted the car and its distinctive **BT1 OFF** number plate.

A few waved encouragement; some, 'gave him the *finger*', and others flew past, over-taking in the hope of a high-speed street-race.

Union Street was unbearably loud with the cacophony of dozens of highly tuned, customised cars; buzzing and screaming irreverently.

Bobby ignored them. He knew better. Heading west, he exited Union Street towards Queens Road.

Debs was sleeping-off the champagne cocktails. She looked like an angel, her strawberry-blonde hair falling seductively over her rosy cheeks.

He knew she had taken off her little black thong in the club because she had put it in his pocket, kissing him provocatively. He was tempted to slide the black taffeta mini-dress up her silky smooth legs and stroke her soft inner thighs, but he decided there would be none of that tonight:

'Women weaken legs, my boy!'

Anderson Drive

Bobby arrived at the Earls Court roundabout and turned left down Anderson Drive, the dual carriageway that would take him over the River Dee onto the lower Deeside Road, where he could have a blast along the quiet country roads on his way home.

It's hard to resist accelerating down that stretch of the '*Drive*'. The downhill, gradual right to left curve in the wide two-lane, smooth-surfaced road is like a race track. Bobby reckoned that at ten past three in the morning he could risk a little right foot, even though the speed limit was forty miles an hour on this main highway in the centre of the fashionable west-end.

He pressed the throttle and the engine barked into life. The little sports car catapulted forward, screaming like a motor bike. Nearing sixty miles an hour, he reached the Cromwell Road roundabout; he hit the ceramic disc brakes, shedding speed, crossing the roundabout at fifty.

Pressing the accelerator again, the engine howled as he exited the roundabout heading down the perfect straight to the lights at Great Western Road.

It was then he became aware of car headlights behind him. His stomach sank; he slowed down.

'Fuck it, the police,'

The last thing he needed was to lose his licence.

The car behind was gaining fast, but there was no flashing blue light.

'Fucking boy-racers!'

Except it was a big car, an SUV, a fast SUV.

It was now right behind him, nose to tail.

Bobby was not about to be overtaken by some fat businessman in a turbo-charged penis extension. He hit the gas, the Type R screamed to 8,000 rpm.

'The pursuing car was still there!'

Bobby slowed a little; trying to get a look at whatever was hanging onto his tail.

"What the hell is that thing?"

Then it happened.

BANG!!!!

Bobby felt the sudden impact to his driver's side: he lost control; the collision awoke Debs who jumped up with a fright, just in time to see the very old and very hard oak tree they were about to hit head-on.

Bobby's hands moved fast - trying to catch the steering. Instinctively, he hit the brakes, but even his lightning-fast reflexes couldn't save them: ***SMACK!!!*** They hit the tree – ***hard!***

Debby wasn't wearing her seatbelt. Her head smashed into the top of the windscreen; she whip-lashed back into her seat and fell unconscious. Bobby's four-point racing harness saved his head, but he was still thrown forward with sufficient force to break four ribs down his right side.

He struggled to breathe through the pain. His right lung subsequently collapsed as he leaned over to see if he could revive his beloved Debs.

Dazed and confused, Bobby did not see the other car stop up ahead, near the traffic lights, even though the lights were at green for go. He did not see someone get out and walk back to the mangled wreckage of his Honda. When his door was opened from the outside, he assumed help had arrived.

He was surprised when he felt a pricking sensation in his jugular; a sharp fingernail pushing deep into his neck; a deep jab, a penetrating bite. Paralysis raced down from his neck; a crushing pain in his chest, no breath, he blacked out.

Debs was still unconscious when she received the same lethal 'bite'.

Bobby Turnbull's promising racing career was over. Debby Glennie's expectation of being the mother of Bobby's children, terminated.

At 3.13 a.m., the couple died, at the same time; just minutes after their car hit the tree.

The stranger threw the syringe into the back of the car and disappeared into the night.

By the time the police arrived, he was long gone.

At 3.15 a.m., a few moments after the death of Bobby and Debby, a second silver Honda Civic Type R raced down Anderson Drive at 70 mph. The driver was a notorious petty criminal and boy-racer. He saw the wreckage of Bobby's car, recognised the number plate but he didn't stop; he had no insurance and was banned from driving for two years.

Aware the police must surely be on their way to the scene, he increased his speed; flying through the red light: a bat out of hell.

Rose Cottage

Ross woke up. It was early, very early. The summer sunlight soaked the bedroom in a dazzling eruption of brilliant white.

At once he was awake, but the seductive scent of his sleeping sweetheart kept him in bed.

Her silky, soft, raven-black hair cast a blanket of perfumed femininity over the pillows. He pushed his face between her delicate shoulder blades, cupped his hands around her soft breasts, took a deep breath of her essence and gently kissed her upper back.

She awoke with a smile. They made love. It was slow and tender. She arched her back, welcoming his firm warmth inside her.

Everyday, nature permitting, they made love as they awoke.

Afterwards, they were ready for anything.

David and Diane Ross were in love: student sweethearts since Oxford where both had excelled academically; he gained a Doctorate in law, jurisprudence and criminology and she, a Masters in natural philosophy and fine art. Both had won sporting blues: brilliant, athletic lovebirds.

Making love was the perfect way to put an edge on the appetite and after showering they needed to eat.

Breakfast was family time in the idyllically named *Rose Cottage*. Dating back some 300 years, the name captured the ambiance, but not the size of the house. Three magnificent reception rooms, six bedrooms, a tennis court, a paddock and ten acres of land used for horses and growing apples; the house had been in Ross's family for a hundred years.

The vista from the large country kitchen, overlooking the River Dee, was breathtaking first thing in the morning. The sunlight glistened on the ice-cool, clear waters which emanate from a source deep in the highlands of the Cairngorm Mountains near Braemar.

The two married lovers sat at the breakfast bar: kissing, basking warmly in post-orgasmic bliss; euphoric, perfectly content together.

A small but welcome distraction arrived.

"Daaaaaaaaaaaadeeeeeeeeeeee"

Johanna Ross threw herself straight into the arms of her adoring father.

"Hello Jo, how are you today?"

"I is fine." Her soft Aberdonian accent featured a hint of a girlish speech impediment, an attempt to be cute. If ever there was the epitome of a little angel it was Johanna Ross, but she never missed a trick to endear herself with her father.

She settled on his knee; he started feeding her cereal and little pieces of toast spread with marmalade.

"Mamma laid?" Jo said happily, as she munched her way through the toast.

"You might say that, Jo," said her father, chuckling.

Jo's little homophonic malapropism caused Diane to get the giggles. She'd been watching her daughter sitting, eating contentedly on Dad's knee and as she herself had been day-dreaming about the morning glories in the bedroom her daughter's inadvertent reference to love-making caused her to crease with laughter. Soon tears ran down her face with the innocent mirth of it all.

"Mummy silly, isn't she daddy, ha ha ha?" Jo joined in the laughter.

Next, a tired apparition appeared, rubbing his eyes. Whereas his sister was already playing the dumb blonde at four years old, Tim, at seven, was a serious, thoughtful boy. Unlike his sister who was blonde, Tim had dark hair and unusual pale blue eyes. He was tall for his age: strong; already displaying the athletic ability inherited from both his parents. He was smart, precocious: he did not suffer fools. In moments like these he considered his mother and his little sister frivolous. Tim was not a morning person.

"What's she laughing at?"

"Oh just a bit of fun in the morning," Ross replied.

"Stupid little cherub," said Tim.

"Is not stupid," Jo hit back,

"Daddy…..what's a cher roob?"

"It's an angel…….." said Tim helpfully.

Jo smiled. She knew she was an angel.

Tim smiled condescendingly.

"An angel with fat, chubby cheeks," he added sarcastically.

Jo's smile became a frown.

"Is not fat! You is fat!" replied Jo.

"Now, now, now, who wants some pancakes and maple syrup?" asked Diane Ross, breaking up the sibling spat.

"ME!!!!!!!!" the whole family shouted simultaneously. Harmony was restored in paradise.

After breakfast, Diane took Jo to nursery and Tim to school.

Ross studied the local newspaper: **The Aberdeen Guardian,** *'Protector of Free Speech in the Granite City',* a parochial broadsheet. On the day the Titanic sank, it famously reported, *'North-East man lost at sea'.*

Today was no exception and featured the usual stories of haddock quotas, the escape of a prize winning bull in the nearby town of Turriff and the visit of Donald Trump proposing to build a golf course on a site of outstanding beauty and scientific interest at nearby Foveran Sands – 'that will upset Diane' he mused.

Ross then read something that caused his inquisitive, criminologist's mind to move up a gear.

'Boy-racer and passenger in death-crash on city's Anderson Drive'

'A young man and his passenger were killed when their car left the road in the early hours of Sunday morning. The names of the victims have not been released'.

Ross wasn't sure why the bloodhound in him picked up a scent, but something registered deep in his subconscious.

He carefully cut out the article with small scissors Diane used for needlework. He put the clipping in his leather *Prada* credit card holder, a present from his wife. Ross had a penchant for design and quality.

The locus and the accident didn't fit; Anderson Drive, a dual carriageway, in a smart residential area, in the middle of the city's wealthy west-end. It was an unusual, possibly unique, scene for a road accident: the speed limit was forty miles an hour; it was well-lit by street-lights; errant youngsters might speed down it late at night, but it was a straight road; unless the driver was drunk, using drugs, or the car was in a terrible state of repair, there was no apparent, obvious reason for a car to leave the road – puzzling...

He made a note to call Traffic as soon as he finished meeting with the Chief Constable.

Ross

Ross was a wealthy man. His father had been a leading lawyer in the Granite City for over 40 years, prior to his death a few years back. Like his father before him, he had bequeathed *Rose Cottage* in trust along with a portfolio of over sixty properties including shops, flats, houses and farms to his son. Ross senior had been financially sagacious with a far-sighted view of the value of property. Applying principles of value adopted from Roman times he had followed the maxim: **'Buy land – they don't make it anymore'.** By the time this collection of property had passed to Ross, the portfolio was worth in excess of ten million pounds, excluding *Rose Cottage*. He had inherited a great deal of other assets: sports cars, antique watches and various stocks and shares, bought many years ago by his father and left to grow into very considerable value. One block of shares purchased in Royal Dutch Shell had risen from a modest investment of five thousand pounds to almost two hundred thousand pounds in thirty years. This substantial personal wealth allowed David Ross to indulge his second great passion (the first being his wife and children). He loved cars; in particular, he loved sports cars. He had a collection, many would envy. An adjacent old barn was now a large moisture-controlled garage where a new Black Lamborghini Gallardo sat alongside two Range Rovers, a Ferrari 250 GTO and a new Porsche 911. He played down his material possessions, urged on a daily basis by his wife to '*get rid of the toys*', as she called them. She was uncomfortable with the playboy image and the downside, the nickname, 'Posh Ross' and the less

complimentary, 'Ross the Toss', from his financially poorer, cash-strapped colleagues.

Ross had been brought up in the Granite City. He had worked hard to get transferred back to his beloved hometown with its golden beaches and close proximity to the highlands of Scotland. After Oxford, it was the police or the bar. His athleticism and hatred of confined spaces meant he needed a career that got him outside and kept him physically active.

He joined the police and shot up the ranks.

The Dalmunzie neighbours were mostly oil millionaires - fortunes amassed from the city's liquid *'black-gold'* in the 70's and 80's. They joked that Ross was the local 'Bobby', an inappropriate term for the youngest superintendent on the Met, seconded to Grampian Police to counter terrorist threats to the North Sea energy industry. The offshore threat was real. The Piper Alpha disaster in 1988 was before Ross's time, but he had studied the legal aspects in the *Orbit Valve* court case. The official outcome was negligence, but he knew how easy it would be for a terrorist organization, especially suicidal extremists, to blow-up an oil or gas platform. The massive offshore structures were highly vulnerable: impossible to protect. The most feared threat was European converts: individuals with many years offshore service becoming Islamic fundamentalists; Caucasian Jihadists - perfect terrorists, unnoticed and undetectable. On a gas platform, a suitably orchestrated leak, sabotage of the shutdown systems; a spark, an explosion....bingo! Unimaginable disaster followed by temporary cessation of oil and gas production in the UK and Norwegian sectors: human and economic catastrophe; hundreds killed; doubling of the oil price; meltdown on the stock markets.

Ross was tracking intelligence on petrochemical attacks including the Buncefield Total/Texaco complex in Hemel Hempstead, where an unconfined vapour cloud explosion was heard as far off as France and the Netherlands. The blast measured 2.4 on the Richter scale; the smoke-cloud had been visible from outer space.

The authorities quickly blamed faulty valves, instrumentation; but the real cause was unknown, a moot point. 5% of the UK's oil supply was obliterated in the blast. 150 firefighters pumped 7,000 gallons of water per minute for several days before giving up, letting the fire burn itself out.

Ross's biggest fear for the offshore industry was a *'cascade'* explosion. Several gas platforms like Shell's Brent field, all lined up in a convenient row, just a few miles apart. Alpha, Bravo, Charlie, Delta: 4 platforms, 500 men; the largest chain-reaction of massive gas explosions conceivable; the resulting fear, panic and uncertainty ending hydrocarbon production in the North Sea forever.

It would destroy the UK economy overnight.

Jihad had been declared against oil and gas production in the Middle East. Al-Qaeda had made several attempts on Saudi installations including the Kingdom's largest, the Aramco Abqaiq facility.

Top activists had been involved, functioning in compartmentalized cells.

Ross had good information the Jihad had reached Europe; the Hemel Hempstead fire may have been the first strike.

The UK authorities had extinguished speculation of a terrorist attack too quickly for comfort; and much faster than the firefighters could put out the fire.

With intelligence contacts all over the world, including GCHQ at Cheltenham, Interpol and MI5, it was intriguing and important work, but mainly preventative.

Ross was getting bored. He needed a real, tangible crime to crack.

He was about to be granted his wish.

The Chief Constable

Ross's Lamborghini rumbled down the long, tree-lined driveway towards the main road. He was heading for a quiet country lane where he could exercise the Lambo's V10 engine and 600 horsepower. If he was stopped speeding he would use the usual police excuse of *'testing and honing his high-speed driving skills'*.

The black supercar devoured the fifteen mile sprint in twelve, howling, screaming minutes; throwing Ross back in his seat, scaring him witless on more than one occasion.

All eyes were on the car as it pulled into the Inchmarlo Golf Club near the wealthy village of Banchory on Royal Deeside.

The Chief Constable was practising his putting. He looked up from a missed putt with what looked to Ross like disapproval, eyeing the grumbling black Italian sports car suspiciously.

"Don't tell me you are one of these blasted boy-racers, Ross?"

"I am test-driving it for a friend." Ross lied.

The Chief overlooked this obvious mistruth. He knew all about Ross's good fortune and his personal wealth. He tried, not always successfully, to put up with the 'Posh Ross' lifestyle.

"What does one of those cost, Ross? Enough to hire half a dozen new police constables, I'll wager."

"Well, sir, it's not just the quantity of the officers, it's also the quality."

Ross was on shaky ground; like all police forces, Grampian was woefully short of manpower.

"Come on then, let's discuss more pressing matters on the course," said the Chief Constable picking up his ball. This was no longer a purely social engagement.

The Inchmarlo architects have created a challenging test of golf. The seventh fairway offers stunning views up the Dee valley towards Her Majesty the Queen's Scottish Highland estate at Balmoral and the imposing presence of Lochnagar (a granite massif featuring spectacular, one thousand foot cliffs).

Against this impressive vista, standing over a long and difficult second shot, Chief Constable Stuart Rennie brought up the subject he wanted to broach with his Superintendent.

Before this, he set up for the two hundred and twenty yard shot to the green. An elevated shot over a pond, the difference in height between the player and the lower green foreshortens the actual distance the ball needs to travel to be home and dry.

The Chief, clearly preoccupied, made the classic and unforgivable error of under-clubbing. His ball flew straight at the green, but just as it should have been landing softly on the short grass, it took an impertinent early bath, diving straight into the pond.

The Head of Grampian Police scowled as if the image of the ball disappearing into the murky depths represented everything that was wrong with society and could never be put right with an under-funded police force.

Ross went next, hitting an easy five-iron over the water-hazard to within six feet of the pin.

"Shot!" The Chief acknowledged the other man's perfect shot with a frown; honest toil was clearly no match for natural talent,

"Ross, have you heard about the death of young Bobby Turnbull last night on Anderson Drive?"

"Jimmy Turnbull's son?"

"Yes, it was reported as a single-vehicle accident. Deborah Glennie was in the car."

"I read about the crash. I didn't know it was the Turnbull boy. I know Jimmy. He's a neighbour at Dalmunzie. Debby is Des Glennie's daughter?"

"Yes. It's a terrible tragedy, they were both killed. I want you to head the investigation,"

"Investigation?" Ross replied with surprise.

The Chief paused pensively before revealing his information.

"It wasn't a single-car accident."

"What makes you say that?"

"He was a racing driver, he had not been drinking; no drugs and the car was new."

"Distracted by his girlfriend? Going too fast?"

"There is something else."

"What?"

"Indications of another car: evidence a second car was involved."

"A race of some kind?"

"Perhaps - that's what we want you to find out, David."

The Chief Constable seldom used first names, even on social occasions; he seemed personally troubled by the affair.

"What is this evidence?"

"I'd rather you heard it from pathology and forensics. They will have the precise details."

The Chief started fishing his ball out of the pond with a long pole that featured a specially designed scoop at the end. The pond was full of small white objects; he was never going to find his ball among the hundreds already abandoned to a watery grave.

"I guess I will have to give you this hole, Ross."

"Thanks, sir." Ross popped his ball into the hole anyway.

The Chief was dwelling on the Anderson Drive incident,

"I hope this does not turn out to be road-rage, Ross. It's becoming a real problem. Certain aggressive elements have decided that possession of a road vehicle is a mandate to insult and attack peaceable drivers - the clenched fist, the obscene gesture, chasing after another driver in a furious rage. How long before it becomes actual bodily harm? You have studied the philosophy of law, David. You know the mind of the criminal, the reasons and motivations behind the criminal act. What's your view on this shocking rise in anti-social behaviour; why do certain drivers insult and attack others as a result of little or no provocation; what is wrong with these people?" The statement contained the man's fears for society. Ross sensed the Chief expected a full answer.

He replied accordingly,

"The precise answer is that jurisprudence, the philosophy of law, and criminology, the study of criminal behaviour, are two, separate academic areas. The first investigates the question of what is and ought to be the law and is related to social philosophy and politics. Criminology by contradistinction examines the social and genetic predisposition to criminal behaviour in an individual or class of individuals; criminology is more psychology and sociology than philosophy. My personal opinion is that any instance of road rage is a criminal act. If it upsets any person; the other driver, a passenger or bystander, then it is a breach of the peace. If it is threatening, as it almost certainly will be, then it is also common assault. Anyone, making an obscene, threatening gesture or displaying similar behaviour is a common criminal. Such a person is possibly unfit to drive a vehicle; they should be banned from driving and prosecuted for anti-social behaviour."

Ross was an academic.

He could have been a judge.

The Chief was slightly taken aback by the complexity of Ross's sagacious response. You don't expect a man driving a black, Italian super-car to make statements of such erudition. He was glad he had a man of this caliber on his team.

"Precisely!" replied his superior.

"You are the man for this case, Ross."

The Pathologist

Ross jumped at the chance to do some hands-on police-work. Gathering intelligence, developing 'what if' scenarios was important, but solving actual crimes, dealing with people face to face was more dynamic, more exciting. There was no problem adding the Turnbull incident to his workload; it was unlikely to take up more than a few hours a day. At least, that was the plan:

The best-laid schemes o' mice an' men
Gang aft agley...

Ross enjoyed 'characters' and there was no greater eccentric than the man who carried out the autopsies in Aberdeen.

Grampian Police engaged the services of Professor John 'Johnny' Henderson to examine the bodies of victims of suspicious deaths.

Standing at just five feet five inches, Henderson possessed the regimented, disciplined demeanor of an army drill-sergeant; an awesome, many would say fearsome, presence; shouting every word he used in conversation.

Henderson had been a leading surgeon and Professor of Forensic Medicine at Aberdeen University for over thirty years. Around sixty years old, slim, in great shape for his age, bald with a bushy grey moustache, he was always immaculately dressed. A dark blue, three-piece pinstripe suit; those half-rimmed spectacles that make the wearer seem to peer down at you with a mixture of superiority and condescension, and a yellow carnation in his button-hole, completed his formal yet foppish garb.

The pathologist was jocularly known as *'Rubber Johnny'*, by police and students alike, a reference to the rubber gloves worn by a coroner and the fact the term was a colloquialism for a condom.

There was just one question you <u>never</u> asked Professor Henderson:

"What was the <u>precise</u> time of death?"

That question guaranteed instant dismissal from his presence, earmarking you as a cretin, forever.

Fortunately, Ross was held in high regard by Henderson who recognised Ross's outstanding academic background, almost considering him an equal - an honour unprecedented with reference to the rest of the police force.

"Ah Ross, has that imbecile you work for sent you along to deal with me?"

"Yes, Professor, the Chief was keen to have me head-up this one."

"Not usually your bag, homicide, is it? Thought you were into terrorism?" The pathologist liked to play with words: experiment with witticisms. Ross ignored the ambiguity, focusing on just one word.

"Homicide?" Ross had not yet realised this was a murder inquiry.

"You look shocked, laddie. Didn't your chief nitwit tell you about this one?"

"I understood it was a car crash, a boy-racer who lost control, possibly in a race with a second car?"

"Nonsense - nothing of the sort - certainly the bodies show injuries conducive with a high speed collision between a moving vehicle and a stationary object, in this case, a tree; but that is not the cause of death, and unless I am wrong, and that is a rare thing indeed, these two were still alive after they hit that tree."

Ross was baffled. How could they be dead now if they were not killed by the crash?

He decided to risk being branded an idiot, venturing forth the inevitable question. Henderson had that look. The look that said: *'Well, ask me the question then?'*

"So...how did they die?"

Henderson took a deep breath; Ross held his, expecting the worst.

The pathologist smiled before stating,

"Lethal injection of potassium chloride!"

"What?" Ross blurted incredulously. Was this some kind of esoteric medical joke?

"Quite," said Henderson enigmatically. "Injected straight into the jugular vein, as in this instance, it stops the heart almost immediately. These two unlucky youngsters were executed, Superintendent; whoever did it, knew we would figure it out. They either wanted us to discover it or just didn't care."

Ross felt he had lost all grasp of reality.

"Are you telling me Professor, the son of Aberdeen's best known businessman, and his fiancée, were deliberately executed in the middle of the city's most desirable residential area?"

"Yes, laddie, I am indeed telling you that," said Rubber Johnny.

The Forensic Scientist

Ross had no sooner left one expert, when he met another.

Dr. Morven Hancock, euphemistically and optimistically known as 'Dr Hand-Job' or 'Dr Hard-Cock' by a few, cheeky male police constables, was senior police forensic scientist. An attractive woman, circa 35 years old, she was tall, olive-skinned with long black hair, usually worn up to promote an image of seriousness. She was both charming and helpful; one of the nicest people Ross had ever met in the police force.

After Henderson's revelations, it was crucial Hancock gave Ross as much detail as possible, including any information on traces of foreign DNA in the victim's car. As ever, she was welcoming,

"Hello, Superintendent Ross, how is Diane?"

Hancock's eyes smiled at him, warmly.

"Great - busy opposing the bypass, preventing the bulldozing of a bird sanctuary and of course running a fast expanding counseling practice, not to mention the two youngsters," Ross replied. She smiled,

"And here was me thinking I was superwoman."

"I am here for the report on the silver Honda Civic." Ross avoided looking into her eyes.

"Yes, I am afraid there is no DNA except that of the two victims and some animal, dog hair."

"Anything that would assist me to piece together what actually happened?"

"One thing is significant," Hancock revealed,

"There is a dent on the driver's door that could not have been made by the impact with any tree. I have analysed the area around the door and there are traces of paint that do not match the Honda."

"I did not see this on the traffic accident report."

"No, the foreign paint is also silver. It's therefore not immediately obvious. I have asked the central lab to run a scraping through mass spectrometry, then to contact the vehicle manufacturers to get an exact match."

"How did you see this paint if it's the same colour?" Ross asked.

"I will show you. Come with me," she purred, enticingly.

A few assistants chuckled as the handsome policeman and the alluring scientist went into a small dark room with no windows. Ross could not see his associate in the dark room, but he could smell her - *Alexander McQueen*, if he wasn't mistaken. She didn't just look great: she smelt great. Ross banished his amorous stirrings. He was happily married.

She flicked a switch. Suddenly the room lit up with a cold purple-blue light. In the centre, a car door hung suspended by two chords.

"Come and look closely at this." Hancock bent forward peering avidly at a small indentation in the door. Ross tried to ignore her provocative posture.

"Do you see it?"

"Not really." Ross felt guilty he was so attracted to this woman.

"Look. You see the darker patch in the middle of the indentation? That is the second type of silver paint. Only visible under this UV light with a special filter," she said proudly, "Optics is one of my special subjects. I have written papers on the applications of lasers and advanced optics in forensic science."

Ross smiled, hoping he looked suitably impressed with her ingenuity.

"It might be from an earlier incident or from someone opening a car door carelessly in a car park?" he suggested.

"It's too big and besides, I cheated. I already asked the victim's family if the driver's door had been damaged. The car was just four weeks old; there was no dent there the day before."

"This other silver car pushed the Honda off the road?"

"It looks very much like it."

"Thanks, Professor. Let me know what kind of car we are looking for."

Ross shook her hand. It was soft but firm. She held on for too long. Hancock was unattached; too challenging for most men.

"I am not a Professor yet, Superintendent."

"You will be - it's just a matter of time."

Ross smiled as he departed; his senses seduced by Hancock's sensuality, her natural female charms, but he was perturbed, baffled by the evidence.

Aristocracy

Jimmy Turnbull had a butler! It was almost beyond belief. A butler! His property stood at the top of Dalmunzie, a very private road; the most exclusive address in Aberdeen. It might have been built by the Romans; running for a narrow half-mile, entirely enveloped by trees, it was as straight as an arrow.

Every 20 yards along the green, thriving hedgerows, discreet entrances opened onto long driveways leading to luxury piles both period and modern. Ross lived at the start of this road. The further you progress up Dalmunzie Drive, the larger the estate, the richer the inhabitants.

Jimmy lived at the very top.

Ross hadn't been up there for a while. It had changed considerably over the past twelve months.

There was nothing discreet about Jimmy. Entering his land was like entering another world; 17th century France - Versailles.

Two large lions-rampant carved from silver granite welcomed the visitor lucky enough to be admitted through the enormous, electric, cast-iron security gates. Peacocks strutted, chatted, called and displayed.

The house or *chateau*, as it now seemed to be, had been rebuilt complete with great columns of white marble framing the ostentatious, regal entrance. Louis XIV would have been embarrassed by the grandeur of the place: maybe not.

The philosopher in Ross considered the consequences of unlimited wealth,

"We burned out all their mansions
In the name of Robespierre..."

A wide sweeping driveway led to Jimmy's palace. Ross couldn't decide if it was *Fontainebleau* or The Hanging Gardens of Babylon. Perhaps it was 'Fountain Blue' because he counted no less than eight large ornamental ponds with geysers of water powering twenty, thirty feet in the air before spreading out, falling in assorted geometrical displays. Brand-new, miniature-tractors and other pristine motorized gardening vehicles moved discreetly about the beautifully-manicured grounds, preening and titivating the horticultural extravaganza.

Jimmy was a king, if such things are measured by displays of wealth and influence.

A new Bentley GTC Convertible Mulliner **"J1M"** in St. James Red with Magnolia leather stood proudly outside the magnate's mansion. Ross stopped to admire the modern replacement for the famously expensive *Azure* model.

Ross walked up the steps to the wide, white marble entrance and was met by a doorman dressed in full Savoy regalia complete with top hat. He held the door open for the police officer.

"Good Morning, Superintendent."

Ross was incredulous at the man's ostentatious attire; peacocks outside and inside the mansion.

"Good Morning," Ross replied

Entering the house, the butler appeared and looked suspiciously at Ross's shoes before appearing satisfied that they were free from stones or mud.

"Come this way, sir."

He walked Ross across an expansive hall paved in the omnipresent perfect white marble.

'What is it about rich people and white marble?'

Ross counted twenty paces before they arrived at the imposing double-doors to Jimmy's offices at home. The butler knocked ceremoniously three times before opening the doors and showing Ross inside.

White marble, as usual, was the predominant feature, comprising the floor, the impressive carved fire surround and the full-size replicas of Michelangelo's *David* and Canova's *The Three Graces* - at least Ross assumed they were replicas. The two statues stood at either side of a vast walnut desk topped with light tan leather and gold inlay. A large throne was pointed at a splendid bay window overlooking the grounds, away from Ross. The butler announced his presence.

"Superintendent Ross, Sir."

The butler retreated deferentially backwards, closing the doors as he left. There was no movement from the throne. Ross wondered how long he was expected to wait for the great man's attentions.

Finally, the chair swiveled around and the stern face of Sir James Turnbull stared at Ross. He looked like a ghost. It was now over forty-eight hours since his son had been pronounced dead; it was obvious he had not slept a moment since.

Jimmy had just one thing to say,

"You get the fucker who killed my son, Ross!"

Ross didn't rush his reply. He knew the other man was mourning. The best Jimmy could hope for now was justice - lawful retribution.

It was a good time to get to the truth,

"I know this is painful, Jimmy, but have you any idea who might have done this?"

Torero Grigio was usually immaculately dressed, disguising his sixty years with expensive Italian suits, fine silk ties, gold cuff-links and handmade leather shoes. Today, he looked every day his vintage; his famous silver hair, unkempt - more like a tramp than a billionaire-in-waiting. Jimmy was wearing blue linen slacks and a white linen shirt. It was the first time Ross had seen the great man without a tie; the informal dress displayed the *Grey Bullfighter's* spreading girth; he was beginning to look more like an old bull than the Matador despite broad shoulders and considerable height.

Jimmy was naturally intimidating,

"*Done* this, Ross? I am getting mixed information from the police force. Was this an accident or not?"

"Probably not,"

Jimmy was used to interrogating employees and advisors. He was not a man to be fobbed off.

"*Probably* not, Ross?"

"Not. Not an accident Jimmy. It has the hallmarks of a hit."

"Ross....."

"I know. It's bad, very bad. The question is why? Enemies?"

"Me or Bobby? I have many. Bobby had none."

"Does anyone hate you enough to murder your son?" The word '*murder*' was not easy to say to Jimmy Turnbull.

"Probably, but they would go for me, I am worth £750 million, Ross, surely kidnapping makes more sense? I would have paid anything to get Bobby back. I'd hand over the whole lot to have him here now. He was my only son; the only human thing I have created. He was my son, my heir and my greatest friend."

"Do you have any idea who might have deliberately killed your son, Jimmy?"

"Ross, if I knew or suspected anyone, I would hire the best Russian hit-man and have the murdering son of a bitch executed within 24 hours. But I have no idea, no idea at all."

The Mont Blanc pen Jimmy was holding snapped under the pressure of his tense, strained grip. Ink splattered over his white shirt. He took it off and threw it on the floor, the blue ink staining the white marble.

"Fuck!"

He picked up the phone.

"Robertson, get someone up here to clean ink off the floor – immediately!"

He replaced the handset.

Ross watched him trying to control events, even now.

As the shirtless *Bullfighter* walked away from Ross, towards the window, the police officer noticed a huge tattoo across *Le Torero's* naked back. It was *Irezumi*, the signature tattoo of the Japanese Yakuza.

What did this mean?

"You are looking at the tattoo, Ross; had it done after I sold *Aberdeen Oil* to Nomura. I realize it's a bit stupid; they invited me to Tokyo and gave me that Samurai sword above the fire. I guess I got carried away; £400 million on a deal can make you giddy."

He broke off, emotional.

"If you don't mind, Superintendent, I think we should leave it there for today; I'd like to be alone for the rest of this week. I built all this for Bobby. His death changes everything. I just don't know what to do..."

Jimmy fell silent, lost in memories.

Ross expressed his sympathies,

"I understand. I am very sorry. I will be in touch."

Ross shook the magnate's hand solemnly and took his leave.

"Just you get him, Ross - just you get him……"

Ross wasn't sure what he'd gained from the meeting; Jimmy was known to be colourful, brash, boastful, extravagant, and a million other things but he seemed as mystified as the police on this occasion.

The tattoo was enigmatic, but then so was *Torero Grigio*, who as a young man of just 13 years had run off to Italy to fight bulls only to discover he was in the wrong country.

A man who had gone bankrupt four times by the time he was thirty, going grey prematurely as a consequence.

A man who subsequently made a vast fortune adopting the famous, local, heraldic maxim:

Vi et Animo[1]

Or, as Jimmy once put it:

'Don't fuck about'

"GO FOR IT!"

---

[1] Literally: 'Strength and Courage' - Ardoe House and Norwood Hall entrance inscriptions.

Tillydrone

Every town has less-than-desirable areas.

Aberdeen has several.

Tillydrone, not far from Aberdeen University, is a no-go area for many residents of the *Granite City*.

The area has become synonymous with drug addicts and ex-cons. Even the police, called upon to visit Tillydrone virtually every day, are wary of certain, aggressive, anti-social inhabitants and the debris of the drugs culture.

Little children run wild along landings; corridors littered with discarded syringes containing traces of infectious diseases, Hepatitis and HIV, as parents indulge in alcohol or drug abuse.

It's a place of little hope where the damned get through each day by easing the pain of reality with anything that induces a mind-altering experience.

The wealthy, healthy citizens of Aberdeen pass-by - going to work or the airport; catching planes to London, onto Houston; getting helicopters offshore: the depravation only visible if an eye is cast to the left or right from an expensive Mercedes or BMW.

Here, Aberdeen's rampant property prices simply mean an increasing gap between rich and poor; fast-appreciating wealth for the few means fast-approaching destitution and despair for thousands.

In Tillydrone, people still know what it means to go hungry; there is no white marble here, you won't find any automatic ice-makers and a water-feature outside your residence literally does mean that someone has been *'taking the piss'*.

Boarded-up windows, un-maintained outer-walls and gaping cracks patently demonstrate the despair and dereliction in this place of forgotten souls.

Anne Daley

Mrs. Anne Daley was an exception to the rule that only drug addicts and drop-outs tend to live in Tillydrone.

She had been born in Tillydrone, near the city's beautiful Seaton Park. She was now in her eighties and had a flat that served most of her needs. It was in a block sold off by the city council with the inducement of grants for renovation. It had the disabled access she needed. After her husband passed away, she was happy to invest her life savings in the purchase.

Mrs. Daley was proud she had lived her whole life among 'real folk'. In the old days, Tillydrone was just a poorer area of town. The people living there were decent. They just had little money.

Now it was different. Now she knew it was not safe to go out after dark. She knew she had to lock her door and be on her guard.

"But who would be interested in an old bag of bones like me?" she reassured her daughter who often urged her to move to an old-folks home or at least somewhere less popular with drug addicts and petty criminals.

Mrs. Daley didn't go out much since she broke her hip. She was increasingly dependent on the motorised wheelchair the local health centre had secured for her, but she was happy just to tidy her flat and reminisce about the old days - the second world-war, when she was considered a rare beauty by visiting American soldiers.

Northfield

Not far from Tillydrone, towards Aberdeen Airport, at the northerly end of Anderson Drive is another infamous residential area, Northfield. One street here is particularly notorious.

It's called Mansion Avenue.

In a flat in Mansion Avenue, Davie Allan, or the '*Hoor-Master*' as he is proudly known, was having breakfast; a tab of ecstasy washed down with a bottle of *Buckfast* - a cheap, fortified wine popular with certain elements. Soon, Davie was spaced out and in love with everyone. An hour later, Gregor '*Gegsy*' Davies and Mark '*The Thug*' Stewart arrived at the Hoor-Master's flat with a cocktail of mind-altering drugs. Davie let his associates or 'pals' into his flat.

"Morning ass-wipes," said Davie.

"Howdy cunt-face," replied Gegsy nodding with a grin. *The Thug,* as usual, remained silent.

They sat in what could be called the 'lounge' on an old, red-cloth sofa that Davie had dragged out of a nearby skip. A small white plastic table, someone's garden furniture until Davie requisitioned it for his own domestic use, supported the Buckfast and a dirty ashtray containing an eclectic mix of pills and tablets. There was also, somewhat bizarrely, a garden gnome Davie had taken a fancy to one night, high on some hallucinogenic substance.

Several copies of *Hungary and Young,* a highly illegal publication of teenage pornography from Eastern Europe lay open on the floor. Semen stains graced explicit photographs of a 'thirteen' year-old 'virgin', displaying her open vagina for the reader's pleasure.

"You're a fuckin paedo, man," said Gegsy, flicking through the pages with obvious interest. "She has'na even got ony hairs on her twat, ye filthy bastard."

"Shut yer face, yer nae fuckin angel," countered Davie, "What are ye packing?"

"*The Thug* has some good shit," said Gegsy.

Mark Stewart produced a handful of small blue tablets.

"It's fuckin Viagra, ye daft bastards!" yelled Davie, convulsing in laughter.

"It's nae fucking Viagra. It's hot shit."

"Ah right, let's hae a go."

All three of them swallowed several of the blue tablets and passed around the bottle of Buckfast.

The Thug picked up *Hungary and Young*, unbuttoned his fake Burberry jeans and started to masturbate.

Davie and Gegsy watched him with no more interest or surprise than if he had been sending a text message on his mobile phone.

Hoories

Upstairs from old Mrs. Daley were two adjacent first floor flats. These had been given disrepair notices and put up for sale by the City Council. They were a real bargain for anyone investing in cheap student accommodation.

A company based in Liverpool called Mersey Properties bought the flats, upgrading them with financial assistance from Aberdeen Council.

Then, a number of young ladies took up residence.

Mrs. Daley assumed these girls were students or nurses, but she noticed they never carried any books, never left their flats before mid-afternoon and, although she was a little deaf, she could hear many visitors coming and going at all hours.

This didn't bother Mrs. Daley too much because once she was asleep she was dead to the world. But she was surprised that when she awoke at 5 a.m. there were still people arriving and leaving at this unusual time of day. All the visitors were men and the girls were cold and unfriendly, *'Young people are afa selfish these days,'* Mrs. Daley said to herself after one girl had totally ignored her, *'Good Morning'* greeting one day. Had Mrs. Daley been an internet user and interested in adult entertainment she could have visited www.doric-escorts.com where she could have seen that the young lady who cold-shouldered her in the lobby was professionally known as Elisha. Her clients rated her:

'19, angelic face, athletic body, £100 per hour, 5-star performer – no holes barred'

This little Den of Iniquity was already known to the Hoor Master and his various nefarious associates, including Gegsy Davies and Mark Stewart. They had visited these very apartments the week before, but were immediately ejected by an enormous black doorman. They were not the kind of customer the establishment wished to attract. The fact they had not booked online, only had fifty pounds, and were clearly high on drugs did not help their case.

Prostitutes, like most women in Aberdeen, could be choosy, because in this oil-rich town men outnumbered women by a factor of three to one.

Seaton Park

Gegsy had struck gold.

The Thug had been offered potent blue pills by a dealer in the city's Seaton area and taken the dealer to meet Gegsy for payment.

The meeting took place in the Gents' toilets in Seaton Park. Gloomy, dank, seedy, smelly, the stone toilet floor perpetually soaked in stale urine, the small white-painted building, adjacent to the River Don, is an infamous meeting place for homosexuals and petty criminals.

Gegsy arrived first. He entered the dark edifice, his boots splashing aside the pungent urine, surprising a middle-aged man administering oral sex to a teenage boy in one of the cubicles. The teenager was having his nipples squeezed, his testicles fondled and his semen swallowed by the well-dressed, silver-haired gentleman.

Gegsy kicked open the cubicle door to witness the boy convulsing in orgasmic pleasure as the prominent criminal lawyer sucked lovingly on the young man's swollen penis. Sticky white sperm trickled down the suave solicitor's face.

Gegsy, high on drugs, was about to kick him on the head when the fellator distracted him.

"Ah, Mr. Davies, nice to see you again…"

"You better get oot of here, man, we're doing a deal," Gegsy advised, half recognizing the lawyer.

"Certainly." The defender of criminal justice spoke with a pronounced, sticky lisp.

He eyed Gegsy with obvious desire.

Had Gegsy been interested, the solicitor would gladly have offered him his willing mouth or eager anus. Sexual desire knows no social boundaries.

"An' you get the fuck out of here as weel, you fuckin skinny homo wank!"

The youth hastily pulled up his jeans, painfully catching his semi-erect penis in his zipper; he exited the building rapidly.

"Tosser!" Gegsy spat at the fleeing youth. He then checked the other cubicles, strewn with used condoms, empty whisky bottles and the ubiquitous syringes, for potential eavesdroppers.

Satisfied the small building was now vacant Gegsy rolled a 'spliff' and waited for *The Thug*. He was really high. A tab of ecstasy, two tabs of acid and now he'd polished off a large chunk of cannabis resin in a highly concentrated joint. The cannabis made him paranoid, on edge. His head was swimming. He sat on a toilet bowl to steady his spinning top. The other two arrived. *The Thug* said nothing; just a conspiratorial nod. Gegsy focused, as best he could, on the unfamiliar drug dealer.

"A'right, mate, how mony hiv yee got and fit the fuck's in these blue bastards?"

The dealer, a student called Rupert Byron or 'Roo' was not from the street like Gegsy or *The Thug*. He was a graduate of economics from Durham, studying at Aberdeen University for a Masters degree in Hydrocarbon Resources. The only reason Roo was in that toilet in Seaton Park was a drug habit, and he could not resist turning a profit.

Wrong place: wrong time.

"They're a combination of LSD, ecstasy, speed, morphine and crack cocaine - the *Full Monty*. A friend of mine makes them at the pharmaceuticals company he works for," Roo replied.

"How mony hiv yee got?"

"There are about five hundred in this bag and they cost £5 a tablet - you can have the bag for £2,000.00."

Had Roo a clearer head and more experience of dealing with the likes of Gegsy, he would never have agreed to this private meeting and he would have known the likes of Gegsy would never carry that much cash - and if he did, that he would never part with it.

"Well, you just gie us that bag an' we'll settle up later."

Roo was uneasy, sensing danger, but he needed the money. He was a student; fees and digs were not cheap. He pressed for payment.

"I'd rather have the money."

Gegsy looked at Mark Stewart and nodded. *The Thug* moved swiftly and clinically bringing his knee up with terrible force into Roo's groin, smashing into his testicles, causing him to scream and collapse in crippling pain. Roo squirmed on the wet toilet floor; vomiting; gasping for precious, life-giving oxygen as *The Thug* went though his pockets and removed the bag of tablets and one thousand pounds in cash.

Roo's entire life was now in Gegsy's hands.

A wealthy background, the very best education, but Roo's party-animal personality, his lack of awareness, had led him to this precarious situation.

Gegsy didn't like Roo.

He was just another stuck-up, privileged 'fuckin tosser'.

Gegsy looked at *The Thug* who instinctively, almost telepathically, understood the silent instruction.

Mark Stewart jumped up - then descended rapidly, stamping his boot down on Roo's head, smashing the helpless student's skull. The student's cranium crunched as it cracked open.

It was a terrible and terrifying attack; no different than if *The Thug* had stamped on an egg or a water melon. He was quite indifferent to what he had done.

They dumped Roo's body on a toilet seat in one of the cubicles.

"That'll gie the fuckin homo's a fright," Gegsy joked.

Roo's pulverized, bloody, death-mask grimaced hideously: a petrified, grotesque *Picasso* – a cubist horror-scene.

The Thug

Mark Stewart, *The Thug*, had been beaten and abused all his life. He was now twenty-five years old and had been taking anabolic steroids and weight training since he was sixteen.

On his eighteenth birthday he had been attacked, as usual, by his father, who'd been drinking all day. *The Thug* had stolen a Mason's hammer and surprised his raging parent, smashing him in the face with the cast-iron tool. Twenty blows later his father was dead, his head pummeled to a pulp in the bloody, lethal counter-attack. *The Thug* pleaded self-defence, claiming the hammer was already in the house. He was acquitted, adjudged not guilty. Ever since, Mark Stewart had been a loaded gun - a veritable killing machine.

This time it was murder, but prison was no problem. They would get out before long.

"I did'na realise what I was doin, man, it was thae drugs."

The victim today was a drug dealer; it was unlikely society would not mourn him.

Individuals like *The Thug* are more common than might be imagined. Highly-damaged, anti-social types can be found at most football matches, every white supremacy march and in most neighbourhoods where crime is endemic.

People like Mark Stewart have no chance of a career, no opportunity to make money legitimately and they own nothing. They have little or no education, so they simply 'don't care' - because society does not care about them.

As a result, they are very dangerous people indeed.

Mansion Avenue

The Hoor-Master was unaware of how Gegsy and *The Thug* had obtained their unlawful stash and any sense of inquisitiveness he might have felt was rapidly obliterated by the 'blue bastards' as Davie was now calling the azure tablets.

"Fuck me, man! 'Am fucking flying – a' could jump oot thon fuckin windae and never hit the grun."

Davie really believed he was floating around the room; he waved his arms to direct his flight.

Gegsy was also in a transcendental state.

Throwing any sense of caution to the wind, he produced the bag of five hundred tablets, and the one thousand pounds, and started arranging the money in twenty bundles of fifty pounds each.

"I fancy some Charlie," said Gegsy "This wee stash'll get us a fair whack."

Davie landed on the runway and cast a bleary eye over the cash.

"Fuck me, man, fa' the fuck did ye get that?"

Gegsy said nothing; he simply tapped his nose knowingly with his index finger.

The Thug, meanwhile, was working his way through the pornography, tasting and smelling the girls. The blue pills were highly potent mixed with the steroids and Buckfast.

"Fuck the Charlie, Gegs, let's gang back to thae hoorie pad and get some fanny."

Davie was living up to his nickname.

Gegsy concurred,

"Ah'right! Put that weapon back in yer kegs, ye big cunt," he smirked at his Neanderthal sidekick.

The Thug had been masturbating for almost an hour without any ejaculate to show for it.

Dressed in jeans, boots and hooded tops, the three doped-up accomplices packed their loot and headed off to the first-floor flats in Tillydrone where the services of young women could be procured hourly for £100.00.

All three of them carried bottles of Buckfast in deep trouser pockets; *The Thug*, as usual, carried a blade.

Great Northern Road

Having spent the late afternoon in the Woodside Bar on Great Northern Road, the three were now drunk. Copious alcohol, combined with the drugs, made reality and rational thought - never a strong point at the best of times with this trio - a thing of the past. *The Thug* resembled Dr. Frankenstein's monster walking, robot-like, in a straight line through any passer-by unfortunate enough to cross his path.

Davie and Gegsy walked like lovers, their arms around each other's shoulders, stumbling along the pavement singing a favourite song of Aberdeen F.C supporters designed to irritate fans from rival teams. It was a bizarre chant and demonstrated the superiority even the lowest citizens of the wealthy 'Silver City' felt over their neighbours in the South;

"In yer Glasgae slum
In yer Glasgae slum
Ye look in the bucket for somethin' tae eat
Ye find a deed rat and ye think it's a treat
In yer Glasgae slum!"

"Ha ha - up the Dons! Ye fuckin Glasgae fuckers!" shouted Gegsy.

Alexandra Terrace in Tillydrone was their ultimate destination.

A police car spotted them walking over the railway bridge on Don Street.

The police officers eyed them suspiciously, but on sighting *The Thug*, with his shaven head, furrowed brow and long muscular arms, they decided not to tackle him in particular without backup.

Roo's body had been discovered a few hours ago, but there was nothing concrete to link Gegsy and *The Thug* to the killing, except that they were clearly out of control and in the general vicinity.

The police car drove slowly past. As it disappeared around the corner, the three suspects ran down the hill and into a block of flats.

The police called for a Black Maria and as many heavy-duty officers as they could summon. They parked near the flat, waiting for assistance to arrive.

The threesome, meantime, had passed through one block of flats, climbed a fence and made their way to the front door of numbers 320-326 Alexandra Terrace, unsighted.

Gegsy, ever-sly, stuffed the bag of tablets into Davie Allen's deep trouser-leg pocket.

"You hang-on to these blue fuckers, mate."

Alexandra Terrace

Number 320-326 Alexandra Terrace stood out like a sore thumb. The blocks of flats on either side had their windows boarded up and were obviously unoccupied, officially at least. The front doors of both adjacent buildings had been removed and old bottles and garbage lay in the lobbies. Number 320-326 was an oasis of good repair in a desert of destruction and dereliction. Bottom left, Mrs. Daley had clean windows and clean net curtains. Bottom right, the flat had been bought cheap from the council, renovated, and leased to some fairly affluent students who were only there Monday to Friday.

The middle floor was totally discreet: new window-frames - the windows themselves were blackened-off with snug fitting blinds. Number 320-326 had a new, reinforced, security door and secure door-entry system.

Gasping for breath, Davie Allen pressed the buzzer for the first floor flats. An expressionless, Birmingham accent crackled over the intercom,

"Name?"

"David Allen," said the Hoor-Master trying to sound posh.

"Fuck off," came the matter of fact reply.

"We've a thousand quid in cash!" pleaded Davie.

A high pitch buzz indicated that although their presence was not welcomed, one thousand pounds cash was irresistible to these peddlers of female flesh.

They entered. At the top of the first set of stairs, the mountainous black doorman instantly recognised them; he was quick to diagnose their condition.

"Are you guys on drugs?" he said, in a calm, quiet voice.

"We've just had a few beers," lied Gegsy.

"Where's the money?" said the black giant.

Gegsy produced a handful of rolled-up wads of cash and offered them to the doorman.

"One of you," replied the Nubian massive.

"You," he said, pointing to the Hoor-Master.

"What the fuck are we meant to do oot here?" snapped Gegsy.

The black giant shot Gegsy a look that even *The Thug* would have winced at.

"He comes out, you go in, one at a time." said the ebony colossus.

"£200." he added.

"Fuck me!" exclaimed Gegsy, handing over four rolls of cash to Davie Allen, "Mak sure she tak's it up the arse for two hunner," he added.

The black doorman shut the door on Gegsy and *The Thug* without a single word.

"Fuckin black cunt," Gegsy said quietly.

Davie Allen entered the pleasure palace and was introduced to Elisha. She was none too impressed; about to tell him to take a hike when he produced the two hundred in cash whereupon she offered him a selection of condoms and told him to wash his genitals in the toilet.

The Thug, now entirely 'out of his face,' swallowed another blue pill, walked back down the stairs and knocked on the door of the students' flat. Luckily for them, they were not at home. He then walked automatically to Mrs. Daley's flat and knocked on her door.

Mrs. Daley was watching Coronation Street and was surprised to hear the knock at the door. An envelope from Christian Aid had been put through her door earlier that day so she assumed it must be Christians at the door, asking for a donation. She could not have been more wrong. There were no Christians at the door tonight. She got her purse, took out a 50p coin to help the poor in Africa, and powered her wheelchair to her front door.

Outside the building the police had mustered ten officers, going door to door, searching for the miscreants. They assumed the three must be hiding in the adjacent empty buildings, not in the veritable fortress of number 320-326. They were wrong.

The Thug entered Mrs. Daley's apartment with his mind in cloud-cuckoo-land and his libido sky-high. He had given that student tosser a good kicking and he'd been drooling over young Hungarian sluts and masturbating all day. He was horny. He knew they had come here for pussy. He was a predator. He wanted his fill. Mrs. Daley was to be his bitch this evening. He grabbed her by the arm, lifting her out of her wheelchair and dragged her to the bedroom, where he flung her on the bed.

Gegsy followed, to see what was going on.

Even Gegsy, high on drugs, didn't have the stomach for what he witnessed in Mrs. Daley's bedroom.

The only compensation was that *The Thug* had forced her to swallow a blue pill and a mouthful of Buckfast.

Mrs. Daley tried to imagine the American soldier she had once made love to and kept a secret.

By the time *The Thug* had finished with her, her mind had quietly dissociated itself from her body.

Mrs. Daley would never utter another word. She was now, to all intents and purposes, a vegetable.

The police finally worked out the suspects must be in number 320-326.

Naturally, the black gatekeeper was not about to open up to the police so they had to remove the door with a battering ram. They rushed into Mrs. Daley's flat to find Gegsy, sitting in a chair, in a combination of trance and shock.

The Thug was pounding his raging erection into the seemingly lifeless old lady on the bed.

A pool of urine surrounded Mrs. Daley.

The wet, yellow stain had an eerie appearance.

It was as if her soul was leaking out of her body.

It was trying to gently seep away - without disturbing anyone.

London, Liverpool Street Station

London was hell.

The contrast with Aberdeen, staggering; the pace ten times faster; patience and courtesy non-existent; bumping, barging, squeezing, frowning - frenzied human happenings - the ultimate rat-race: stress personified.

The regular, monthly visit to the City for Ross to meet the senior officers in charge of Fraud, Money-Laundering, Anti-Terrorism and Public Order (AT&PO) had come around again. For convenience the tripartite meeting was held at the Bishopsgate Police Station, adjacent to Liverpool Street Railway Station.

Ross was stressed-out. Check-in on departure at Aberdeen had taken two hours. Two hours for a fifty minute flight!

Superintendents Harry Moore (Fraud) and Sally Shepherd (Money Laundering/Terrorism) together with Chief Inspector Maruuf Syed (AT&PO) were already in meeting room one; a great deal of ground had been covered by the time the Scottish contingent, Ross, arrived. Shepherd and Syed were two of the busiest officers on the Met.

Ross had barely warmed his chair when a call came through, scrambling all anti-terrorism personnel.

A red-light flashed, pulsing silently above the door as a concise, urgent loudspeaker made the clarion call,

"Code Red! Gatwick Airport!"

Shepherd and Syed sped from the room.

Only Harry Moore didn't grab a hat and make a beeline for the door.

It was a different world.

"Well, Ross, I bet you miss the cut and thrust."

"Perhaps I should tag along?" Ross replied.

"I doubt it. The fire brigade and the military will be there in their millions. Too many cooks.....coffee?"

Harry Moore was not your normal copper. Recruited from Barclays Bank on a stupendous package, he'd worked front and back office across the investment banking sector; probably the only man in the Met who understood derivatives, commodities, swaps, hedging, arbitrage and futures trading. He'd made millions in the late eighties and early nineties, burning out at 39, joining the police very late aged 40 in 2002. After 9/11, the global meltdown in technology shares and international stock market disasters, the Met was a welcome cup of certainty for the former investment banker. Harry had nothing to prove; he was a hobbyist, amusing himself spotting both obvious and furtive cases of insider dealing and the usual City scams. He was well-connected, a personal friend of senior staff at leading financial institutions.

"Is it drinkable?" Ross was suspicious of police coffee.

"I made it myself, Ross, the finest organic Costa Rican roast. Fancy a cigar?"

"No thanks."

"Mind if I do?"

The answer to this question from anyone else would be, "Yes, I bloody well do mind," (smoking in public places was now banned in Scotland), but Harry was such an affable, inoffensive, old Etonian that anything he did was pardonable; besides, Ross needed his help. Harry filled up two white Denby china coffee-cups; cream first, then the thick, black coffee. He stirred slowly with a silver spoon he carried around in a leather pouch, engraved: *HM.*

Taking off his tie, Harry leant back in his seat and took a long draw on his cigar, slowly releasing the smoke high in air, away from Ross. Sipping his coffee, he smiled,

"So how is life treating you in Jock-land, David?"

"Well, it's become interesting lately. I could use your help, Harry. I need a contact in Nomura. Who would be responsible for energy-sector acquisitions, specifically, buying oil and gas assets?"

"That's pretty specialized. I am meeting Charlie Butterfield at Deutsche Bank in half an hour. He knows everybody. I will get a name at Nomura for you and try for a meeting over lunch?"

"Fantastic, Harry. Let's go and see Charlie now."

"Steady, David, let's finish our coffee."

Harry looked at his gold Rolex Submariner, pretending to be chronologically diligent for Ross's benefit. In no hurry, he took another long drag on his cigar. Crime would still be there in fifteen minutes. Besides, he wanted to make Ross an offer,

"Fancy selling me your Ferrari, David?"

"The 250 GTO?"

"Don't tell me you have another Ferrari?"

"No chance, one is enough to live down."

"Well, sell it to a good home?"

"Sentimental value, Harry..."

"Million quid, Swiss bank, no capital gains."

"Tempting, let me ask Diane. We might be interested."

"Excellent." Harry smiled contentedly.

Nomura

Investment banks are the best place to work in the world. Ten years ago, trainee computer programmers and trainee traders were making one hundred thousand pounds a year. Now, hedge fund managers can easily earn in excess of ten million a year. *Money, money, money*: from the minute you walk in the door of Nomura or a hundred similar City establishments you are entering an Aladdin's cave of unimaginable wealth.

Harry's contact at Nomura was a gentleman called Murray Raw, a tall handsome man in his thirties with golden blonde hair and green eyes. He had that easy, nonchalant air that comes with being wealthy. It's easy to be relaxed when you have no mortgage, a private jet, twenty million in cash, and salary and bonuses exceeding five million per annum.

Nomura's fabulous offices are located in the impressively named 1 St. Martins Le Grand, EC1. The gothic building is traditional Victorian monolithic grandeur. Inside, glass, marble, wood and water features abound. Wherever and whenever money wants to impress, you will find marble and water features; a legacy from all the great ancient civilizations no doubt. The Japanese investment bank's power and affluence includes its own Nomura art gallery and a recent, opulent, two million pound refurbishment of the staff canteen. The canteen is even more impressive than the art gallery – an exquisite kaleidoscope of vivacious, brightly coloured, contemporary, culinary design - modernistic and Machiavellian.

The meeting with Raw took place in one of the many grandiose boardrooms.

Ross, as usual, cut to the chase.

"What can you tell us about Jimmy Turnbull?" he asked Raw.

"Jimmy is a successful, Aberdeen-based hydrocarbon entrepreneur." Raw spoke with perfect BBC English; received pronunciation, no R in Aberdeen.

"Tell me about *Aberdeen Oil* - I understand Nomura bought the business?" Ross pressed Raw.

"Not quite. That was the original plan, but several of our Directors got cold feet. Too far outside our expertise, too risky," replied the investment banker.

"I thought Jimmy made £400 million?" said Ross.

"He did, but in the end, we just acted for him. The buyer was a Japanese consortium, who sold-on almost immediately to a company based in Monaco."

"I need details. I want you to show us your files."

Murray Raw was flabbergasted at the request.

"Impossible, Superintendent; that is strictly confidential. No-one would ever deal with us again if we disclosed such details."

"Do I need a warrant? Suspected money laundering?" Ross stated bluntly.

Harry Moore intervened, spluttering, choking on his latest cup of fresh filtered coffee. This was not how he did business. He preferred a nod and a wink. He calmed the waters,

"Murray, this is a murder enquiry, a young man and woman. Not just a murder, but a possible assassination, a hit. We really need to know everything about this one"

Raw nodded. Coming from Harry it sounded reasonable.

The banker made a concession,

"Ok. I will get the files and leave them here for half an hour. Then I will return and answer your questions. Should you choose to read the files, then I know nothing about it. I just forgot I left them here, okay?"

"Okay," said Ross.

The files were thick and complex and could not possibly be assimilated in thirty minutes. It seemed Jimmy Turnbull had sold the business to a Japanese consortium, Kyoto Oil, but just two weeks later, the business was sold to Monaco Oil, a company registered in Greece, operated by several Russian Oligarchs based in Monte Carlo.

The file included several noticeably irate faxes from lawyers claiming the assets were not as stated; terms like '*inconsistencies in proved, possible and probable reserves,*' were bandied about: a plethora of legal threats were obvious.

Murray Raw returned and sat down.

"Find what you were looking for?"

"Not an amicable transaction?" replied Ross

"It was far from amicable. The Russians discovered the assets were overstated and overvalued. On discovering the errors, or *alleged* misinformation, it was suspected the Japanese sale was artificial - to make the assets more attractive and desirable; in turn, giving the Russians confidence to buy at a high price. Jimmy has friends in Japan, and looking back, it's not impossible the sale was suspicious. My senior directors were extremely relieved we did not buy the assets; overvalued apparently; short by almost 50% and the deal carried hidden, punitive, abandonment liabilities."

"The Russians wanted their money back?" Ross asked Raw.

"Yes, Diputz Rekuskok, the Russian oligarch heading the purchase of *Aberdeen Oil,* wanted to sue Jimmy for £250 million, the likely loss on the deal; the shortfall. But litigation proved too complicated and Jimmy's cash, by that time, was in offshore trusts."

"Ha ha, 'offshore trusts' - ironic oxymoron: Oily-garchs?" Harry interjected, seemingly amused by the affair. Murray Raw ignored Harry's banter. He remembered the whole business vividly. It was close to a disaster. The bank had faced a law suit from Monaco Oil and Murray's bonus and job had been on the line.

"It got messy. We faced an action for negligent misstatement; shades of *Caparo* and *Hedley Byrne*; very expensive and terrible publicity. In the end, Rekuskok, decided to make it personal; he doubtless had a few skeletons in his own cupboard and wanted to avoid litigation. He told Jimmy to stay out of Russia and Monaco until he covers the losses. Jimmy told him to '*kiss his ass!*'"

Ross considered Jimmy's Yakuza tattoo. It was almost a joke that the name Yakuza derived from the worst possible hand in the Japanese equivalent of the card game Black Jack. How ironic to deal a bad hand to a company based in Monte Carlo.

Had Jimmy paid a terrible human cost for his slight of hand? Had his son been killed to square the deal?

It was unlikely Ross could bring a Russian oligarch to trial in Aberdeen. If it was a professional hit, the hit-man would be hard to track down: impossible to place in Aberdeen on the night of the murder.

Dead-end.

Ross thanked Murray Raw and apologized for his heavy-handed request over the files. Harry shook hands with the banker and made a quip about *'still having all his fingers'*. Harry somehow got away with such comments.

"If you guys ever fancy a job in compliance we are offering big bucks right now," Raw waved them off.

"It's tempting, great place to work," said Ross. Ross meant it. Even the receptionists at Nomura look like catwalk models. He was sorry to leave London. It had been interesting; as ever, a fascinating glimpse into big business and big money.

Ross contemplated investment banking and the City. Beneath the veneer of fabulous wealth: art galleries, marble, expensive offices, received-pronunciation - was it just legalized, taxed, loan-sharking on a grand scale? And the stock market – a casino without the safeguards? Certainly, the investment bank appeared to have been engaged primarily to give *Aberdeen Oil* a higher-class of salesman. The policeman's philosophizing was interrupted by the less reflective, more pragmatic, ex-banker,

"Well, David, what about that Ferrari, how about £1.2 million and two weeks timeshare for life at La Sport, St Lucia?"

"Okay, Harry. You have a deal. Diane has been nipping my head about the GTO for years."

"Splendid. Have a cigar."

Ross accepted it this time, as a courtesy.

Ross had discovered a probable motive for Bobby Turnbull and Debby Glennie's death: retribution for a dodgy sale of overvalued assets to dangerous people. He had also sold his old Ferrari for a small fortune.

'Not a bad day's work'

The Sheriff Court, Aberdeen

Aberdeen Sheriff Court is located at the top of the city's main thoroughfare, Union Street, in an area called Castlegate. The court buildings are constructed of traditional Aberdeen granite and are a dichotomy: a visual paradox to the new visitor.

Outside the court is usually gathered a collection of individuals in shell-suits, smoking cheap cigarettes and wearing hooded tops or fake Burberry caps. These are the accused persons; the clients of the criminal court defence lawyers. Inside, by contrast, is a grandiose edifice resembling an opera house or a theatre resplendent with deep-pile red carpeting, pitch-pine woodwork and delicate plaster cornicing. It's a grand place indeed.

On the right-hand side as you enter is an area that might easily be the café at the National Gallery in London. Formerly a gap between two buildings, this interesting space has been cleverly crafted into a meeting area for legal counsel. The grey skies above have been sectioned off by a glass roof canopy and the exposed exterior rough-granite walls of the two conjoined buildings are used to great effect to create the impression of some great hall in a medieval castle. Effective use is made of beech-wood and glass in the tables and chairs that adorn the floor of this fine area. A steep set of stairs descend magnificently to the luxurious meeting area below populated by the learned men and women wearing long black gowns. Some might say, these 'legal-eagles' resemble a flock of large ravens gathering to make the most of a seemingly endless, bountiful harvest of state-sponsored criminal legal-aid.

Continuing along the sumptuous red carpet, towards the courtrooms themselves, you will find, to the left, a splendid light-wood and glass kiosk where the helpful duty officer will inform you of the business of the day, including highlights, such as murder trials conducted by the visiting High Court sitting with a jury.

Today, he will tell you that two Aberdeen lads are being summoned, accused of the murder of one Rupert Byron and the rape and grievous bodily harm of a Mrs. Anne Daley.

This trial is taking place in court 6.

The High Court, Aberdeen

In court six, the two co-accused stand in the dock trying to look as remorseful as possible.

Defence agent, Jason Jameson, the *Silver Fox*; tall, tanned, elegant, around fifty years old with grey hair and a lisp - a lisp that seems to mysteriously disappear when he is in full flow in front of a jury – addresses the court confidently, entering pleas on behalf of his clients: *"My clients plead not guilty to the alleged indictments and further claim a defence of non-insane automatism should they be judged to have committed any of the alleged acts on the charge sheet. There is nothing, actually, conclusively, connecting either of the accused to the murder of Rupert Byron, save some weak circumstantial evidence, and in any case, my clients were so clearly under the influence of hallucinogenic substances to the point that they had no connection between mind and body. These substances were consumed innocently, under the mistaken belief the blue tablets were Viagra, therefore it cannot be said they took these mind-altering drugs deliberately or recklessly.*

*The result of this is that my clients could not possibly be held to have the requisite **mens rea** or 'intent' to be guilty of any of the crimes with which they are charged; crimes which they, in any case, deny."*

The Advocate-Depute (the state prosecutor in capital offences) who had thought he'd heard everything, had to repress a burst of outraged laughter at this preposterous defence. He immediately requested that the jury be dismissed so the pleas in defence could be debated in private with Lord Simpson, the trial judge. The court was cleared while the two lawyers and the Judge held the legal debate.

"My Lord, the accused are known violent criminals with a history of drug dealing and drug abuse. We cannot allow them the possibility of escaping justice on this ludicrous defence," pleaded Charlie Reid, HM Advocate.

"I take your point, Mr. Reid. We must ensure a fair trial for the accused, but we must also ensure a fair trial for the victims and for society. Mr. Jameson, do you earnestly and honestly stand by this defence?"

"I do, Your Lordship. We have a reliable witness who swears under oath that he supplied 'blue pills' to the accused persons and that he told them the aforementioned pills were Viagra. He further told them that these tablets would be of benefit for their later trip to a house of ill-repute." The suave defender of justice was convincing, compelling.

"Does your witness understand that if it can be shown that he knew the pills were not Viagra and that these pills can be proved to be a significant cause of this crime then he could be charged as an accessory, or indeed, the actual perpetrator of these evil acts?" stated Lord Simpson.

"Yes, My Lord. The witness is aware of the importance of his statement being truthful." Jason Jameson replied, untruthfully.

The Hoor Master was protecting his friends, but he certainly would not have agreed to his disingenuous statement if he had thought he faced any charge greater than perjury. He had been assured perjury would be impossible to prove because there were no witnesses; Roo was dead and Jameson was obviously silent.

"Very well, we will proceed and accept the pleas and allow the jury to consider the defence of non-insane automatism. However, please remember this is a difficult and technical defence, Mr. Jameson. It must be shown the drugs were a causal factor; innocently or mistakenly consumed, and that the accused experienced a total dissociation of mind and body. In other words, they had no idea what they were doing," Lord Simpson concluded.

"I am aware of that, Your Lordship," Jameson replied victoriously. He had spent hours coaching Gegsy, and, with more difficulty, The Thug, on how to answer any questions thrown at them.

Gegsy Davies, a regular client of the lower, Sheriff Court, had quickly engaged Jameson's services for fairly obvious reasons, not least of which was the fact he held the power to instantly end Jameson's successful career in public scandal.

Charlie Reid sighed as the jury was reconvened.

Lord Simpson began by explaining the defence of non-insane automatism.

"Ladies and Gentlemen, I feel I must say something to you about the meaning of the term **non-insane automatism**. It is similar in some ways to the defences of insanity and diminished responsibility

except that these latter defences require a medical history of proven mental illness. In a case of insanity the accused has a defence because his or her mind is incapable of the normal control and restraint due to a mental defect. Usually, if this defence is successful, the accused will be found unfit to stand trial and will be committed to a secure mental institution. Diminished responsibility is short of insanity but similarly requires a proven mental aberration. If successful, it reduces murder to culpable homicide. However, the defence of diminished responsibility is not available for psychopathic personality disorders or for crimes involving drink or drugs[2]. To recap then, both these aforementioned defences are based on what is known as an internal or **intrinsic** mental disorder. By contradistinction, non-insane automatism does not require a history of mental illness. The accused can be of normally sound mind hence the term 'non-insane'. In pleading non-insane automatism, the accused is claiming to have lost all power to control his mind due to an external or **extrinsic** causal factor. An external factor might include a mind-altering drug. Due to this extrinsic cause, the accused is claiming that, although he may have committed the criminal **act,** he had 'no mind' and is therefore what is known as an '**automaton**'. It is crucial to the defence that this external factor must not have been taken in the knowledge that it could have a detrimental effect on the mind of the accused. In other words, voluntary consumption of mind-altering drugs or excessive alcohol fails the test. The ingestion must be either involuntary or via a genuine error. In the case of a mistake, the consumption must be based on

[2] **Galbraith v HM Advocate (2002) JC 1**

*a reasonable belief that the substance consumed was innocuous. For example, the purchase and consumption of a sandwich from a reputable high street store, surreptitiously and unexpectedly, containing LSD, might be allowable as a genuine, unforeseeable, mistaken ingestion of a mind-altering substance. I hope this overview assists you to grasp the meaning of **'non-insane automatism'**. I will now call upon Her Majesty's Advocate to make the case for the Crown as the prosecuting agent in this trial."*

Gegsy was called to the witness box.

The Thug had been removed from the court temporarily to prevent him from hearing Gegsy's story.

"You are Gregor Davies?" asked HMA.

"Yes," said Gegsy. This was to be, pretty much, his only honest reply of the day.

"Can you please tell the court what you were doing on the 7th of July 2006 around midday?"

"When?" said Gegsy.

"On the day Rupert Byron was murdered and Mrs. Ann Daley was assaulted and raped by your co-accused, Mr. Mark Stewart."

"I cannae remember. I had taken some bad shit," said Gegsy, sticking to script.

"Do you remember what happened before you took the drugs?"

"We went to get the Hoor Master to ging doon tae the hoories at Tilly."

There was definite, muffled laughter from at least one member of the jury.

"This is a serious matter," interjected Lord Simpson, "Please answer sensibly."

"You mean you went to the flat of Mr. David Allen in Mansion Avenue with the intention of his joining you on a trip to a place you knew to be a brothel in Alexandra Terrace in Tillydrone," suggested HMA.

"Aye," said Gegsy, nodding.

"Exactly what happened when you got to the flat and met Mr. Allen?"

"He gave us Viagra and I canna remember onything after that," said Gegsy.

"He told you the blue pills were Viagra?"

"Aye,"

"Do you remember leaving the flat and walking to the Woodside bar on Great Northern Road?"

"No."

"Do you remember running from a police car?"

"No."

Her Majesty's Advocate changed his attack.

"Mr. Davies, you are asking us to believe you found a public bar, where you have been many times previously; recognised a car as a police car and located a flat in Tillydone you intended to visit; yet you are claiming you did not know what you were doing and that you remember nothing about it?"

"Aye - I cannae remember onything," said Gegsy

"Very well, let's have Mr. Stewart on the stand," said the exasperated prosecutor.

Unfortunately for the prosecution, Gegsy and *The Thug* had said nothing when arrested and cautioned, or later when questioned by the police. Gegsy had been too stoned and too shocked to talk and *The Thug* never spoke anyway. They had not even given their names until several hours later. This absolute silence simply assisted the defence of non-insane automatism - at the very least the two accused had indeed been: *'away with the fairies'*.

Silence in Court

Mark Stewart, *The Thug*, took the stand.

"You are Mr. Mark Stewart?" asked HMA.

Mark Stewart said nothing. He simply looked at prosecuting counsel with his expressionless black eyes. Mark Stewart had no empathy, no sympathy and no soul. These had long since been stolen from him by his father in early-life experiences.

"Mr. Stewart, you must answer the question," repeated the prosecutor.

Jason Jameson stood up and made a request to address the court on behalf of his client,

"Mr. Stewart has a very nervous disposition, My Lord. He has had a particularly traumatic life, including experiencing the death of his own father in self-defence of his own life."

"What you mean is that Mr. Stewart killed his father," interjected Charlie Reid, already sensing this case was going to be difficult.

Jameson was quick to set the record straight,

"My Lord, that is an unfair, inappropriate comment. Mr. Stewart was found entirely blameless of any crime in the case of his father's tragic death where he was justifiably defending himself after being repeatedly abused for many years at the hands of a violent drunkard."

The defence agent's words were not entirely untrue. *The Thug's* father, some would say, had got what was coming to him. Mark Stewart winced slightly at the mention of his father. Somewhere in the recesses of his damaged mind, he remembered the misery and brutality of his childhood. It could be argued that Mark Stewart's father had caused the death of Rupert Byron and the rape of Mrs. Anne

63

Daley. After all, the constant rage and indifference to the suffering of others *The Thug* displayed hadn't been there at birth. It was not until his fifth birthday, when his father had punched him in the face so hard that several of the boy's teeth had been knocked out, that Mark Stewart had started to suffer, and began to detest humanity. On that occasion the five year-old boy had simply wanted to go outside to play. His drunken father had been watching horse-racing and was disturbed by the five year-old's innocent request. His response was a brutal attack on a defenceless child and now society was paying for not protecting that child from abuse.

"Can I request the prosecutor's comment is immediately withdrawn?" Jameson demanded.

"I hereby withdraw the comment, Your Lordship." said Her Majesty's Advocate Depute in resignation.

"The jury will disregard the comment," said Lord Simpson.

Jason Jameson was often criticised for siding with nefarious rogues; protecting them from legal retribution. Often this criticism was warranted, but he represented his clients effectively, deserving his reputation as the best criminal lawyer in town.

"I have a statement here made by Mr. Stewart, under oath, in response to questions submitted by the Procurator Fiscal. I am happy to read out these questions and answers to the court in the presence of Mr. Stewart, who, I feel sure, will acknowledge the veracity of his answers," said Jameson.

The Thug looked blankly ahead. It was unlikely he had ever heard the word 'veracity', let alone understood its meaning.

"Are you saying that the accused is incapable of speech?" asked Lord Simpson.

"No, My Lord, Mr. Stewart can speak but has great difficulty reasoning or talking when he feels pressurized; in some ways he is like a child."

"Very well, Mr. Jameson, you may speak on behalf of the accused, but the jury will have every right to draw its own conclusions about Mr. Stewart's silence. If they feel your client is being deliberately silent, in order to withhold or conceal the truth, then they may conclude that he is being evasive, and this may prejudice his defence."

"With regard to my client's speaking difficulty, would it assist the court to know that as a young child Mr. Stewart was punished for talking? I have some old reports from the child protection agency that testify that as a child my client was made to suffer the appalling indignity of having a clothes-peg clasped to his tongue, often all day, when his father felt his boy was being a garrulous nuisance. In addition to the obvious psychological effects, this has given Mr. Stewart a speech impediment that makes forming certain words extremely difficult," Jameson was masterful, "There are also reports of physical torture and extreme sexual abuse."

Mark Stewart looked down at his feet. His defence was taking its toll. He had, hitherto, removed his childhood memories from his mind. Now, he started to recall the beatings, losing his teeth at five years old to that terrifying blow from his own father; having a clothes-peg clamped to his tongue for asking to go out to play or for a particular Xmas present or just to go to the toilet. This was just the surface of the abuse Mark Stewart had undergone. His father would not let him use the toilet as a punishment for drinking too much lemonade. He had also used the young boy for sexual relief, when his equally abused wife had left home.

Mark Stewart's entire childhood was one of pain. He recalled crying in pain almost all of the time. As the memories flooded back, Mark Stewart, *The Thug*, sat down and refused to stand up.

As he was led out of court, several of the women and one man in the jury were close to tears. It was obvious the man who seemed like a monster had suffered more than anyone could imagine. Rupert Byron had simply died. Mrs. Daley had been raped, but Mark Stewart had been tortured almost every day of his childhood life. Mark Stewart was also a victim: a product of hell itself.

"We will take a break at this point," said Lord Simpson, "We will start again in twenty minutes."

Her Majesty's Advocate

Charlie Reid, Her Majesty's Advocate, sat down and opened a bottle of mineral water in the luxurious rest area. A few legal practitioners said their *'Hellos',* but he did not hear them. He had thought this was a clear-cut case, but like so many trials this was not simply an instance of bad people, doing bad things. It was a tragedy - a legacy of abuse resulting in terrible consequences. His confidence was shaken. How could he push to convict Mark Stewart having heard all that? He decided to focus on Gregor Davies and if that failed there was always Davie Allen. After all, Gegsy Davies seemed to control Mark Stewart, and Allen must have known the nature of those blue pills. The Viagra was just a story, surely? The others had not been abused as children? Surely there were people out there who were simply bad and needed to be punished? He thought about Mark Stewart again. He had been punished every day of his early life and

what had that accomplished? Unjustified and entirely improper punishment had created a monster.....his train of thought was interrupted by a police officer carrying a cup of coffee.

It was David Ross.

"Hello, Superintendent, what are you doing here?" asked Charlie Reid.

"I thought I'd check out this murder and rape trial in court six. It seems like a series of appalling, unprovoked crimes. My wife is joining me to hear the next session. She likes to try and understand the psychology of the perpetrators as you know."

"There will be no winners in this one, David," said Charlie Reid, wearily getting up to return to the reconvening tribunal.

Diane Ross was seated in the 'cheap seats' at the back, on the left-hand side as you enter the courtroom through the beautiful, new solid-wood oak doors. Her husband joined her and they held hands as he sat down. They always held hands.

"All stand!" shouted the clerk of the court as Lord Simpson entered. Simpson reconvened proceedings,

"Mr. Jameson, I will hear your deposition on behalf of Mr. Stewart. I will expect to see a medical report backing up your claims about his difficulties talking and I would like to see these CPA reports you refer to."

"Certainly, My Lord, I have them here," said Jameson, passing the files to the judge.

There were no surprises in Mark Stewart's testimony. He had taken the pills thinking they would make him have a better time with the girls. He said he could not remember anything after he took them. He claimed he knew nothing about attacking Rupert Byron or Mrs. Anne Daley. In the absence of any

witnesses (excepting Jason Jameson's presence in the toilet cubicle, which he was not about to admit) there was nothing to place Gegsy or *The Thug* in the toilets in Seaton Park, except for circumstantial evidence: traces of Rupert Byron's blood and brain tissue found on Mark Stewart's boots, and Rupert Byron had about his person, several blue pills of the same composition as those found in Davie Allen's flat and in the blood of Gegsy and *The Thug*.

Jameson dismissed this circumstantial, albeit real and material, evidence by suggesting to the court that the accused could have visited the toilets in a state of complete automatism, stepping in the blood, at any time, after Roo was killed, and before his body was discovered. Anyone who visited the toilets that day, after the murder, might have Roo's blood or soft tissue matter on their footwear. Similarly, the blue pills were a tenuous link because many druggies in that area could have taken the same. Fortunately for the defence, Davie Allen had taken the bag of around 500 pills into the flat with him. When he heard the police breaking down the door, he did the obvious thing. He flushed them down the toilet bowl. So the police had no idea that Gegsy and *The Thug* had a motive for the killing of Rupert Byron. Certainly, Gegsy had £800.00 in cash and the Hoor Master had £200.00, but they explained this was down to a good day on the horses, unlikely, but possible, and again circumstantial.

The case, therefore, rested heavily on the witness testimony of David Allen, aka the Hoor Master.

Davie Allen was called to the stand where he took the oath, although it's doubtful this meant anything to Davie. He was in court every other week and lied on every occasion he appeared.

The Hoor Master

"You are David Allen, 698h Mansion Avenue, Aberdeen?"

"Aye, Your Lordship," said Davie, smiling. A few laughs came from the public benches and the jury.

"I am not His Lordship, Mr. Allen. I am the Prosecuting Advocate acting for the Crown," said HMA modestly

"Aye – you are like the PF – sorry, man," said Davie, making 'PF' sound like a profanity.

"Mr. Allen, you are not on trial today for murder. You are a witness for the defence and it is my job to ensure that what you are saying, on behalf of the defence, is true."

"Aye man, it's true," said Davie sincerely.

"If you could wait until I ask you specific questions," said the Prosecutor. "These blue tablets which have been much spoken about and are a major part of the defence – where did you obtain these?"

"Fae a guy in a bar," said the Hoor Master.

"And what was this person's name?"

"Nae idea," said Davie.

"Come now, Mr. Allen, you are not telling me that a stranger in a bar offered you blue tablets comprising LSD, Ecstasy, Speed, Morphine and Crack-Cocaine and he did not know you?"

"He was fae Dundee, a male nurse. He says they wis Viagra, man," said Davie. "He was just up here for the day."

"How much did you pay him for the tablets?"

"Nothing, I just telt him aboot the hoorie pad in Tilly and he says 'Thanks, man,' and gies us the Viagra." Davie was now believing his own story.

"This man told you it was Viagra?"

"Aye, he says 'this'll gie thae hoories a pink flush,' and he telt me he got the Viagra at the hospital."

"A pink flush?" said Charlie Reid, immediately regretting the question.

"Aye, ye ken, how the lassies cheeks gang pink when they cum, man," said Davie grinning.

Davie knew how to play to the gallery.

Several jurists had to disguise smiles. Diane Ross was amused at the apparent innocence and consideration of Davie's comment. The idea that someone like Davie cared about giving a prostitute pleasure was a glimmer of hope in this dreadful business. She could think of many law-abiding men who could not care less about their partner's sexual satisfaction. She squeezed her husband's hand.

Charlie Reid, Her Majesty's Advocate, didn't know whether to laugh or cry. He remembered his job, his duty to the crown, and got tough.

"Mr. Allen, this is a murder trial. Please just answer the questions without the amusing anecdotes."

"Andidotes, man, fit antidotes?" said Davie.

Muffled laughter emanated from the jury despite the fact they knew this was a deadly serious matter. There was now a danger of this becoming farce.

"Ladies and gentlemen, please be silent. Anyone laughing in court will be removed!" barked Lord Simpson, "Mr. Reid, please frame your questions more appropriately. Mr. Allen, please be aware that if I deem it that you are being deliberately disruptive, you will be held in contempt of court and will face prosecution yourself," he added.

The courtroom fell silent.

"This is better than a movie," Diane Ross whispered to her husband.

David Ross was reflecting on the trial. The focus of attention in any criminal trial inevitably falls on the accused. The victim in a murder trial obviously cannot be there in person, so the only way of representing the victim is to have the grieving family members in court, but this just causes them further grief and angst. The jury will therefore be influenced by the behaviour, on the day, of the accused. If he is pitiful or funny then the jury will sympathise with the accused. If he looks dangerous and threatening then they will not sympathise with him, but either way at least the accused gets the chance to speak and be seen. The victim is silent. Ross considered this focus on the accused a serious flaw in the judicial system, particularly in rape and murder trials. Mrs. Daley was now in a geriatric ward; her nervous daughter had refused the chance to make a victim statement on behalf of her mother who had not spoken or eaten since the attack and was being kept alive by drip feeding. Her life ruined, it was hard to portray her misery to the court. Ross already knew this trial was a disaster for the prosecution and the victims of crime. He had realized, years ago, that the criminal courts were an exercise in damage limitation: *the hidden social sewers of society*. He looked at his wife and smiled back, without having heard her words.

"How many tablets did he give you, Mr. Allen?" continued HMA.

"I am nae sure, man, ah think it was aboot six," replied Davie.

"Isn't that rather a lot to be giving you free of charge?"

"Ah think he was awfa grateful, he had'na had it for a while," Davie quipped.

"Mr. Allen," said Lord Simpson, furiously. "This is your final warning!"

"Ok. He just put his hand in his pooch and gies me half a dozen,"

"What did you do with the tablets?" asked Reid.

"I took one that night and kept the rest to have with the lads the next day,"

"What was the result of taking that initial blue pill?"

"It gave us a real hard-on, man - it was that hard, it fair hurt," smiled Davie, lying beguilingly.

Despite their best efforts, two members of the jury laughed. It helped break the tension: ease the stress of the situation, and there was something about Davie Allen; an instinctive animal charm.

"That's enough," said Lord Simpson.

"We will break for twenty minutes."

Eventually, after the recess, order was restored. The jury was reminded again that they must not get involved with witness attempts to seduce them or make light of the matter.

Charlie Reid continued his questioning,

"Mr. Allen, I am sure we all want to go home soon so perhaps we can progress a bit faster."

"Sure, man. Nae sweat."

"You told the police that Mr. Stewart and Mr. Davies arrived at your flat around 3 p.m., at which time you had just risen?"

"Aye, man – yes that's right."

"You each consumed a blue pill and decided to visit a supposed brothel in Alexandra Terrace in Tillydrone?"

"I cannae remember onything after I took that blue bastard. I mean the blue pill," said the Hoor Master.

Davie had been well briefed by Jameson as to when his total alienation of reason and memory should have begun. The prosecutor pressed him,

"How did you feel after you took that blue pill? Happy, sexually aroused, sleepy; like you could fly?"

"Sorry, man. I just cannae remember," said Davie.

"Do you remember visiting the Woodside bar?"

"No."

"Do you remember seeing a police car in Don Street?"

"No."

"Do you recall telling the guard at 320 Alexandra Terrace you had one thousand pounds in cash?"

"No."

"Then how is it, Mr. Allen, that when the police found you in the first-floor flat, the alleged brothel, you immediately gave your name as Davie Allen? If your mind was not working correctly - how did you know your own name? And how did you remember the address of the supposed brothel in the first instance?"

"No idea. I can't remember."

"I put it to you David Allen that you knew very well these pills were not Viagra. I put it to you that, together with Gregor Davies and Mark Stewart, you knowingly and recklessly consumed hallucinogenic drugs, proceeded to go on a drinking binge and on entering 320-326 Alexandra Terrace, and having been refused entrance to the brothel, Mark Stewart and Gregor Davies entered the lower flat belonging to Mrs. Anne Daley where Mark Stewart brutally raped her and I put it to you that you are lying under oath to hide the truth and protect the accused who had taken these drugs in the full knowledge that they were not Viagra, but some combination of LSD, Ecstasy, Speed, Morphine and Crack-Cocaine."

"I am sorry, man. I really thought they wis Viagra and I cannae remember a thing aboot it," said Davie. It was a line he had practised a thousand times,

"All I can think is that there must have been some bad shit mixed in wi' thon Viagra." Davie was a liar, but he was not stupid.

David Allen, the Hoor Master, was excused and Gegsy and *The Thug* were put on the stand to hear the case against them.

The Case for the Prosecution

Charlie Reid, Her Majesty's Advocate Depute, stood up to make his closing speech on behalf of the Crown to the jury:

"Ladies and gentlemen of the jury, it is my duty on behalf of the Crown and that of my learned colleague, Mr. Jameson, on behalf of the Defence, to help you reach the right conclusion. This is not a battle between two sides fighting for a victory. It is an opportunity for the truth to be discovered and after all the facts have been disclosed then you must decide what you feel is the appropriate course of action to be taken.

Mr. Jameson, Lord Simpson and Her Majesty's Advocate are your guides leading you carefully and precisely to your destination – the correct verdict.

The Crown considers this to be a clear case of murder and rape. In the first case of murder, blood and brain tissue from the victim's body were found on Mr. Stewart's boots. The victim died from a blow to the head, possibly from a kick or a stamping blow.

Mr. Stewart is known to have a violent and temperamental disposition.

74

Both accused had taken the same blue pill containing the same cocktail of illegal substances that were found on the person of and inside the victim's body.

The accused were in possession of a large quantity of cash; they were known to be in the vicinity of the locus of the murder around the time of the murder and as we know they were later involved in the rape of an old lady. The act of rape was actually witnessed by police officers.

All the evidence suggests that Gregor Davies and Mark Stewart, either, went on the rampage, killing Rupert Byron, <u>after,</u> taking these drugs, or, they robbed and murdered Mr. Rupert Byron and <u>then</u> went on the rampage with the spoils of that murderous adventure.

Either way they are clearly guilty of his murder.

I cannot see any other reasonable explanation for the material evidence, the circumstances and the events of that day.

Mr. Jameson has pleaded the defence of non-insane automatism on behalf of the accused. This defence is effective <u>only</u> if the accused were not aware the alleged 'Viagra' was in fact a concoction of mind-altering drugs and also it must be shown they took due care to ensure the tablets consumed were indeed Viagra.

I do not believe for one moment the accused believed these tablets were Viagra and I certainly do not believe it has been shown they took any steps to ensure the source of these tablets was from prescription or a similar lawful, medically certified source.

Non-insane automatism is an obscure defence and although it has been attempted before it has never succeeded because there is a strict requirement to prove a total dissociation of mind and body. Put simply, this means that the person must have absolutely no idea what they are doing. Their bodies must act as if they had no mind. It is unlikely therefore the accused could visit a bar where they are regulars, sing football songs, recognise and run from a police car, find a house of ill-repute and talk their way into a place with a notoriously strict security guard if they had lost all powers of rational thought and reason. Remember that intoxication itself is not a defence in law to a criminal act.

In conclusion, I assert that Mr. David Allen is lying to protect his friends, Gregor Davies and Mark Stewart, who, either before or after knowingly taking illicit drugs killed Rupert Byron; and in the case of Mark Stewart, obviously raped a defenceless old lady.

There is only one verdict here today and that is guilty as charged, with the appropriate life sentences."

Charlie Reid sat down. He had kept it brief and simple. He knew he was right, but he dreaded the speech to follow.

At this point the jury would agree with him and return a verdict of 'guilty'. No doubt about it.

In a few minutes time, all that could change.

The Criminal Lawyer

Jason Jameson, the *Silver Fox*, stood up. Plentiful, grey locks swept back across his head, coupled with a permanent sun-tan, he looked more like a movie-star than a criminal lawyer in a small town in the North-East of Scotland. An impressive figure, standing at around six feet tall, he had wide shoulders and a noticeably small waist with no sign of any superfluous body fat. For a man of fifty he looked fantastic. He was also a fantastic actor and his best acting emotions were sympathy and remorse: sympathy expressed on behalf of his clients towards their victims because his job was mainly mitigation. In other words, his clients normally pleaded guilty, so his job was to minimize the sentence. His speeches invariably started with the words: *'My client appreciates that he has made an error and takes full responsibility for his actions; he is deeply, deeply sorry for the trouble he has caused and is taking the following immediate steps to ensure that it never happens again....'*

But not today!

Today, he was going to win a great victory and he would become the most celebrated criminal lawyer in the country.

Like all great orators he started with a pause...

He held the pause for a full ten seconds, looking every member of the jury in the eye, hypnotizing them. Ten seconds is an eternity in a packed courtroom during a murder trial. Several members of the jury were already so impressed with Jameson they should have been removed for personal prejudice. Sun Tzu:

'The war is won before battle commences'

77

The Defence of Non-insane Automatism

The *Silver Fox* smiled warmly at the jury,

"Ladies and gentlemen of the jury, as you know, this is a murder trial. Fifty years ago a person convicted of murder would be taken to a place a few hundred yards from here, the Gallowgate, and hung by the neck in a barbaric ritual and spectacle that has now, in these more enlightened times, thankfully, been abolished.

In the old days, innocent people were often wrongly convicted and killed just to satisfy society's need to see justice done and to satisfy that same society's blood lust. Make no mistake about it, ladies and gentlemen - wrongly convicting someone of murder is little short of murder itself. In the past it was actual murder, when an innocent person was unjustly executed, but even now you are robbing that innocent person of their freedom and reputation forever.

*The stigma of a murder conviction can be even worse than the life sentence in prison. It is for these reasons that we require the Crown to prove the accused are guilty beyond **all** reasonable doubt. If there is even the slightest doubt then you <u>must</u> acquit, because they are then **not guilty**."*

The *Silver Fox* paused, reflecting on the absolute truth and massive significance of this revelation before continuing:

*"Not only is there extreme doubt in this case, but the circumstances suggest that even if the accused were by some amazing coincidence connected with the sad and extremely regrettable death of Mr. Byron, then they were **not responsible nor culpable** for any of their actions on that day."*

Jameson specifically addressed this last comment to Rupert Byron's mother. He was so sympathetic that she believed his oratory to the extent that she wondered who could possibly have killed her son.

The defender of justice continued,

"The toilets in Seaton Park are a place no doubt visited by many people. It has been said that homosexuals and drug users visit and use this building, but so, no doubt, do many innocent parties. It is not a crime to enter a public convenience. It is fair to assume that Mr. Byron had been in that building for some purpose because his body was discovered there. It is also possible Mark Stewart was there at some time after Mr. Byron was attacked, but this does not make Mark Stewart guilty of murder. We simply do not know what happened in those toilets that day. We can make guesses or assumptions, but there will always be reasonable doubt about what actually happened and for this reason alone we cannot condemn either of the accused based on purely circumstantial evidence."

"Let me now turn to the most unfortunate incident regarding Mrs. Anne Daley. As I hope I have demonstrated, Mr. Stewart has had what can only be described as a tragic upbringing. He has been beaten, abused, even tortured, his entire life."

"Mr. Stewart is the product of a selfish society. Sadly we are all too busy and too preoccupied with our own problems to ensure the children of strangers are protected twenty four hours a day. We all hope the authorities and agencies will do this job on our behalf, but they, too, are stretched and have limited resources."

"The result of this lack of proper care are young men like Gregor Davies and Mark Stewart who have essentially fallen out of normal society and continue to be neglected even as adults. They have no role-models apart from abusive parents; they have no educational qualifications because they have never had the encouragement or the peace and stability to study; and in the end, they do not have the stable personalities required to secure a job and a family."

"The rape of Mrs. Daley is an appalling tragedy, but so is the life of Mark Stewart, ladies and gentlemen. All I can I ask of you is not to add to this young man's tragedy, without giving him the benefit of the doubt – the benefit of all reasonable doubt."

Jameson paused again for reflection and dramatic effect, before continuing,

"Drugs are without doubt the curse of our society and of course the most common factor in many crimes of the type we are deciding today is the drug called alcohol. Most violent crime would be ended today if we could remove alcohol from society, but instead its circulation is encouraged because, I assume, of the vast amount of money it generates."

"My point is this, ladies and gentlemen; please do not be prejudiced because drugs may be involved in this case because anyone who has consumed alcohol has taken a mind-altering drug, it just so happens that alcohol is a <u>lawful</u> mind-altering drug."

"Finally, you will recall that Mr. Reid said the defence of non-insane automatism has never succeeded in Scots law. Well, that is both true and yet misleading at the same time."

"The defence has been accepted as a valid one in leading cases such as **Ross**[3], but the facts did not match the strict criteria in that case. In <u>this</u> case the facts most certainly do match the criteria. The defendants sincerely believed they were taking Viagra to prepare them for some amorous pursuits. They had no idea they were taking something that might seriously affect their mood or judgement."

"It is this unanticipated, unaware consumption of a mind-altering drug that makes the consequences so dangerous. After ingestion, when the drugs take effect, the mind is unable to comprehend the changes it is experiencing. It is these unexpected and unanticipated effects of the drug on the unwary brain that some believe, cause the mind to temporarily cease functioning altogether, leaving only the subconscious motor functions to automatically operate the body."

"The hapless victim becomes a mindless robot with no conscious mind. In Scots law, this mindless state means the accused cannot be guilty of a criminal act because they do not have what is known as **mens rea,** or in other words, there is no guilty mind. They have, in effect, no mind. Without mens rea there is no crime in Scots Law."

Jameson paused for the last time.

His incredible grasp of psychology and medical science caused some of the jury members to nod in agreement. Several of the women thought he was Dr. Kildare. If only they knew the truth.

Her Majesty's Advocate shook his head in disbelief at his charming adversary's audacity and thespian genius.

---

3 Ross v. HMA, 1991 S.L.T. 564

"Ladies and gentlemen, I apologise for having taken more of your time than I anticipated, but I would rather stand here forever than see a single innocent person convicted of murder or rape."

"In this case there is not only considerable doubt, as I trust I have amply demonstrated, but there is also a complete defence."

"I ask you therefore to bring in the only possible verdict and that verdict is one of **not guilty.**"

Jason Jameson sat down and looked at Charlie Reid. Charlie Reid felt sick. He tried not to show it.

It was obvious to any professional with experience of the criminal courts that the accused were guilty beyond any reasonable doubt, but Jameson was quite brilliant, and Reid feared the worst.

Lord Simpson

Lord Simpson directed the jury,

"Ladies and gentlemen, I think the case has been eloquently presented by both the Crown and the Defence. It only remains for me to explain to you your role in this trial and the verdicts open to you. You are not here to decide on matters of the law. That is my job. You are here to decide on the facts. If you do not understand the law, then you must ask me for an explanation of the law, if this is preventing you from coming to a decision based on the facts. If you believe, based on the facts, that the accused persons are guilty of murder, and as Mr. Jameson pointed out, your belief must be 'beyond reasonable doubt', then you must bring in a verdict of guilty.

If you honestly believe there is some reasonable doubt as to the facts of the case against them, then you must find them <u>not</u> guilty.

In the case of the charge of the rape of Mrs. Daley, it is rather more complicated. If you believe that Mark Stewart had no controlling mind, to the point that he had no mind whatsoever, and that this was due to an external factor, of which he had no knowledge, then he has a defence in non-insane automatism and this is a complete defence. If he had no mind, due to no fault of his own, then he is not guilty.

Similarly, if you believe, based on the facts, that one or both accused caused the death of Rupert Byron, then the same defence of non-insane automatism is available, but only if you truly believe the facts support this. Much of this will depend on the extent to which you find David Allen a credible witness and how much weight you give to the circumstantial evidence.

Finally, should you feel that the accused cannot be found, 'not guilty', but the case against them has not been proven beyond all reasonable doubt, then you may, under Scot's Law, find them 'not proven', but I must advise against this third verdict because it is generally considered unsatisfactory to all parties."

"Please now retire and consider your verdict."

The Road to Hell

David Ross drove home from the High Court in philosophical mood. The result had been controversial. Old Mrs. Daley's relatives and friends had threatened to 'get even' with Mark Stewart, Gregor Davies and Davie Allen.

Her Majesty's Advocate, Charlie Reid, had uncharacteristically lost his temper and asked for the jury's verdict to be disallowed by Lord Simpson as 'incompetent'.

Lord Simpson, after a heated debate with Reid, threatened to hold him in contempt of court. A crowd had gathered outside, threatening Jason Jameson, who needed a police-escort to assure his safety. Gegsy's 'two-fingered' salute to the press photographers gave the iconic impression that the legal system had been conquered, once and for all, by the accused 'criminals'.

Driving home, Ross was thankful he could leave it all behind and return to the paradise of his marriage and his family home. His beautiful wife, Diane, sat next to him, kissing the back of his hand. She was curiously happy with the verdict. She felt Mark Stewart in particular deserved a break after his appalling and horrendous childhood, '*It would be a terrible travesty of natural justice if he was now to be jailed for life after being tortured as a helpless, young boy*'. She had a beautiful and compassionate heart, he could not criticise her for that, but he saw the other side of the verdict. Criminals would see this as *carte blanche* to run riot, safe in the knowledge there was a strong chance of acquittal. The public would scream for more stringent laws and harsher punishments. The press would blame the police and the criminal prosecution

system. Lord Simpson would be severely criticised and Jason Jameson would become infamous; a hero to the myriad misfits and growing number of anti-social individuals in society. The future looked bleak; animosity and hatred escalating between the law-abiding majority and the lawless minority. Tolerance and leniency would be the losers in this war of attrition; the criminal justice system would be eroded by the endless accusations and recriminations.

Ross could already see and hear calls for the restoration of the death penalty from cranks and extremists. Justice had to be seen to be done and that had not happened today.

The natural sympathy of fifteen compassionate individuals had been the accidental catalyst for what could become the kind of loss of faith in law and order that leads to anarchy.

'The road to hell is paved with good intentions'

Rose Cottage

Rose Cottage was beautiful that evening; a perfect mid-summer sunset; the sky a light baby-blue, purple-pink and orange-red. Summer nights were never black in Aberdeen; daybreak was early, around 4 a.m. A sexy and fecund time of year; life in evidence everywhere, Rose Cottage was an oasis for wildlife: barn-owls, deer, sparrow-hawks, foxes, blue tits, great tits, coal tits, red squirrels to name just a few; the whole place was immersed in the wonders of nature.

David and Diane Ross were celebrating their tenth wedding anniversary and because they had two young children they were celebrating at home. Diane had dressed to please her husband in a long, gossamer-silk, black dress. It stuck to her, displaying her perfect curves in the finest detail.

A stunning woman, a little above average height, around five feet seven inches with disproportionately long legs, her backside was a perfect hemisphere. She had a tiny waist and wonderfully pert breasts: an athletic yet feminine physique; testament to her many sporting achievements as a young woman, winning medals for both swimming and sprinting. Her hair was raven-black; her dark blue eyes turned green when she was angry or particularly aroused. He called her 'Succubus' because of her magic eyes and her bedroom talents. A few freckles around her upper cheeks gave her a youthful countenance, earning her the pet name, 'Baby Cheeks'. She was the other half of his whole life.

The two married lovers stood drinking champagne by a crackling open fire in the small rear lounge that overlooked the river; a snug by name and snug by nature.

Rose Cottage was old, with thick stone walls. The snug had a solid feel; rustic and homely. An exposed granite wall housed a lovely original old cast-iron fire surround. The remainder of the room was painted dark red and featured a couple of large comfortable sofas on a dark, natural-wood floor. French doors led out of the snug into an antique conservatory, recently renovated and modernised to include a mini-observatory with the latest optical and refracting telescopes. To create the maximum atmosphere the upper section of the conservatory withdrew back inside the roof of the house via a motorised contraption revealing the glittering parade of flickering diamonds cast in the dark red-blue night-sky above. This heavenly display contrasted beautifully with the luxurious flames devouring the copious wooden log crackling in the open fire.

The couple moved to the conservatory.

Diane strutted to look into one of the telescopes.

Peering into the eyepiece she pushed out her perfectly sculpted gluteus maximus provoking a response from her husband who never took his eyes off her perfect behind.

"How is your Uranus looking this evening, Baby Cheeks?" he quipped.

"You tell me, Big Boy," she teased him, slowly moving her hips from side to side.

"What can you see with your oculars?"

"Infinity and beyond," she replied.

"Is that Nietzche or Buzz Light-year?"

"Same thing; both thought they were Supermen. Buzz was cuter."

Ross was contemplative, watching his gorgeous wife's pert buttocks as she peered into the telescope, outer-space-wards,

"Do you realize that if time and space are infinite, then there are infinite possibilities; leading to the inevitability of identical events occurring in parallel worlds, universes and galaxies..." he proffered.

"Is that Nietzche or Buzz Light-year, Zarathustra?" She knew it was not Buzz.

"Meaning, if you believe in an infinite Universe and infinite time, then somewhere else, right now, I am watching your gluteus maximus and thinking about cunnilingus," he concluded, sagaciously.

"Ooh, lucky space-girl! But time and the Universe are not infinite. The Universe came into being a finite period of time in the past and will end, at a finite time in the future. Infinity is a concept not a reality: reality is all about 'big bangs'." Pressing her point, she wiggled her booty, provocatively, looking at him over her shoulder; she winked before returning her baby blues to the eyepiece. He smiled,

"Do you like big bangs?"

"Ooh yes!" she replied.

Diane was unusually tall this evening thanks to the four inch high-heels of her latest extravagance, Manolo Blahnik Brazil Velcro Sandals in black velvet. Her '*Manolos*' pushed her backside up and out, accentuating her booty, bringing out the stallion in her lover.

"Just you keep looking in there, Baby Cheeks. I have business with your ass."

He massaged her firm, round buttocks through the sheer, silky dress as she pushed her uber-ass into him encouragingly, moaning softly. His touch became more intimate, his fingers moved between her legs tracing out the lines of her labia; his thumb teased her anus. "Don't move," he bade her softly.

Looking into the telescope, her mind drifted out into the distant nebula. She smiled, eagerly anticipating her darling husband's next move. Even though she knew exactly what would transpire - each event, every touch, every word would be enjoyed; savoured; as it always was between them.

Her lover dropped to his knees and lifted the long dress, displaying her beautiful calf muscles and fine ankles. Kissing the backs of her legs, he started just above the ankle, working his way up to her thighs. She continued looking out into the ever-expanding darkness of the universe, drifting dreamily, her wetness increasing; the beginnings of her first orgasm slowly building.

Carefully, he revealed her breathtaking backside. It was decorated in a black velvet thong, stylish, matching her elegant designer high-heeled sandals. The tiny g-string was designer dental floss; just enough to wrap up her most precious parts; sufficient to delay the ultimate pleasure for her: maximise the excitement for him.

He moved slowly up the back and inside of her thighs, carefully caressing her delicate skin with his lips and tongue; he looked up at the tiny pout between her legs: sexual heaven in black velvet. Massaging her wondrous crotch with the top of his head, he gently nibbled her inner thighs.

He took a mouthful of chilled Veuve Clicquot; his wife smiled and purred as she looked deep into the night sky. Ross was a stud and a great lover. He was considerate; his wife's pleasure, his first priority. She enjoyed contrasts, a variety of sensations, so he knew she was going to like his next move. His mouth full of cold champagne, he carefully pulled her thong to one side, tight across the middle of her right buttock.

Putting one hand on each butt-cheek, he pulled them apart revealing her breathtaking, pink-paradise.

He paused to look at this wonder of nature, this azimuth of erotic art before slowly releasing the chilled bubbly, first into her anus and then, more generously, into her hot stickiness. She gasped, pushing her champagne-filled pudendum back into his face; he licked out all the fizzy contents; a cat that's just got the crème de la crème.

He licked her eagerly to a shuddering, cosmic orgasm.

Quivering and glowing, her tongue instinctively dashed deep into his mouth; an intimate, loving French kiss of gratitude - pure sexual lust; their evening of passion just beginning.

"Did you have a Big Bang, Baby Cheeks?"

"Infinitely," she purred contentedly; happily contradicting her own theory of time and space.

Intellectual sparring was ever-present between these two love-birds, inevitably leading to ever more intense love-making. They never quarreled; they debated and made love; simple and simply perfect.

Walking hand in hand away from the telescope, they discussed law and order. Diane provoked her husband; controversial, impishly.

"I am glad they got off with it today."

He could still taste her in his mouth, a taste he could not live without; the nectar of the succubus. He knew this was a purely hypothetical discussion preceding the next act of love-making, to follow very soon judging by his wife's rosy cheeks and flashing emerald green eyes.

"You are playing Devil's Advocate," he replied.

She allowed a sandal to drop from her left leg and started running her bare foot up the inside of his thigh, teasing him, watching him get harder.

"Not me. The Devil's Advocate was in court today, acting for the defence."

She smiled and continued,

"Those boys were just the conduit; society is to blame for those crimes. Society failed to protect Mark Stewart; the other two are victims of social neglect. It's no good sending in the police to arrest them after the event. If they had a proper upbringing, decent parents, good housing and education they would never have been in court. If you were not a fascist official of the police state you might agree with me." She moved forward a little, rubbing his erection using both her bare feet; cupping it delicately with her insoles; she was an expert at such little pleasantries.

Ross was distracted, but he chastised his wife's wayward thesis,

"That's idealistic nonsense and you know it. You know quite well that some people are just plain evil. The Yorkshire Ripper, the Moors Murderers and many more. They were not the product of social depravation. They were just depraved."

"I thought you liked depraved?" she replied, displaying extraordinary pedal dexterity, successfully unbuttoning his trousers; withdrawing his throbbing erection using only her tiny, painted-red toes. He looked at her, captivated: the button nose, the freckles, those green eyes, dark-blue before she had climaxed; the long, soft black hair with a hint of natural henna: her incredible scent. She was surely some ancient spirit of femininity, reincarnated in the most beguiling form imaginable. Ross knew his wife was no normal woman. She was remarkable: he was in awe.

91

He took a mouthful of champagne and relaxed as she moved her insoles up and down the expanding shaft of his aching hardness.

"Ok, my Lord and Master, I will concede that there are exceptions. There are genuinely evil people, but those boys are products of a societal illness. The real issue is that the people at the top don't care; they are isolated from the consequences, hiding in tax-havens, sitting on yachts in Monaco or villas in the Bahamas, protected by security guards and close circuit television. Criminal law is ninety per cent damage limitation. It's cheaper to prosecute and incarcerate pathetic offenders than it is to give low achievers a decent standard of living."

"Is that the end of your little polemic? Up the revolution! The proletariat is uprising," he replied.

"I see you are up-rising," purred Diane Ross.

She moved forward on all fours looking up at him with her impudent, enlarged pixie-green eyes.

His shaft in her left hand, she pulled back its wrapper making the swollen head even bigger. She made small circles with the end of her right index finger around the tip of his glans. She knew this drove him crazy with pleasure. The Succubus adopted a catlike posture, sticking up her round, pert buttocks facing away from him. She knew he would want to see and touch her sex, but he wasn't getting to. It was her turn to take control. Maintaining a firm grip with her left hand on his warm erection, she put her soft moist lips to his tight scrotum and started licking beneath his testes occasionally letting her tongue touch his anus, driving him crazy with the sensation. She licked his perineum and his hard balls until finally she started her blow-job.

Giving pleasure was a pleasure for her.

Love-making was a symphony and sucking him to a climax was the crescendo.

She began by licking the thin, shiny membrane of his taught, pulsing, purple velvet with the back of her tongue looking up at him, wide-eyed, from the depths of her lustrous, long black hair.

He focused on restraint; not coming too soon; easier said than done as she started probing the underside of his enlarged bulb using only the end of her tongue.

She was ready to take him in her mouth.

She began by sucking his throbbing cherry-head like a lollipop. She used long, slow, sensual sucks; loving, totally committed. It was no chore. It was her delight. She was his wife, his equal, and, when she wanted to be - his slut. She opened her throat and took his full seven inches in her mouth massaging his membrane with her tonsils, demonstrating her deep throat abilities.

He was unlikely to hold out much longer.

Working his shaft in her mouth and his tight scrotum in her left hand, she removed the one false nail she maintained on the middle finger of her right hand, exposing the short, manicured nail deliberately kept this way for a special purpose.

He sucked her middle finger before she carefully pushed it deep into his anus stimulating his prostate; faster and faster; deeper and deeper - she licked and sucked. He erupted, volcanically; screaming:

"Ooooooooooohhhhh Woooowwwwwwww!"

A torrent of sperm pumped up his pulsating manhood: exploding; a massive orgasm of brilliant white semen. She captured it in her mouth; licking, sucking the excess from his sensitive, swollen velvet organ.

He screamed; bucking involuntarily; spasms of excruciating pleasure; her firm grip squeezing his pulsating, sperm-drenched penis, she sucked him hungrily like the succubus she must truly be, teasing out every last drop; the source of her two beautiful children; the epicentre of his sexual love for her.

She loved sucking his cock.

She took a mouthful of champagne and passed it from her lips into his mouth, kissing him deeply, massaging him with her sticky tongue.

"Now that's what I called depraved," she said proudly.

Her eyes sparked like emeralds.

He was emotional, tearful - in love.

"Honey, I love you more than words can ever say."

"I know," she purred, "Now have a glass of this champagne and fuck my brains out, you horny bastard!"

The Press

The Aberdeen Guardian carried the following
headlines and story the next day.

'MURDERERS AND RAPIST WALK FREE!
<u>NOT PROVEN</u> VERDICT SHOCK.
APPALLING CRIMES GO UNPUNISHED!'
'LOCAL MP CALLS FOR REVIEW OF LEGAL
SYSTEM.'

Aberdeen citizens were stunned to hear the verdict
reached by a jury of 15 at the High Court yesterday.
Two men were effectively acquitted of the murder of a
young male student and the rape of a defenceless,
wheelchair-bound old woman, despite being caught
red-handed by the police.

Legal loopholes, obscure legal defences and
Scotland's notorious NOT PROVEN *'third verdict'* has
enabled these two monsters to escape justice and
roam our streets tonight - free to commit similar
atrocities. This story, including the views of leading
citizens, is on page seven today - where we ask the
question:

*'Criminal justice in Scotland, who does it protect,
the victim or the criminal?'*

Belmont Street

Peter 'Pete' Auld had been out for a few drinks with colleagues from work. A physical education teacher at the city's prestigious Robert Gordon's private school for the children of the well-heeled, he was an affable guy; 28 years old, tall and slim with blonde hair and a little goatee tuft of beard; he looked like movie-star heartthrob Brad Pitt.

Belmont Street and the adjoining Academy Centre are Aberdeen's trendiest areas, restored and upgraded to give a rustic, authentic feel, comprising cobbled streets and pedestrian only access. Several magnificent churches have been transformed into bars and nightclubs and the old City Academy has been changed from a schoolhouse into restaurants, bars and shops. At weekends, there is a farmers' market; various stalls sell fish, fruit, flowers and a plethora of candy sweets and cheap fluffy toys.

The only blot on this thriving landscape is the omnipresence of the ubiquitous street beggar. Seemingly everywhere on the streets of Scotland's major cities, they sit slumped, begging bowls in their lap, in a vacuous, heroin-induced stupor as shoppers and passers-by ignore them completely.

To a stranger, from another more civilised culture, this must appear a very strange propinquity indeed - wealthy, healthy shoppers oblivious to the misery and destitution existing so close as to be visible in their own peripheral vision.

Belmont Street is devoid of shoppers in the evenings when it becomes an area of a thousand bars. Pete and his friends had been in several of these experiencing a *Gorilla Fart*, an *Anal Probe*, some *Witch Tits* and an *Elbow in the Boobs*.

He had also enjoyed a particularly delightful *Tight Snatch*, then *Masturbation* and he had swallowed several large *Orgasms*.

Yes, Pete and his fellow teachers had been playing a drinking game, ordering the silliest cocktails on the menu. The mixture of Vodka, Rum, Schnapps, Pernod, Gin and other alcoholic beverages left Pete feeling dizzy, and because he had a football match at 9 a.m., the following morning, he decided to drop out at midnight, go home and get some sleep.

Pete headed off up Belmont Street towards Union Street where he could flag down a taxi. He crossed Union Street and headed down towards Market Street, hoping to catch one ahead of the crowds amassing further up the road. As he passed the *Virgin Records* store he vaguely noticed four youths in hoods, lurking in the doorway.

The next thing Pete noticed was his own nose bursting open in an explosion of red blood and excruciating pain.

Blood poured out so fast and thick that he was temporarily blinded. Within minutes his white shirt was crimson red. Now in shock, he needed urgent assistance.

No assistance was forthcoming.

If you see a man with a profusely bleeding nose, late at night, smelling of alcohol, swaying backwards and forwards, crying for help - would you stop and assist him? Probably not and neither did anyone else that night.

Three of the four youths drew out their mobile phones and replayed the short video they had just captured of their fourth member smashing Pete in the face with a fist.

Pete could only vaguely hear the malicious taunts,

"Fucking, *happy-slapping*, mate!"
"Aye - fit a fucking twat!"

Pete collapsed, sobbing, trying to stem the blood with his sleeve. The pain in his nose and head was unbearable. He threw up in the gutter.

"Disgusting!" said a couple of young women stepping over Pete as if he was a beggar or a heroin addict.

Pete couldn't get a taxi that night. No taxi driver would allow him in their car. One concerned citizen did, finally, flag down a police car. Pete was arrested for a breach of the peace and taken to Aberdeen Royal Infirmary where he waited a further two hours to have his nose repaired.

He missed football the next day.

The video of the hooded attacker brutally smashing Pete's nose to a pulp was on www.happyslapper.com the next day for the entertainment of assailants everywhere and much to the amusement of the four youths.

Pete sat in his lounge staring at the television. It was switched off. He had six stitches and a splint on his nose. He was in pain and finding it hard to breathe.

In his right hand was an aluminum baseball bat.

Danny 'The Fanny'

Danny 'The Fanny' Thompson was auditioning a new girl.

He was smoking a Double Corona Cohiba Havana Cuban cigar, his favourite at around ninety dollars each. This was despite the fact that smoking was now banned in all public places including lap dancing bars.

Danny couldn't care less. It was his club.

They could stick their smoking ban up their ass!

The air was suffocating; thick with the pungent aromatic tobacco smoke. The Latvian girl in front of him was struggling to cavort erotically in the claustrophobic booth filled with the stench of the fumes and Danny's appalling body odour.

Danny 'The Fanny' enjoyed this exquisite torture. He had initially opened his lap dancing club for two reasons – naked women and money.

He still loved the money, but he was bored with the women. This one was new to lap dancing and 'just off the boat' from Latvia. She was actually a sweet girl looking to make money from her perfect body to send home to her family and hopefully meet a nice guy to marry. Danny had seen hundreds like her and he was sick of them. She was dressed as a schoolgirl in a small black pleated skirt and little white blouse tied at the front just below her pert, natural breasts. Her long hair was bunched in two pigtails. She was 5 feet 8 inches, slim, long legs, long blonde hair, green eyes, very beautiful, but Danny couldn't care less. He was immune to female charms; mildly curious to see her 'gash', as he referred to the female genitalia, but beyond that he just wanted to know if she would assist with his latest business venture.

Danny was expanding. Lap dancing wouldn't pay for his new villa in Marbella, but beautiful, fresh girls willing to do 'extras' might. He had a technique for quickly assessing if a new girl would go further than just exposing her body and pressing her breasts in the punters' faces; he was just biding his time, putting up with her until then, "Hurry up and get yer kit off," he barked, impatiently.

Mirka was upset at his comment, but tried not to show it. If she was going to be a stripper she would be an artist. A promising medical student, she could not resist taking a year out to seek her fortune in Europe's oil capital. Swallowing her pride, she accelerated her performance. It was almost impossible to be sexy for this disgusting man.

Danny was now about fifty. Small, fat and smelly, he resembled his namesake, Danny DeVito; only larger and fatter with a Scottish accent and without the comic genius. He always wore short-sleeved shirts that were a size too small. He liked to think he was slimmer and fitter than he really was.

Tonight, Danny was wearing black trousers and a black silk *Gucci* shirt. His belly-button was clearly visible through buttons five and six of his shirt. Buttons, one to three, were also undone, exposing his thick, black hairy chest. The button on his trousers was under so much pressure from his swollen gut that it might fly off at any moment. A patent black *Gucci* belt helped ensure the whole ensemble was protected from the stresses and strains exerted by his excessive, subcutaneous blubber. A thick gold chain hung around his neck; gold jewellery decorated his right wrist and right hand. Danny liked how gold looked against the dark hair that covered his entire body.

"I go faster," said Mirka.

She whipped off her top and Danny noticed she had fabulous breasts, so firm they hardly sagged at all; emerging straight outwards as if two oranges had been implanted into her rib cage.

"Are you sure those are real?" Danny asked suspiciously. Implants were no longer in vogue. Customers wanted 'natural' girls - sweet and innocent.

"I am a very genuine," said Mirka, who had not yet mastered the indefinite article.

As Danny was clearly bored, Mirka was hoping she could just take off her skirt and keep on her thong. She felt sure that the real customers would be nicer than this fat, smelly brute. She would take off her knickers for these nice customers, but not for him.

Her skirt fell to the floor.

Danny was impressed. He had seen so many crotches that he only got vaguely interested if the girls looked unusual or, even better, underage.

This one, he thought, could pass for sixteen or seventeen.

The little pouting part between her legs seemed tiny, almost immature; money in the bank. Danny was waiting to see what was under her little white thong.

Doing her best to gyrate her hips at a safe distance, she was out of luck if she thought she could escape taking off her pants.

"Right let's have the money shot," snapped Danny, dismissively.

"I am a sorry?" replied Mirka.

"Your pussy, let's see your pussy!"

Mirka froze. She thought this would be easy. It wasn't. Only her boyfriends had seen her 'little Mirka'. She had never shown it to a stranger. Although proud of her body, her vagina had so far remained private.

Danny feigned a smile.

"I won't bite it."

"Ok." She thought she might cry.

Slowly, she pulled down her pants exposing the little pink outer lips of her labia majeur. Unusually for a stripper, she was unshaven, and she had platinum blonde pubic hair. And it was 'natural'. For Danny this was a windfall. It was like discovering the old table and chairs your Grandmother left you are Chippendale. This woman could be worth a fortune.

Mirka carefully threaded her platform boots through the legs of her thong and stood with her hands over her pubis looking sideways, rather ashamed.

"Well..." said Danny, *The Fanny.*

"I sorry?" said Mirka.

"The money shot!"

Mirka looked blankly at her new boss.

"Come here, turn around and bend over..." said Danny with exasperation.

Mirka didn't like the sound of this one bit, but she had come this far, she told herself, so she must be brave. She moved closer and turned around.

"Bend forward, put one hand on each ass-cheek and pull 'em apart. I want to see your asshole," said Danny charmingly.

Mirka wanted to walk out and go straight back to Latvia. She did not want a big house in the UK anymore. She wanted to go home and see her family and her old boyfriend Timur.

"For fuck's sake, do you want to make money or not?" pressed Danny.

Mirka thought about the money as she put her hands on her buttocks.

Her fingernails were beautifully manicured with clear gloss varnish decorated with tiny silver beads in the shape of an inverted V.

Danny could smell her perfume and her sweat.

He wanted to fuck her, not because she was beautiful, but because she was shy and frightened and he was excited by the fact that she obviously found him repulsive. He decided that he would fuck her in the next few weeks.

Resigned to her fate, Mirka reluctantly pulled her ass-cheeks apart and leaned forward exposing her anus and her open vagina to Danny.

Danny felt like a God.

Mirka's anus was pink just like her vagina. Her vagina glistened under the small halogen spotlights, her natural moisture making her pussy-lips look as shiny as the little beads on her fingernails.

"Just hold that position for a few minutes," said Danny enjoying himself.

Feeling degraded and violated, she recalled the first time she had inserted a tampon during her first period. She was eleven years old and had felt so dirty putting that thing inside 'little Mirka'. It was an appropriate memory for what happened next.

Danny was a pervert, but he was also a shrewd businessman. He needed to know if Mirka would be useful only as a dancer or if she could also be deployed in his new scheme. What happened next was Danny putting his toe in, to test the water.

Danny's cigar was a big cigar, wider and thicker than the thumb on an average male adult. Danny's thumb was like Danny, 'fat', so his cigar was about the thickness of his own, fat thumb.

He took the cigar out of his mouth.

It was wet and sticky because you don't just smoke a cigar - you suck it and chew on it. He took this wet, sticky, saliva-covered roll of hard-packed Havana tobacco and pushed it straight up, inside Mirka's unsuspecting little pink vagina.

It went in about two inches, about the length of his thumb.

Mirka was initially stunned.

It was so unexpected as to be unbelievable.

She jumped forward and turned, looking at him, hatefully; ready to cry and stab him through the heart at the same time.

This disgusting, fat, smelly pig of a man who had told her there was never any touching in this business had put his thumb in her most special private place; her face glowed red.

Danny lifted up his cigar to show her he had not actually touched her with his thumb or any other part of his body. The end of his cigar was now considerably wetter and stickier than it had been when it left his slobbering mouth.

He knew he had taken this as far as he could at this stage and put his hand into this shirt pocket.

"Ok. Take this." He handed her a fifty pound note.

"And if anyone tries that when you are working, you tell me and we will have the fucker arrested," he joked.

Mirka grabbed the money, picked up her clothes and made a hasty exit in the direction of the Ladies. She was going to have the bastard killed.

When she was in the Ladies toilet, however, and after she had had a little cry, something unexpected came over her.

Sitting on the toilet, she started to stroke 'little Mirka'; squeezing her right nipple, frantically rubbing her clitoris within ninety seconds she had a spasm of intense pleasure, beginning in her clit and bursting outwards and upwards across her whole body. She squeezed her nipple uncontrollably, almost crushing it as she came.

Shocked, but feeling more comfortable, more in control, she looked at the fifty pound note. This was a week's wages in Latvia; she had earned it in five minutes and had a spectacular orgasm into the bargain.

She smiled. She would do this job and make a lot of money. She would still have that fat, smelly pig killed, but not quite yet.

Danny relaxed in the booth. He put the cigar up to his nose and took a deep inhalation. The rich tobacco aroma was now laced with the scent of Mirka. It was a strong female smell of musky sex: strawberries, licquorice and honey. Danny squeezed his unexpected erection, his first in six months. He was almost impotent so it was a great occurrence. He licked her juice off the end of the cigar and put the sticky butt of the cigar back between his lips. It tasted sweet and sour. Mirka was going to be good for business and good for Danny. He got up and walked to the bar, his penis as hard as Aberdeen granite.

"Give me a bottle of Dom Perignon," he instructed the barman.

The barman, who had never sold or indeed opened a bottle of the champagne that sold for one hundred and fifty pounds in the club, looked gob-smacked.

Danny spotted Mirka emerging from the toilets wearing a long, white, skin-tight dress and glowing warm pink.

"Two glasses," His cock drilled into the bar.

"Come and have a drink with the boss, on the house, angel," he said to Mirka.

Mirka looked at him and thought about the fifty pound note in her purse. She had never tasted real champagne in her life.

"Ok. I have one drink. Then I go," she said.

"No problem," said Danny 'The Fanny'.

Danny was looking forward to working with Mirka.

Mirka had taken her first steps towards becoming a highly desirable call-girl.

A Moment of Bliss

Diane Ross had established a thriving business based on the correct assumption that many successful, responsible people need to talk, and the best person to listen is a professional; an understanding, intelligent stranger; an expert with no vested interest or bias.

People use business partners, friends and spouses for advice, but sometimes they are too close to stand outside the box. With a doctorate in philosophy, she was able to draw upon the erudition and sagacity of Socrates, Plato, Aristotle, Aquinas, Kant, Nietzsche, Schopenhauer and her personal favourite Epicurus.

The latter great thinker was the 'Daddy' of them all. Epicurus expounded a philosophy of simple humanity and self sufficiency. All a person needed to be happy is freedom from odious individuals, freedom from meaningless drudgery and the permanent company of true friends. She used these tenets to good effect with her many clients suffering from *dis-ease*.

A simple cure for unhappiness is to *stop doing* what makes you unhappy; *stop dealing with people* who make you unhappy and *do something simple* that does make you happy: talking to friends, going for a walk.

Of course this was idealistic and many clients were too materialistic and too driven to be satisfied with simple pleasures so she offered consolation across areas as diverse as taxation and growing old.

'*High taxes* were to be celebrated because they were, after all, a corollary of great financial success. The higher rate taxpayer is a great patron of society. Paying tax is as great an achievement as making a large donation to a charity.'

'*Growing old* is an opportunity to allow the mind to dominate the base animal passions and the restless distractions these passions invoke. The mature mind is more settled and productive.'

It was interesting work, but intellectually demanding because her clients regularly challenged her suppositions and propositions.

At the subtle end of the scale these challenges included:

"I see what you mean, but...."

Or, at the more aggressive end:

"Quite frankly: that's bollocks!"

As a philosophical counsellor, she had to concentrate on everything she said. The secret was never to suggest or claim anything easily contradicted or overly subjective.

Self-made businessmen and lawyers were the most challenging clients and the most reluctant to pay their bills.

Today, Diane was having her afternoon off. No clients, no children and no husband for the next two hours. Much as she loved David, Jo and Tim, it was still great to get a few hours alone.

She had a long and luxurious bath, and then, that greatest of all luxuries beckoned, an afternoon nap.

Walking around her house naked was natural and exciting, but she could no longer do this when Tim, her seven year old son was at home; he would rightly be greatly embarrassed.

But he was not at home, so she walked around, butt-naked, feeling free, daring and sexy.

She threw back the covers and dived onto the huge bed; happy and horny. The brand new, soft cotton sheets felt and smelt gorgeous. Stretching out she rubbed her nipples and her pubis forward and backwards on the pristine sheets.

"Mmmm…lovely..." She was very content.

Not quite sleepy, but very aroused she reached into the bedside cabinet and removed her *lapin d'amour*. Lying on her belly, she lifted her hips up a little and inserted the vibrator carefully set at its slowest, gentlest setting. Drifting, drowsy, her mind wandered; *kissing her husband, their tongues entwined, hot, soft, eager and sweet; he kissed her neck, her upper back, her hardening nipples…*

It was so real, he was almost there beside her. The beads rotated inside her as she unfolded the 'Rabbit's' two little 'ears' to kiss her swollen lips.

Daringly, she started to think about the young men she had seen in court accused of murder and rape. Davie Allen was quite sexy, in a rough, uncouth way; and the big guy, Mark Stewart, had a sad vulnerability that made her want to mother him.

The Thug suckling her like a baby while Dave Allen licked her from behind, the rabbit worked its magic; she burst in an all-over, full-body orgasm, her nipples tingling with pleasure.

In her afterglow, she made a resolution to help potential criminals and disadvantaged children.

Her family had made a fortune from diamond mining in Africa in the eighteenth and nineteenth centuries. She was certain they had also been involved in the appalling slave trade, shipping Black Africans to the plantations in America.

Dirty money…

To avoid inheritance tax her parents were giving away large portions of their estate in advance of old-age; about twenty million was coming her way.

She resolved to spend this money helping the likes of the three young men she had seen in court. She would set up a trust to manage several special schools. These schools would provide the very best education, accommodation and nutrition for as many deprived children as possible.

Hopefully, other patrons would follow her example and crime would finally be tackled from the 'bottom up'. She smiled at this little pun as she put the clever device back in the drawer, beneath her underwear.

She set her alarm to give her exactly one hour's sleep.

At least the Ferrari had been sold to Harry; that car was a million pounds trapped in a useless gaudy, status simple.

It was time to live by the teachings of the great Greek philosopher, Epicurus.

All she needed was her darling family and to sleep easy at night.

With the problems of society solved, she fell into deep, blissful slumber.

Mirka

Mirka was lucky. A few days after Danny had 'recruited' her, she discovered her first client was a real gentleman.

She had never worked a 'punter' before; he had never been with a call-girl before, but the pressure had got to him and he connected to the *Pandora's Box* that is the Internet. Inserting the keywords 'executive massage Aberdeen', he discovered Danny Thompson's latest business venture.

Danny was no creative genius. His lap dancing club was called 'The Slippery Pole' and his new escort website was called www.sexynight4u.com

It all seemed rather too easy to the first ever customer. He sent an email from an anonymous hotmail account suggesting a meeting place and a time. The webmaster replied with amendments, prices and guidelines. He replied, suggesting she simply came to a flat he kept in town for when he worked late and needed to be in the office early the next day.

His wife never questioned his overnight absences from home. He was a very busy man.

The webmaster suggested champagne and a bath to begin with and after that it was up to him. Two hours with Mirka was priced at £300.00. An overnight stay was £500.00. The webmaster explained that these were introductory offers and about half the true market rate for a woman like Mirka. He was to give her cash in advance and treat her with respect.

He made a real effort, tidying the flat and running a bath full of bubbles. Several bottles of Moet et Chandon Rosé lay chilling in the fridge.

He could not remember when he had made such an effort for a woman; butterflies fluttered in his stomach. Nervously, he wondered whether he should cancel the whole thing, except he was unsure that he could. Before he could reach for his laptop, the doorbell rang; a soft, anxious, Eastern European, female voice on the intercom indicated his guest had arrived.

Mirka walked in; he was mesmerised. He had never seen such a woman in real life, unable to visit lap dancing clubs because of his position, having her there in his flat was like a dream. She was a stunning woman and he wondered why she was doing this when she could easily be a model.

"I am Mirka, how are you doing?" she said.

"Hello, I am Tommy," he lied. She smiled. She was new to this, but she was not a fool. It was obviously a false name.

"Would you like a drink? Please have a seat? Now, how much do I pay you?"

He was all-thumbs, gibbering like an idiot, but she thought he was very sweet.

"Thank you. Three hundred, if you please and you can also pay me a bonus if you are very satisfied."

The bonus was her idea. She intended to please.

He handed her three hundred pounds and suggested that she leave by midnight because he had to be up early in the morning. The champagne was popped and conversation began to flow.

Fifteen minutes later (time is money), Mirka let her long black dress fall to the ground and he looked at her aghast: in wonderment. Wearing a tiny white g-string and purple platform sandals, her naked breasts stood straight out from her body defying gravity.

Legs like stilts, cheeks flushed pink; Mirka's thick, long blonde hair shone like gold in the candle light.

He was astonished, infatuated.

Moving to the bathroom, she bathed him with the lightest of touches before squeezing in beside him; they made love in the bath. It was the most exciting few hours of his life.

Mirka really liked him. He was kind, gentle and funny; she was sure he would give her a big tip.

She encouraged him to drink the champagne and she was so disappointed when the first bottle was finished, he felt compelled to open another.

Sucking him to a thundering torrent of an orgasm, she made love to him by sitting on his face. She came quickly, moving backwards and forwards over his soft mouth and his darting tongue. Mirka had a great time, but was careful to secure her bonus before he fell asleep.

"Let me stroke your hair, darling. It will help you get a nice sleep, Tommy. Perhaps if you are happy you will give me a bonus?"

He was giddy; her taste was in his mouth; her seductive, addictive, scent everywhere. He had not had champagne for years.

He found his wallet and gave her another £200.00. She was worth it. She was worth two thousand pounds.

Satisfied, he lay on his bed as she massaged his temples and stroked his hair until he fell asleep. He slept like a baby; dead to the cares of the world.

Mirka felt very bad about what she did next, but Danny had told her she would get all the money, if she delivered as instructed. She took out a digital camera and took a picture of her own face and naked upper body next to the face of the sleeping man.

The illusion was of him kissing her nipples.

Next, she searched through his wallet for his details. She found his name and address on his driver's licence and credit cards.

As a gift, she left her panties under his pillow.

Contented she had done a good job, she let herself out of his flat to the taxi waiting for her below.

The next day he received an email to his work account; not the hotmail account he had used to protect his anonymity the day before.

The email message contained a link: www.sexynight4u/busted.

Closing his office door, he clicked on the link with trepidation.

To his horror, he saw himself looking like a corpse. Next to his head were two perfect white breasts with the pinkest of nipples and the face of an angel with green eyes and golden blonde hair. He felt nauseous. The email advised that a second message would follow shortly with advice on how to get the picture removed from the website.

'Failure to make payment on time would result in the link being disclosed to the newspapers and local television news!'

A Slippery Slope

Half an hour later he got a text message on his mobile phone. It was from 'M'.

So sorry! I help you. Meet me today please.

His immediate reaction was anger, but he was an experienced man. He replied to her text, *'Come to my flat at 7 p.m.'*

She was already waiting at his door when he arrived. She looked genuinely upset.

"Tommy, sir, I am a so sorry about this matter."

"Come inside, quickly." He bundled her into the foyer of the apartment block.

One of the residents walked past and gave a look of disapproval at this unlikely looking pair. Mirka was wearing tight denim jeans that revealed her entire abdomen and a tiny black t-shirt with the word '**Slut**' on the front. She had the idea that this was somehow ironic and fashionable. He was just embarrassed.

The tight t-shirt emphasised the fact that she was wearing nothing underneath and the jeans were so low that surely she was bereft of any knickers. Her high-heeled sandals made her a full six feet tall.

Despite his feeling of hatred and betrayal he found her incredibly attractive. She had a wonderful, fresh, feminine smell. He led her upstairs to his apartment where they stood looking at each other.

"Did you find my panties what I was leaving you as a gift?"

His heart sank.

Had his wife been at the flat today? If she had, he was finished. Mirka walked to the bedroom and bent over. He watched her, immediately aroused. What a fabulous rear this incredible woman possessed. She reached under the pillow and handed him the panties.

"Thank you," he said, "but I think you should keep these. I am married."

"Of course, I am silly," she replied

"Now you said you would help me."

"Yes. I feel very bad about what Danny is doing. It is dangerous I think also for me. I might be deported or something and I am thinking that you are a nice man."

"Who is Danny?" he asked.

"Oh, he is the Mr. Big behind this idea for making money by scaring men by putting photographs on the internet. I think it is stupid, but he promised me much money."

"And how will you help me?"

"Well," she said, smiling at him coyly,

"If you help me then I will not need Danny anymore and I will tell you his name and where to find him and I will delete the internet pictures and the pictures on the camera."

"You know how to do this?" he asked, somewhat surprised.

"Oh yes. I am not just a pretty face, as you say," she said happily.

"And you are not afraid of Danny?"

"No. As we say in Latvia, 'it is cutting the middle out of the man'!"

"You mean – 'cutting out the middleman'?"

"Exactly, if he is getting nasty, I have friends in my country that he will not want to be meeting. They can be very persuading with the bat for the baseball."

He was not sure he wanted to be involved with these miscreants, but his hands were tied. He needed the pictures deleted and he was none too sympathetic about the fate this Danny would suffer at the hands of Mirka's friends.

"So what do you want?" he asked Mirka.

"Well, I think you are finding me most attractive, yes?"

"Yes," he said, looking at her admiringly.

"Ok. Well, Danny will ask you for ten thousand pound and then for more," she confided. "He will never remove the pictures."

He felt his stomach churn. How could he possibly hide a payment of ten thousand pounds from his wife?

"I am suggesting this. I will be your woman. I will be discreet. You will let me stay in this flat and you will give me one thousand pound a month for buying the food and also you give me presents and tips. And I will look after you." She looked pleased and even winked.

He had no idea how this would work, but he had to agree. He had to have those pictures deleted.

"Ok" he said, "deal!"

"Fantastic, Tommy, my darling." She threw her arms around his neck and kissed his lips.

Moments later they were making love and Mirka was enjoying multiple orgasms in the arms of her new benefactor, whom she had taken to calling, "Daddy."

He was still a professional and made sure that all the facts were at his disposal.

"What is Danny's full name?"

"It is Danny, 'the Fanny,' Thompson."

He suppressed a smile.

"And where can I find him?"

"He is owning the Slippery Pole lap dancing club in Charles Street."

"Ok."

With that, he relaxed and enjoyed another evening of pure bliss with the marvellous Mirka.

Beggars and Hoodies

There was a new 'Hoodie' in Aberdeen city-centre that night. Dirty old denim jeans, second-hand training shoes and a black hooded top, two sizes too large, he kept his head low as he walked to his destination like a fast-moving, urban, punk-monk.

At the junction of Belmont Street with Union Street, he sat down outside the finest luxury jeweller in town. Ironically, several beggars sat in a line beneath a large imitation Rolex watch. Cartier and Patek Phillipe time-pieces, costing in excess of ten thousand pounds each, glittered in the windows.

Of course, this merchandise was safely behind metallic security blinds, but it was a perfect illustration of the proximity of extreme, conspicuous wealth and desperate, pitiful poverty in the city.

The Hoodie took out a fake Burberry cap and adopted the half-lotus yoga position, the cap on the pavement at his feet. Head slumped forward, he appeared doped-up on heroin or methadone, but this was no junkie. This Hoodie was here for a specific purpose and it was not begging.

The time on the large Rolex was around ten and the young people of Aberdeen were out exercising their favourite *passé temps* - drinking alcohol. For many, it was their only pastime, except watching television.

As they marched, strode and staggered past the row of street beggars, interactions could be heard as follows:

"Got any change mate?"

The familiar request came from a soliciting beggar and received a number of standard replies, including,

"Get a fucking job, you sponging bastard!"

And,

"Fuck off, junky scum!"

These were at the negative end of the scale.

A positive response was the non-verbal 'clink-clink' of coins falling into the Nike or Burberry beggar's cap.

One street beggar that night was being particularly, aggressively loquacious; his incessant,

"Got any change, mate?" like a broken record.

He was annoying many passers-by, several of whom had threatened to,

"Stick his Nike cap up his arse!"

The new Hoodie, by contrast, was having a highly successful 'inauguration'.

Benefiting from the animosity directed at his seated neighbour, he'd amassed over thirty pounds in an hour when the reason for his presence arrived in the doorway of the *Virgin Records* store opposite, directly across the road from where he was sitting.

He stood up and emptied his plentiful bounty into the Nike cap of his irate neighbour who responded with,

"Fit the fuck?" before gathering up his new found wealth, calling it a night, and dancing with delight into the distance.

Philanthropic Hoodie crossed the road, in the direction of the four shady individuals lurking in the doorway opposite.

He walked within a few yards of the foursome who appeared to be smoking some illicit substance in the corner of the doorway.

As they became aware of his presence, the leader challenged the hooded newcomer.

"Fit the fuck are yee gawking at, cunt?"

The interloper produced a digital flash camera, firing a photograph within a few inches of the profaner's hooded face. The entire entrance area, about four paces by five paces, was instantly illuminated by the brilliant white flash.

The nearest hooded gang member, blinded by the light, was defenceless when the photographer produced a fist bound in copper wire and smashed it into his face, shattering his nose and removing his front two teeth, before running off down the adjacent steps to his parked car below.

Running down the steep set of granite steps that descend from Union Street to the area known as, *The Green*, below, he placed his feet carefully; if he fell now, he was a dead man. Smooth and treacherous, worn down by millions of pedestrians over hundreds of years of heavy use, the sixty-five stone steps were a dangerous escape route; easy to slip and fall with disastrous consequences.

The three remaining Hoodies pursued him, hollering the usual unimaginative profanities.

"Yer a fucking dead man!"

Heart pounding, nearing his car, he pressed the remote control, opening the doors he jumped in and started the engine. To the surprise of his *sequiturs*, he did not flee the scene.

Instead, he re-emerged from his car holding an aluminium baseball bat.

One pursuing Hoodie was ahead of the others and he was about to pay a price for his enthusiastic desire for revenge. Dropping down low, the hunted turned hunter, driving the baseball bat hard into his pursuer's shin, he stopped him dead in his tracks.

His victim hit the deck hard, clutching his broken leg in agony; another flash; a picture taken of a face contorting in pain from the violent blow.

The other two pursuers decided that discretion was the better part of valour. They pulled up short of their associate, content to shout abuse and taunt the baseball bat yielder. One picked up and threw a bottle, missing the baseball bat owner by inches.

The avenger simply pointed his camera at them and took a few more flash photographs before slowly getting into his car and driving off, leaving the thugs beaten and frustrated in his wake.

Later, Pete uploaded his photographs to www.happyslapper.com

The message next to the pictures of the severely injured hooded reprobate simply said:

'Which of you assholes is next?

Revenge

A week into the arrangement with her benefactor, Mirka was holding up her end of the bargain. Exhausted and sexually satiated, she left his flat at midnight.

Her taxi was waiting outside as usual.

As the taxi pulled away, a second car followed discreetly behind; a black 1988 Jaguar XJS Convertible with white leather and ebony wood veneer. A big cat stalking its prey; creeping along: silently, stealthily; totally unnoticed by the unsuspecting passenger in the taxi.

Mirka arrived at *The Slippery Pole*, and after checking Danny was not about, she headed straight for his office.

Her 'Daddy' had managed to stall Danny with excuses, *'time to raise the cash'*, but the *'Fanny's'* patience had run out; he was ready to disclose the affair to the press. Danny knew he had stumbled onto a great prize. So, tonight, Mirka had no choice. She had to remove the incriminating photographs.

She started the ftp connection to the internet site.

Connection established...

Her elegant finger moved to press **delete.**

Unseen, a thick, hairy hand grabbed her wrist, forcing her arm painfully up her back. His signature disgusting smell informed her, Danny had arrived.

"Do you think you can cross me, you Russian bitch?"

"I am not Russian; I am from Latvia. I was checking the connection to the site was okay," Mirka replied.

"Is that why you spent the evening with that punter without telling me?"

"He called me and asked me to visit him."

"So where is the money?"

Mirka produced the cash bonus her new friend had given her the week before. She was saving her bonuses.

"Good try, bitch, but I can smell a rat when I see one. You thought you could cut a deal."

Danny was hurting her; breaking her arm.

"No. Please..." she begged.

"Let's give lover-boy something to think about!"

Danny had a secret. A few months earlier he had attended Harley Street in London for a novel operation to cure his impotency: a series of penile implants now graced his flaccid member.

The prosthetic was a two-part device made from elastic and fibro-cartilage with polypropylene rods and silicon implants. His *corpus spongiosum* and *corpora cavernosa* had been repaired and renewed allowing maximum blood flow into his hitherto useless organ. A plentiful supply of stimulants had been prescribed to bombard his neurological system with nitric oxide, ensuring he achieved a solid result. Post-surgery, he had enjoyed several stupendous erections, but he had never actually penetrated anyone with it; that was about to be remedied.

The process of achieving a deliberate erection was slightly bizarre, and he was about to discover if the five thousand pounds had been well spent.

Mirka was helplessly bent over his desk and he took full advantage of the situation.

He pushed her right arm as far up her back as he could without breaking it off.

Mirka screamed in agony.

Distracted by the pain, she had no chance to stop his other hand tearing down her hipsters, revealing her bare backside and her pink sex.

Danny, a sadist extraordinaire, was now very horny. He reached into his pocket and produced several tablets of Phentolamine and Viagra, swallowing the lot with a mouthful of whisky.

His monstrosity emerged through his open zipper. The prosthetic worked by squeezing and releasing the internal rod; similar to two, small diameter, used toilet roll cartons, one inside another – an inner and outer cylinder of polypropylene reinforced silicon. There was a sound like muscle tearing as the device snapped into place. The prosthetic and the drugs gave Danny a full eight inches of blood-gorged, rock-

hard erection; an erection that was now destined for Mirka's defenceless pink wetness.

Danny grabbed the digital camera that was next to the computer and thrust his synthetic manhood violently inside Mirka.

"How do you like that, you blonde bitch!"

There was a chance that Mirka might have liked it if it had not been Danny and his intention had not been violent rape.

Her arm was in great pain, her insides were on fire and all the time the air was heavy with Danny's appalling body odour.

As he pumped violently, deep into the unfortunate Mirka, he began to sweat, making the foul stench emanating from his hardly-ever washed body so noxious and nauseating that Mirka started to retch until she finally vomited onto Danny's desk.

"You filthy bitch! You will pay for that."

Danny was enjoying himself. His penis implant was working a treat. He was fucking Mirka senseless; he was a predator and she was his prey; a virile god with his sacrificial sexual lamb.

He pulled his swollen contraption out of her and decided to go for the kill. Pushing hard, he penetrated her virgin anus. Trickles of blood surrounded his synthetic phallus as Mirka started to bleed; she screamed out loud as her rectum was torn apart; the music in the club drowned her cries; no assistance came to save her.

Danny took a photo of Mirka, tears of pain running down her face, and then a second showing his penis tearing at the sensitive flesh around her anal sphincter. He spurted some seminal fluid inside her ass, enjoying the feeling of her internal muscles massaging his glans. The fact her muscles were in

spasm from pain, not pleasure, did not concern Danny. She was a tart and a bitch; she was lucky to be alive.

He pushed her head into the pool of vomit and took a photograph of her sobbing, head-down, covered in the disgusting sticky fluid that had recently been the half-digested contents of her stomach.

Marching her to the back door of the club, his hand still thrusting her arm up her back, he threw her into the dark and dirty back passage.

Mirka walked home crying. People pointed, laughed and gave her a wide berth. She was utterly humiliated.

The next day her 'Daddy' got an email with the link: www.sexynight4u.com/yourbitchgetsit

He opened the link with dread and beheld a shocking image. His beautiful mistress: brutally, anally raped and tortured by a faceless monster.

There was also a message:

'The price just went up to £20,000.00'

A calm, collected man, he was not given to outbursts of anger or rage. It was a positive personality trait that had made him the successful senior public servant he was.

However, these photographs activated a sense of injustice in him so great that he simply could not stem his fury; his hand smashed straight through the screen of his computer.

Staring at his bleeding, throbbing hand, he spat out just three words through clenched teeth:

"Danny, 'fucking', Thompson!

Punishment

The fist flew past Ross's head.

It was close, too close.

Sweating profusely, he launched a counterattack, three roundhouse kicks; right leg, low to the thigh; left leg, mid-section to the ribs, then fast up to the head; turn, jump, right heel, spinning-kick to the head.

It was all happening in a flash. The other man's knee came into Ross's ribs, but it was a glancing blow, easily evaded; Ross countered with a jumping axe-kick, bringing his left heel, hard down on his opponent's collar bone. Gasping for air, pouring with sweat, the two men paused.

Applause!

It had been a fantastic contest, the current Scottish Taewondo champion against the former European champion. Ross had been out of full training for several years, but he had prepared hard for this bout; just as well, because Robbie Tester was a super-athlete, not as technically brilliant as Ross, but incredibly fit and impossible to stop, a truly indomitable spirit, the essence of the five tenets of Taekwondo, the Korean martial art famous for its acrobatic kicks and demonstrations of explosive destructive power.

Ross bowed and shook the other man's hand.

Tester returned to teaching the class and Ross moved around the students, observing and advising.

"F=MA!" barked Tester, citing Newton's second law of motion to a group of students.

"You cannot increase the mass of your hand or foot so we work on maximising the acceleration."

"Maximum acceleration leads to maximum force!"

He nodded to a student who put four separate, one inch blocks of wood together on the 'mule'.

"Once you can generate enough acceleration you can do this."

In a blink of an eye, he flew threw the air, smashing all four blocks with the 'sword' edge of his right foot - 4 inches of wood sliced like butter.

Spontaneous applause!

"Ok, let's see you lot punch!"

"Ha-na, tul, set, net, ta-sot, ya-sot, il-gob….!"

He counted loudly to ten in Korean as the students alternated punches between right and left clenched fists.

One student got confused and lost the count.

"Get down; give me fifty press-ups!"

The student frowned, but did as he was told.

It was intensive training.

Ross moved on to supervise another group of students practising one-on-one sparring - hand to hand combat. He gave them a few pointers,

"Press down on the balls of your feet, don't duck, keep your guard up, bend at the knees - pick your spot……"

The various students attacked, defended, counter-attacked; getting bruised and winded in the process.

Smack!

A nasty crunching sound suggested that someone just took a painful blow. Ross went to investigate the bloody accident.

A tall, good-looking man adopted the crouched position, the custom after a stray blow caused actual injury to an unlucky combatant.

Ross dismissed him and sent him to fight an experienced black-belt at the other end of the hall.

"So what happened here?" Ross asked the bleeding party.

"I caught him in the ribs with a side-kick and he smacked me on the nose. I never even seen it coming. He is a karate guy, bit of a psycho."

"It doesn't appear broken. Go and put a cold compress on it," Ross replied.

The student went off to the changing rooms to attend to his injury.

Ross walked slowly over to watch the karate interloper.

At the other end, the karate kid was taking a hammering from the Taekwondo black-belt. One kick after another hit him in the ribs and on the face, but he was unflinching.

The karate guy had a nasty gash in his nose from a previous fight, but he had no fear. He just stood there taking punishment. Ross noted that he wore a white-belt, the mark of a novice, but what a novice. The veins on his neck stood out as he absorbed one blow after another. As the black-belt started to tire the novice made a move. It was a simple reverse punch, but it caught the black-belt in the ribs and he went down.

Ross was amazed, but he decided he needed to teach this novice a lesson.

This guy needed to learn restraint and respect.

The ex-European champion bowed to the tall, blonde visitor, noting the look in the other man's eyes: determination, total self-belief. They started to rumble. Ross blitzed the newcomer with a barrage of kicks, forcing him back up against the wall, almost knocking him off his feet but his opponent stood up, undeterred. It was obvious the karate guy was new to this, but his spirit was enormous.

Ross kept up the attack, hitting him with dozens of glancing blows, just enough to bruise and wind, never excessive: perfect control. His opponent soaked it up, waiting for a chance.

Then, as Ross began to tire, the 'novice' made his move; that same, simple, low reverse-punch aimed at the ribs. Ross blocked it, but it was close and it was fast: hard, dangerous. The man's arm seemed to be made of steel.

They bowed as the bout, and the session, ended.

In the changing rooms, Ross watched the karate guy. Naked, he had a superb physique: lean, mean, sinewy, tough muscle. Ross thought he looked like Brad Pitt in *Fight Club*.

"So what brings you here?"

"I just started Karate and I wanted to see how Taekwondo compares."

"And how does it compare?" asked Ross.

"It's great, but I think it takes too long to learn all these fancy kicks?"

"Yes, it takes years. That reverse punch of yours is a real surprise," Ross complimented the newcomer.

"Thanks. It's all I practice, thousands of times a day."

Ross smiled,

"My name is Ross." He held out his hand.

"Pete. Pete Auld." The newcomer accepted the policeman's greeting. The 'karate guy' had a powerful, decisive grip.

Ross watched him leave.

There was something about the 'karate guy'.

A great man to have on your side in a tough spot: a formidable opponent.

Vigilante

Pete Auld was promoting his views, building on his heroic actions. He registered the website www.vigilanteforce.co.uk and set to work featuring recent examples of appalling anti-social behaviour, ASBO recipients, and of course, he named and shamed the happy-slappers he had attacked and photographed.

He linked to: http://aberdeen-action.blogspot.com, hosted by a public-spirited group of citizens calling for more police, increased sentencing of violent criminals and greater protection for the potential victims of crime. Within days, Pete was getting hundreds of hits and emails of support. Among the many unacceptable anti-social acts featured on his site, Pete included the following examples:

Police in Aberdeen have launched an investigation after a pensioner suffering from cancer was the victim of a "happy slapping" attack, BBC News, August 2006

A man who broke his antisocial behaviour order just days after it was served on him was yesterday warned he now faces prison. When he saw two officers arriving at his home, he lunged at them with a corkscrew. He shouted: "I'll kill them!" lashing out at the constables, The Aberdeen Press and Journal, August 2006. And, most infamous of all,

Aberdeen citizens were stunned to hear the verdict reached by a jury of 15 at the High Court yesterday. Two men were effectively acquitted of the murder of a young male student and the rape of a defenceless, wheelchair-bound, old woman, despite being caught red-handed by the police, The Aberdeen Guardian, July 21, 2006.

For his website, Pete had researched and provided details of personal security alarms, pepper mace sprays and canine repellents. Illegal in the UK, these could be imported via the internet. He described how home-made protection could be manufactured using perfume vaporizers filled with bleach. He suggested that a baseball bat or golf club should always be carried in the trunk or back seat of your car.

Pete now attended Karate, Jujitsu, Aikido and Taekwondo classes. His reverse punch was already a rib-breaker.

Martial arts and weight-training every day was exhausting, and even though Pete was young and fit he needed supplements. Research on the internet led him to liquid Anodrol, a liquid form of Oxymethobol, an extremely potent anabolic steroid. Applied as a cream, rather than injecting or digesting, it offered protection against liver damage and other adverse side effects normally associated with anabolic steroids. Rubbing a little into his arms and legs, twice a day, produced astonishing rapid muscle growth.

He could now easily tear a phone book in half; his tolerance to pain was massive and his sex drive was insatiable.

Working on his website, he was constantly logged-on to internet sex-sites, masturbating continuously. He did not need to sleep.

Before he was attacked by happy-slapping yobs, Pete had been an easy-going guy, trusting and fearless. Now he was becoming lethal. Ready for anything, he would not hesitate when challenged. If threatened, he would break limbs first: ask questions later. He packed a knuckle-duster, a rubber peace-maker and several high-pressure take-down sprays.

A baseball bat, several golf clubs and an ice axe in his car completed his armoury.

Midnight, Saturday; most people were out drinking; seeking a good time. Pete was looking for a different kind of entertainment. Slowly he proceeded along the beach boulevard, notorious for boy-racers, in his new Isuzu Rodeo truck. Numerous boy-racers screamed past in small, noisy, customized cars. Two cars gave Pete a two-fingered salute before pulling in and parking a few hundred yards away, overlooking the beach.

Pete followed them.

He drove slowly over to where they were parked and *straight* into the back of the black Mini Cooper, smashing its rear windscreen with his truck's bull-bars.

He sat and waited for the action to begin. Two youths from the Mini and another two from the adjacent Citroen C3 burst out and started kicking Pete's truck.

Pete wound down his windscreen.

"Get away from my truck, you little shits!"

His voice was deep and menacing.

The youths stopped and looked, but he was only one and they were four, so they rushed him.

Pete couldn't wait to engage these hooligans. The first youth received a blast of bleach vapour spray in his eyes, screaming in agony as the follow-up reverse-punch hit his ribs. The second one was even more unlucky, a gold knuckleduster catching him full on the jawbone.

Pete was becoming artful in his vigilante violence; experimenting and enjoying the danger.

The other two hesitated, now wary; so Pete walked over to the Citroen and smashed the front windscreen with a five-iron, motivating the remaining two youths to charge. A simple karate front kick settled the first one and Pete threw the last boy-racer over the barrier and into the sea. He was as light as a feather after 10cc's of liquid Anodrol. A life-belt was lifted off its holster and launched at the flailing youth who managed to grab it and stay afloat.

Before departing the scene, the vigilante slashed all the tyres on each car with a hunting knife. It felt good. Once you were strong enough and got the hang of it, violence was fun and very satisfying.

As usual, Pete took photographs then drove away, unhurriedly.

The night was still young so he headed for the centre of town where he knew dozens of drunken, anti-social individuals would be terrorizing the law-abiding majority.

Pete looked forward to redressing the balance...

Jason Jameson

Jason Jameson was reading. He only read two subject matters - law and homo-erotic material. Tonight, it was a bit of both, but primarily law.

He was studying the latest Scottish Criminal Court Reports for a particular reason. A fellow lawyer had been convicted of an offence and it was being bandied about town as 'statutory rape of a minor'. It was nothing of the sort.

The girl was 14 and the proven offence was in fact, '*sexual activity with a child.*' The offender had received six months in jail, but far worse than jail would be the destruction of his career in law.

The circumstances were far from clear-cut. The unlucky, guilty lawyer had been in Edinburgh, defending a client. After a grueling few days in court he had gone to a nightclub on his own. Very good-looking, late thirties, shoulder length blonde hair, a surfer and playboy, women pestered him wherever he went, drooling over his well-defined muscles and golden blonde locks.

A precocious, leggy 'model' in a micro-dress and teetering high-heels had approached 'surfer-boy', seducing him with her big eyes, luscious lips and sickly-sweet girlish purr. The playboy-lawyer assumed she was yet another hot, randy eighteen year-old so he took her back to his hotel room for champagne and a night of sexual pleasure.

In the morning, the girl had sobered up and told him she was fourteen. She had also decided that he had lured her to his room and seduced her. She had absolved herself of any guilt and shame by transferring all the blame to the legal-eagle.

Jameson knew women were forever crying rape; in constant denial of their own lust: *their disgusting female sexual desire.* The girl's father had called the police and the rest was history. Jameson made up his mind quickly about the girl, *'Cock-sucking little slut.'*

Jameson had a crush on the Greek God. He despised all the horny little 'moistened bints' who monopolised his handsome heartthrob's attentions. He was sure he could persuade his colleague that true, lasting satisfaction could only be achieved between men: intellectual, physical equals - devoid of feminine inanity. Jameson's misogyny was a great asset in defending rapists or sex offenders: exposing the supposed victim for what she really was:

'A dirty, lying whore; they were all just eager holes - gagging for it.'

He used more precise, acceptable language in court, of course, but usually the women involved had been drinking, were sexually experienced and provocatively dressed. He believed most of them had it coming to them.

'They should be grateful for the attentions of a man in the first place.'

The *Silver Fox* had been called in to appeal his colleague's case, and he didn't want his adorable brother-at-the-Bar to be languishing in a cell for a moment longer than necessary,

'Bloody ridiculous - little tart was practically on the game.'

He quickly reviewed the facts of the case. She had gained entry to the over-eighteen-only club using a false ID card. That was enough to prove she was a liar. She was alone: cruising for male flesh? From the list of alleged sexual acts, she was no shrinking violet.

She understood, without any explanation, advanced sexual terms such as 'rimming'.

But why had her father decided to take it to the police and make his daughter go through the horrendous indignity of testifying and cross-examination in court? Surfer-boy was no angel. Despite his angelic looks, he had a reputation. He liked them young and he liked it rough. Maybe he had pushed too far, too hard, slapped her about, actually hurt the girl?

The facts, of course, were purely incidental to the case Jameson would construct around them.

As he digested and pondered the evidence, he fantasised about his colleague; tight buttocks, firm muscles, long blonde hair, drenched in massage oil.

His name was Phillip Good - Phil Good, 'Feel Good', 'Fill Me Good'. Jameson was aroused.

An etymologist, the *Silver Fox* loved words.

The fashion was towards eponymy in many professions; the government advisor, Lord Adonis, how pretentious, or Damian Grammaticus; the rather-too-aptly, grandiosely named BBC correspondent. Perhaps, he, too, should join the trend: *'Jason Judiciary'* or *'Victor Veracity'* – *there was, after all, one High Court Judge actually called 'Mr. Justice Justice!'*

Jameson's mind could deviate in a hundred, simultaneous directions before returning to a single, critical conclusion: multifarious, flexible, logical and ruthlessly clinical – the epitome of a brilliant, criminal courtroom lawyer.

He stood proudly in the large bay-window of his impressive study, a gin and tonic in a thick, crystal tumbler in his right hand. A log crackled in the real fire behind him. He liked the sensual smell of a burning log.

The study was on the first floor, facing the considerable front garden of his prestigious Rubislaw Den mansion, the best address in the city centre. The room was lavishly furnished in deep blues, golds and reds. Jameson was successful and rich. He adored luxury and opulence.

His incarcerated colleague needed help fast so *J.J.* decided to engage the services of one of his many happy clients, a well known burglar who also happened to be good looking, muscular and very popular with the ladies. He would send him to Edinburgh to have a liaison with this Fion McPhee, where he could pump her for information, perhaps arrange a threesome and take some incriminating photos for the purposes of persuading her to reverse her testimony.

The criminal lawyer was just about to re-examine the precise wording of the *Sexual Offences Act* when he noticed something unexpected; a large vehicle reversing up his front driveway - right up to his very front door.

He received all manner of people, at all times of day, but he was not expecting anyone at ten p.m., that Friday evening.

Most of his 'after-dark' visitors entered from the rear.

A man dressed in black, wearing a baseball cap, got out and rang the doorbell.

Jameson watched from above. Unsure what to make of it, he walked to the hall, looked at the security camera and pressed the microphone button,

"What do you want?"

"Is that Mr. Jason Jameson?"

"Yes. What do you want?"

"We have an urgent delivery. You will need to accept it in person, sir. It's extremely valuable."

"Come back tomorrow! I am busy."

The visitor was persistent.

"Sorry, sir, I have strict instructions to hand this over to you tonight."

Jameson considered the possibilities. He had enemies, but he also had grateful friends. A recent client, now resident in Cyprus, had promised to send him original, ancient Greek artifacts after a brilliant, successful defence to a charge of money laundering.

Avarice and inquisitiveness got the better of Jason Jameson.

He walked downstairs dressed in a Harrod's dark-blue, silk dressing-gown to confront the stranger.

He opened the door to see the back of the newcomer, leaning into the vehicle, struggling to pull out some apparently heavy object wrapped in a blanket.

"Could you possibly give me a hand, sir?"

Jameson, reluctantly, but curiously leaned into the vehicle to help remove the heavy object.

"Mmooooommmmfffff…"

The criminal lawyer briefly recognized the smell of chloroform. He valiantly fought its inevitable effect, but the hand holding the saturated cloth to his face had an iron grip. Within seconds he was out cold, bundled into the back of the vehicle.

The stranger entered Jameson's house, removed the videotape from the security camera, extinguished the fire, put off all the lights and locked the front door. Five minutes later the house looked unoccupied, as if the great defender of justice had taken a last-minute vacation.

The *Silver*, blue-silk-attired, *Fox* awoke in a large room; a warehouse, the pungent stink of rotten fish assaulting his cultivated sense of smell.

He was sitting on a chair. He tried to move, but he seemed to be strapped in.

No sooner had he regained consciousness when he felt a jab in his right forearm.

A feeling of euphoria came over him; he felt excited, ecstatic, then he felt warm, glowing and relaxed; very, very relaxed.

"Hello, Jason." It was his mother, she'd returned to him from her eternal, resting place.

He was five years old, very excited and happy to see his mother again.

"Tell me all about the Seaton Park murder, Jason..." said his mother.

He wasn't sure whether he should tell his mummy that he had been a very naughty boy, but he felt he must.

"Well, Mummy, I was meeting a lovely, friendly boy in the toilets for some yummy, sticky honey from a pink lolly when this bad boy came in and told us he was having a powwow and so..."

Jason poured his heart out to his long-lost mother...

Footdee

Aberdeen beach is a beautiful sight first thing on a summer's morning. Despite the best efforts of the developers to ruin this area of considerable natural beauty, the beach remains a lovely, awe-inspiring vision at six a.m., when the tide is far out and the sun is rising over the North-East of Scotland. On these rare occasions the normally choppy North Sea displays an almost dead calm. The sun is reflected on the water like a mirror image; the sea imitating a tranquil lake or *loch* as it's known in Scotland. Numerous, burbling channels; a million tiny, glittering streams carry the salty, crystal-clear sea-water off the beach back to the huge clear-blue expanse stretching all the way back to Norway, several hundred miles away. The golden sands are held in place by Jurassic fencing: old, giant wooden beams running from the sea-wall to the sea; *Groynes,* brooding over the beach, protecting it from the watery invader, year in, year out; these sentries of the sands give the landscape an intriguing geometry, captured to great effect by local artists fascinated by the play of light on the water at this time of year.

At the far end of the beach, and adjacent to Aberdeen harbour is the old settlement of Footdee ('Fitty'). This tiny hamlet was once an independent fishing village; now it is amalgamated into the main town of Aberdeen. Toy-like cottages huddle together along the seafront with ceilings so low that it's almost impossible for a modern adult to stand erect inside the rooms. The people of Footdee must have been very small indeed, two or three hundred years ago.

The streets and walkways of Footdee are made of *Cassies*, large stones from the beach; it's a pedestrian only, conservation area.

The residents take huge pride in the appearance of the place; it is widely decorated with flower-baskets and other ornate features.

Footdee is arranged as a square. One edge sits facing outwards overlooking the harbour. Here, an open expanse of concrete separates the houses from the harbour water, serving as a walkway, car park and turning area.

A small French restaurant called *Silver Darlings* is located nearby.

Lucky diners at this extensively glazed, gourmet seafood restaurant can look out to sea or watch the boats, entering and leaving the harbour, glide past, lit up like Xmas trees, while they eat a delicious evening meal of West-Coast scallops and white chocolate mousse.

Like all old fishing communities, Footdee has strong historical links with the Church. Not so long ago, entire communities were decimated when fishing boats were lost at sea leaving grieving widows and starving children dependent on the support of neighbours and the church.

Nowadays, the fishing industry is almost a thing of the past; the fishermen ordered to tie up their boats to preserve exhausted fish stocks.

Big Jack McKay

One noticeably large detached house in Footdee overlooks the harbour. It was built by a successful skipper and owner of a fleet of the best fishing boats in Aberdeen over a hundred years ago. It is now owned by a successful skipper who was paid a small fortune by the EU to stop fishing and scrap his boat. This is the home of Jack McKay or as he is usually known, 'Big Jack'. Big Jack amongst other things is a devout Christian and his life revolves around the teaching and preaching of the Word of Our Lord. He lives in this idyllic house with his wife of thirty years, Mary; his two daughters, Sarah and Rebecca; his two sons, Michael and Samuel and their dog, Samson, a black Labrador.

Big Jack is loved by everyone. A giant of a man at six feet three inches, he is almost as wide as he is tall and it's all muscle; the result of working on a fishing boat from the age of fifteen till fifty when he was finally forced to call it a day.

The former skipper is philosophical about the demise of the fishing industry; it could be a terrible job with long periods at sea. Even in recent memory he had lost friends and brothers overboard to the cruel sea. Jack was troubled that Spanish and Portuguese boats could still fish the UK waters, while our own boats could not, but he knew mankind was weak; its judgment flawed. In the Kingdom of Our Lord all these human errors would be set aside. There would be fish and fishing for everyone; the waters would be calm and no-one would be lost overboard - our eternal soul is immortal, impervious to the pain and decay of human flesh.

With The Lord by his side, Big Jack McKay was happy to be alive. He smiled as he reflected on the grace of Our Lord. On this beautiful Sunday morning, Big Jack had been up since 5 a.m. He had a modest breakfast of porridge and fruit and some strong coffee. Stimulants were probably ungodly, but he was partial to coffee and good red wine. He had to watch himself with the wine. One evening, Big Jack had fallen into the harbour after drinking too many bottles of a rather excellent Californian Cabernet Sauvignon with an old shipmate when Mary was away, visiting her sister in Fraserburgh for the weekend.

At 6 a.m., every day he took Samson for a walk. Usually they would head down to the beach, but today they were off in another direction. Once outside the house, Samson immediately took off at great speed in the direction of the sands, chasing after gulls and various other seabirds, but Big Jack stopped him in his tracks with the sheer power of his voice.

"SAMSOM, GET YERSELF BACK HERE!"

Samson skidded to a halt, turned on a sixpence, and shot straight back to his master with the athletic prowess of a greyhound.

Big Jack had a wonderful voice. Delivering a sermon he could hold the assembled flocks' attention as if they were actually sitting in the palms of his enormous hands; but the really impressive thing was his singing voice. Had he not been predestined to be a fisherman, he could easily have been a world famous bass-baritone. His singing voice was quite simply awesome. Children at his sermons stood transfixed in wonderment as this giant mesmerised his church with a richness and perfect pitch that would have rivalled the great Wagnerian opera singer, Hans Hotter.

Today, dog and man were heading to Torry to visit the hall where he would later that day deliver a sermon. He did get a little nervous in advance of his talks so he liked to familiarise himself with the surroundings and practise his sermon, over and over, until he could do it without even looking at the Good Book for reference. This was important because Big Jack was something of a celebrity in his community and people came from far and near to hear him talk, and of course, to hear him sing.

Normally, he would preach at Footdee's own very quaint and well attended chapel that stands, almost secreted, in the epicentre of the community, but today he was a guest speaker at another church and such was their faith in Big Jack that they had given him the key to their hall so he could practise all morning until he was word perfect.

Samson was placed on a thick, black leather leash and together they strode purposefully and briskly out of Porca Quay, up York Street towards Torry. Torry is another old town that has acceded to the main city of Aberdeen; like Footdee its history lies firmly rooted in the fishing industry. It lies south of Footdee, across the harbour, on the other side of the River Dee.

They walked along Waterloo Quay and Regents Quay where dozens of large offshore supply and support vessels lay moored to the docks. These enormous ships were part of the booming offshore oil industry and it was obvious from the sheer scale, quality and modernity of these vessels that the oil industry was not just thriving, but positively awash with money.

"Aye, it's a fair business, eh, Samson?"

Big Jack put the rhetorical question to his canine companion. He was sad the fishing industry could not be blessed with the same good fortune as the oil industry, but he comforted himself with a few thoughts from the good book:

"It is easier for a camel to go through the eye of a needle, than for a rich man to enter into the kingdom of God: Matthew 19:24,"

Big Jack boomed out the passage and smiled. He loved God, and he loved reflecting on, and spreading, the Word of God. They reached Market Street, named after the fish market (now also gone) and turned left, heading south, towards Victoria Bridge, taking them over the River Dee to Torry and the Hall of Worship.

Even before they arrived at the bridge it was obvious a fearsome commotion was occurring ahead.

Like most North-East towns, Aberdeen has a problem with seagulls. Actually the term 'sea' gull is a misnomer because many of these gulls have never been anywhere near the sea. They are town gulls who have colonised vast areas of the city, considering any high building, a 'cliff-top' nesting site.

Aberdonians refer to these screeching banshees as *'flying rats'* because of their disgusting anti-social habits, some of which would offend the dignity of an average self-respecting rat. The gulls are scavengers, growing to enormous size because of the plentiful supply of food. They will eat anything. They eat what we discard even when we wrap it up and dispose of it carefully. They tear open plastic bags full of garbage to get at the stinking contents within; they will swoop down and remove the deep-fried battered haddock out of your very hands as you are enjoying your takeaway fish supper.

They have been known to dive-bomb and knock over a fully grown adult to make him drop his food and they work in teams.

But the worst thing is the noise. In the mating and nesting seasons, when chicks are about, the noise is unbearable. From first light, they scream at each other with what can only be described as an 'ungodly' wail. Many reasonable citizens, driven to distraction by the noise, want to have these gulls destroyed and Big Jack McKay was not in disagreement.

Some of these beasts had grown almost as large as Samson; and his dog, who was no coward, would think twice about taking on more than one of the huge, beady-eyed, yellow-beaked devils.

It was no surprise then to Big Jack that the appalling and ghoulish screams up ahead were emanating from a flock of giant white gulls, apparently involved in a mass brawl or more likely, a crazed feeding frenzy.

The preacher and ex-skipper assumed the bins of a nearby fish processing factory had been raided by a gull; a gull subsequently hijacked by its associates: full-scale, gull-war had erupted.

But, this was an unusually fearsome disturbance even for the infamous Aberdeen 'sea' gulls. The huge grey and white beasts appeared to be attacking each other to secure the consumption of some irresistible, bloody, stinking delicacy.

As Big Jack and Samson started over the bridge, they noticed the alluring feast was not on the bridge itself, but appeared to be under the bridge.

Something or someone was hanging from the bridge.....

The Bridges of Dee

The discovery by Big Jack McKay was of biblical proportions.

Had the sky been red, it was Dante's *Inferno*, Munch's *Scream* and much more.

There are numerous bridges over the River Dee. The first, where Big Jack and Samson stood, is at Victoria Road and connects Torry with Aberdeen.

The second on Wellington Road is the Queen Elizabeth Bridge, about a mile west, inland. It leads to Aberdeen Prison amongst other things.

Running parallel to this is an abandoned suspension bridge called Wellington Bridge that dates back to 1831. Aberdeen City Council closed this bridge to vehicular traffic in 1984 and erected three metre high pallisade fencing at either end to prevent public access. This interesting bridge is now listed as an Ancient Monument. It can be seen clearly from the adjacent Queen Elizabeth Road Bridge and is a much overlooked landmark.

The next bridge, half a mile further inland, sits high above the river. This is the main railway bridge. Whereas the other bridges are constructed of granite or concrete, except the old suspension bridge, the railway bridge is a massive steel structure towering above the water with no public access.

Further up the river, traveling west, are two more road bridges, the Old and the New Bridges of Dee.

To travel anywhere, out or into Aberdeen, you must cross one of these bridges.

Many people use the areas around the river: there are football pitches, cycle tracks, golf practice, dogs being exercised by their owners and rowing boats on the river – it's a hive of activity.

This Sunday, the road bridges all had one thing in common. They all appeared to be closed. A single roadwork sign at either end stating, *'Bridge Closed,'* prevented traffic crossing. Unusually, however, there was no tape preventing anyone walking over the bridges and no sign of any actual construction or repairs being undertaken.

There was, however, considerable commotion, not just on the Torry Bridge where Jack McKay and his dog Samson were standing, but also around the disused Wellington Suspension Bridge and the nearby imposing Railway Bridge. These bridges were engulfed by flocks of screaming, diving, hysterical gulls. The reason for this avian frenzy was about to be discovered by Big Jack McKay, or to be more accurate, by his faithful and fearless dog, Samson. The black Labrador dashed past the *'Bridge Closed'* sign, making a beeline for a fat, malevolent gull pulling apart a pink fleshy morsel on the pavement in the middle of the bridge. Samson, filled with righteous indignation, charged towards the gull, snarling and barking, exposing his razor-sharp, white canines at the feathered fiend. The gull looked at the dog dismissively, casually considered its options and nonchalantly flew a few yards, up, onto one of the ornamental lights that decorate the sides of the Victoria Road Bridge displaying all the arrogance associated with its species. Samson was left sniffing at the pink, meaty scrap forsaken by the gluttonous bird. The dog was tempted to eat the temporarily abandoned meal, but decided against it, perhaps because the gull had been there first; gulls are notorious carriers of *Clostridium Botulinum* (the bacterium that causes botulism), something probably subconsciously recognised by a sagacious dog.

Jack McKay was just a few seconds behind his dog, keen to prevent a confrontation between his black, furry-friend and a flock of belligerent air-borne devils. Instead he found himself under attack from the aerial monsters. It was all he could do to retreat to the other side of the bridge, dodging the diving gulls as he ran over the bridge towards Torry, in a scene reminiscent of Alfred Hitchcock's, *'The Birds'*.

Safely out of the interest range of the crazed gulls, Big Jack moved upriver to get a view of what was causing this airborne hysteria.

Worse than his bleakest imaginings of Hell; hanging from the bridge was what appeared to be a 'scarecrow', the body of a man hung upside-down in the form of an inverted crucifix.

It was facing away from the bridge, upstream towards the next road-bridge; its hands secured behind its back.

A strut stretched the thing's legs wide apart, and almost too horrible for words, the clothing had been cut; torn around the genital area. .

It was this unfortunate creature's genitals that were providing the greedy gulls with an unexpected, gratuitous, gory feast.

Blood oozed from the creature's femoral artery, soaking the entire body in crimson blood, pouring out into the river, twenty feet below.

Jack McKay was too far away to see the gulls had removed the testes, most of the penis and the majority of the soft flesh around the groin. He had to look twice, not believing his own eyes.

Perhaps it was a student prank? - But what about the blood? And if it was not real, why would the gulls be so attracted to the thing?

He ran to the nearby call box and dialed 999.

"Police, ambulance, it's an emergency - send someone immediately.......it's a terrible, terrible thing..." he sobbed, with panic and pity for the tortured soul suspended from the bridge.

This was the first of several similar calls the police received around 7 a.m. that morning.

The second call was from a Mrs. Margaret Mutch who discovered the body hanging from the old Wellington Suspension as she walked across the adjacent Queen Elizabeth Road Bridge. This time it was hung upside down, but there was no strut holding the legs apart. It was facing the road bridge and the gulls had eaten off much of the face. The eyes and the tongue had been completely removed. The clothing had not been removed, but one arm fell outstretched towards the river.

The third call, from a Mr. Sandy Clark, rowing on the river, reported three black bags hanging high above him from the Railway Bridge. They were surrounded by swooping, screaming seagulls. On closer inspection they were not black bags; all three objects were bodies, hung by their feet, and again the gulls were making short work of any exposed flesh.

The police, ambulance and fire brigade arrived as soon as they could muster suitable numbers for very early on a Sunday morning, but the bodies did hang there for at least thirty minutes to an hour before the areas could be cordoned off and the public held at bay.

Long before this, huge crowds had gathered. The pretence of closing the bridges had caused hundreds of motorists to amass and furiously investigate the cause of the tailbacks and traffic jams. Cars were abandoned as road-rage gave way to morbid curiosity.

Many who witnessed the spectacle were crying, some were vomiting and many were in need of medical attention for shock.

Hundreds of photographs and videos recorded the scene for posterity and the purposes of the media.

The television news and the newspapers were going to have a field day. If the purpose of this appalling crime was exposure then it had achieved that and more by eight o'clock that Sunday morning.

The Bodies on the Bridges

Ross arrived within forty-five minutes of Jack McKay's phone call. It was not exactly the blissful awakening he normally enjoyed on a Sunday morning. Dressed in shorts and a t-shirt, he raced into town pushing past the crowds to meet the officers at the Torry Bridge. A small portable crane was being used to winch the body up. The structure supporting the creature was suspended by thick steel mooring rope looped around the centre ornamental iron lamppost on the right hand side of the bridge as you cross from Market Street. It had proved impossible to heave it up without mechanical assistance.

Ross stood-by watching, as the remains were slowly wound upwards.

The gulls continued to swoop. Sensing their food was being stolen, their fury increased. Officers used electric-shock batons and flares to disperse the aerial menace. Eventually the body was dragged up over the side of the bridge.

Ross was not prepared for the hideous, bloody gore that was his first experience of the thing.

A large black plastic sheet was quickly thrown over it as one officer stunned a persistent gull with his electric baton to keep it at bay; it wobbled and rocked, but as usual with these animals, it recovered, flapping off to a safe distance. A medic cleaned the thick, crimson blood off the thing's face so that it might be identified. Ross stepped forward and looked at it. It was a sorry sight, but at once he knew the creature.

It was Mark Stewart, *'The Thug'*.

Ross had never felt sorrier for anyone.

A life of misery and violence had ended in appalling circumstances. He leant forward to examine the face. It was largely unmarked. The gulls had focused on the lower body: unspeakable!

Crouching close to the head of the body, Ross almost died of fright.

"Help me...."

It was just a faint whisper, but Mark Stewart was still alive...

He managed to say no more and was rushed away in an ambulance.

Ross got back into his Range Rover and raced to the scene of the next discovery, just half a mile upstream, on the Wellington Suspension Bridge.

It appeared that the second body had been taken up river and hoisted from below - direct access to the bridge was impossible to any normal person.

It was still hanging there because the police were waiting for the council employee who had the keys to the padlock that secured the high, spiked gates - the bridge itself was covered in barbed wire to stop trespassers. A crowd gathered on the adjacent bridge as ghoulish observers used mobile phones to inform friends about the incident; flash photographs were being taken every moment.

Ross shouted at the police sergeant in charge.

"Get those people off that bridge and get the fire brigade to cut through these chains with a torch - NOW!"

The gatekeeper finally arrived just as the firemen cut-through, opening the heavy metal gates.

Ross prepared to run out onto the bridge.

"STOP!" The shout came from the council employee. Ross turned, ready to savage the minor bureaucrat.

"It's not safe. The floor of the bridge is rotten," said the man from the city council.

Ross put a tentative foot forward; the wood beneath gave way, falling into the river below.

"You could probably make your way along the outer frame; at the edge, by holding onto the handrails," suggested the man.

Ross nodded to the man and signalled to a group of firemen to follow him across. They carefully shuffled sideways along the outer iron-frame to the point where the body was dangling below.

This time it was secured by nylon rope. Ross guessed that one man could have crawled along under the bridge with the rope. The rope had been looped over a steel beam and then the body pulled up from below and finally secured by the man on the bridge[4]. One thing was for sure. They must have had a boat, and there had to have been more than one of them.

Again it was impossible to pull the body up because they were standing on such a precarious perch. The coastguard sent a small boat up-river.

---

[4] Visit the scene - the remains of the rope can still be seen hanging from the suspension bridge

They cut the rope and let the body fall aboard. Ross made his way back to the riverbank and waited for the barge to come to meet him. A few minutes later he boarded the craft.

"It's a right mess," warned the Coastguard, "I've seen bodies pulled from the sea after a few weeks that looked healthier."

Ross was forewarned, but it was still a shock.

The tongue had seemingly been pulled forward and stapled to the·chin. Only the tip of the tongue and the staple remained. The mouth was held open by several steel bolts forced between the upper palette and the base of the, mostly eaten, outstretched tongue. The gulls had consumed the remainder of the tongue, the lips and the eyes. The empty, bleeding, eye-sockets were particularly shocking. There was a small bullet hole at the top of the forehead where the scalp originated.

Despite the mutilation, it was obvious from the tanned skin, silvery-grey hair and movie-star-perfect jawbone that this was, or rather had been, Jason Jameson, *The Silver Fox*.

"What's that in his hand?" The Coastguard asked, joining in the detective work. The hand was clenched shut, holding a small leather pouch, bound fast with silver electrical insulating tape.

Ross removed the tape and snapped the fingers open. It was a gruesome task.

He emptied the contents onto the deck,

"Twenty pence coins, thirty of them, thirty pieces of silver? You better wait here until the pathologist arrives. He will want to make a full examination before we move him again."

The Coastguard nodded, looking at the monstrosity again.

"I think there is something in his mouth."

Ross put his gloved hand deep into the back of the throat and pulled out a metallic talisman. Similar in size to a St. Christopher, it featured the image of a skull not unlike that found on the Jolly Roger. Ross had no idea what it was.

He placed the talisman on the chin of the former criminal lawyer, "make sure the pathologist sees this," he told the Coastguard.

Ross washed the blood off his gloves in the river as he watched Chief Constable Stuart Rennie arrive.

"Extraordinary, Ross, beyond belief," said Rennie.

"Three more hanging from the Railway Bridge," Ross informed his superior, "we couldn't get at them until the signalling guys can guarantee they have stopped all the trains."

They drove to the next locus in their respective Range Rovers. The Chief's was white and courtesy of Grampian Police. They drove to nearby Polmuir Road, pulling into a builder's yard, the nearest point of access to the railway line. It was a walk of some 200 yards along the line to get to the bridge.

Under instruction from the attending detective police seargent, the fire brigade had already pulled up the three bodies by the time the two men got to the crime scene. In a similar state to Mark Stewart and Jason Jameson, one body had genital mutilation and deep incisions to the femoral artery; the other two were fully clothed and generally unmarked apart from the seagull induced injuries to the lips and eyes. All three had the same small bullet hole at the top of the forehead, '*Shot and bled to attract the gulls...*' Ross concluded instinctively.

Despite copious quantities of blood, the policeman immediately recognized two of them - Gregor 'Gegsy' Davies and Davie 'The Hoor Master' Allen. The third man, the one whose genitals were dismembered, was a mystery.

Ross looked at his Chief Constable,

"Who is this poor devil?"

The Chief Constable shook his head. Ross looked through the clothes and discovered a business card.

Slippery Pole Gentlemen's Private Club
Daniel C. Thompson
Chief Executive and Founder

Ross did not recognize the owner's name or the establishment. To the Chief's apparent surprise, Ross pulled an identical talisman out of each throat and placed them on respective chins to save Professor Henderson a job, "mean anything to you, sir?"

The Chief inspected the unusual skull emblem.

"Not a thing. It has a cubist quality to it."

"I think I have seen enough to write it up," Ross suggested. "If it's okay with you, sir, I am going home to have a shower."

"No problem. I think I will wait and say hello to Henderson and Hancock," replied the Chief.

"Oh yes, Hancock," mused Ross, "I wonder what she will make of all this."

Ross left his superior officer staring at the three bodies. The Chief Constable appeared lost in his own thoughts. *'Probably never even imagined anything this horrific could happen on his patch,'* thought Ross.

With that melancholy reflection, Ross headed home to wash and have breakfast with his family.

He didn't sleep well that night.

The Press

Ross picked up **The Aberdeen Guardian,** vexed by the simplicity of the headline:

Slaughter!
'Brutal Murder or Just Desserts?'

Three notorious suspects recently acquitted of murdering a young man and raping a helpless old lady were found dead, hanging by their feet over the River Dee yesterday morning.
The three, known anti-social misfits, were joined by an infamous defender of criminals and the owner of strip clubs: alleged manager of call-girls.
Stop Press - The Aberdeen Guardian has received an anonymous tip and awaits full details of the dying men's confessions.

Ross was not surprised that the local rag had misused 'desserts', but he was perplexed to see the newspaper not just reporting the facts, but apparently giving its approval to the retribution implied in the nature of the crimes and the subjects executed. He was extremely pissed-off the paper seemed to have considerably more information than the police. No-one had told Ross about these 'confessions'.

Dougal Shand was News Editor at **The Aberdeen Guardian**, Aberdeen's local newspaper. It was a broadsheet and despite its local focus it was, generally, a quality publication. Shand had worked at several larger newspapers before settling in Aberdeen where he could be close to the sea and the mountains. He was an educated man with a degree in English Literature from Edinburgh University.

157

Ross had met Shand at several police press conferences and considered him a good journalist, a man of obvious talent who could easily run the newspaper if he had the inclination. Shand was not surprised when he was told that Superintendent Ross was in reception and he was genuinely happy to see him. He guided Ross through the incredibly noisy open-plan office, past the myriad cubicles, to his own larger, open office-space surrounded on three sides by a higher quality of sound-screen.

"So, Superintendent, what can I do for you?"

"Confessions...?" Ross was tired and even more concise than usual.

"Ah yes. I think we jumped the gun on that one. The news desk got a call from what was described as an 'educated sounding voice'. I have the full transcript here on our system. I will read it to you," Shand offered sheepishly,

"*Sunday, 30 July 2006, 11 p.m.*

'They confessed to murder and rape. The confessions will be sent to you presently. Violent criminals can no longer escape justice.'

Notes: Educated English Accent, Male 30-50 years, unemotional."

"That's it? It could be a crank." Ross was not pleased an anonymous call from an unknown source had been given such credence by a quality newspaper.

"I'll confess we got carried away. The whole thing is fantastic, totally unprecedented. I was here all day yesterday. I have not slept for 36 hours. CNN, Sky and ABC are interested. From a news point of view, Aberdeen could become the crime capital of the Western World." Shand was excited by the prospect.

This was not what Ross wanted to hear. He had moved to Aberdeen to live in peace and tranquillity. He did not relish presiding over a media circus portraying the city as Bedlam, "Unless this source can be substantiated and corroborated within 24 hours, I want you to print an apology, telling your readers the call was a hoax. If you do get details of these confessions you will not publish anything until we study them first. I don't want to get heavy-handed, but this is a deadly serious matter as you will appreciate."

Dougal Shand nodded. He preferred to have the cooperation of the police; he suspected he'd overstepped the mark with his sensational headline. Ross offered him an olive branch.

"Go home and get some sleep."

"Thanks."

Ross shook hands with the newshound, exchanged a few pleasantries, left the building, and dashed across town in his Black Lamborghini to the City Infirmary.

He needed all the information Mark Stewart could give him.

Hanging On

Mark Stewart was clinging on to life by the finest of threads; kept alive by dozens of tubes and wires and a bewildering array of instrumentation and machinery. Beneath the sheets, his legs were held apart by a contraption designed to protect the area where his genitals had once been.

Ross discussed the patient's precarious position with the consultant in attendance.

"Can I talk to him?"

"Not a chance. He was pumped full of drugs and lost almost every drop of blood in his body. On top of that, there is the massive psychological and physical shock. If he pulls through he will require a lifetime of physiotherapy and psychiatric assistance. It might have been better for him if they had killed him."

"They intended he should survive?" Ross replied.

The consultant picked up the notes by the bed.

"We could get very little blood to test, but what there was contained high concentrations of non-synthetic Scopolamine from a natural plant source, probably *Nightshade*. An interesting and dangerous substance; in the wrong hands, it turns the victim into a mindless robot. This *Burundanga,* as it is called, is used widely in Haitian Voodoo Zombie rituals and elsewhere as a truth serum. Under its influence, the victim is unable to put up any physical resistance. It suggests Mr. Stewart was alive and conscious throughout the ordeal. His captors possibly wanted him to experience his terrible fate, perhaps?"

"Would he have been aware of what was happening? Could he identify who did this?"

Ross was grasping at straws; worth a try.

"That is unlikely. Scopolamine deactivates the memory processes. The victim might be aware of what is happening, in some kind of detached or distant way, at the time, but there would be no memory of the events. The drug is used, illegally, to rape, abduct and rob unsuspecting victims in places such as Colombia and Haiti. It is extremely unusual to find it in this form in this country."

"Thanks, Doctor."

Ross left Mark Stewart in his vegetative state. It was obvious he would get no further leads from what was left of *'The Thug'*.

Lunch at the Foyer Restaurant

Ross met Professor Johnny Henderson for lunch.

The bridge bodies had been subject to emergency post-mortem autopsies.

The results were extraordinary.

Henderson was to explain the full details and discuss the implications with Ross.

They met in The Foyer restaurant in Crown Street. It was an apt location. The Foyer lies about 800 yards down Crown Street, on the right hand side. It is at No.82: opposite No.85 Crown Street: a unique building - a temple; home to several Masonic lodges.

Ross had never spent more than twenty minutes with Henderson and he was surprised by the latter's suggestion that they should lunch together.

The Foyer is a stylish, modern restaurant housed in an old granite art gallery. It features solid, cut-glass topped dining tables and an abundance of Scandinavian light wood features. Modern art is hung at various opportune vistas and the restaurant features its own modest, yet impressive, art gallery. It's a trendy, understated establishment.

Pausing in the foyer of the Foyer, Henderson pointed to the inscription carved above the large doorway of the Masonic building opposite.

"How is your Latin, Superintendent? - AVDI, VIDI, TACE!" boomed Henderson.

"HEAR, SEE, BE SILENT," replied Ross.

Henderson gave the full maxim.

"AVDI, VIDI, TACE SI VIS VIVERE IN PACE?"

Ross obliged with the full translation,

"LISTEN, OBSERVE - SAY NOTHING IF YOU WOULD LIVE IN PEACE."

Henderson massaged Ross's ego,

161

"Impressive. All those years at Magdalen were not wasted then."

"Latin and the law were my subjects, Professor."

"And how is your chemistry, David?"

"Well, I could use some H_2O, I am parched."

They followed a young waitress to a table near the front window where they sat and studied the menu, "Sparkling mineral water and a cappuccino and......." Ross paused, waiting for Henderson.

"I will have a glass of Pinot Grigio. In fact, make that a bottle and two glasses."

Not a lunch-time drinker, Ross was uncomfortable at Henderson's presumptuous order.

"Don't worry, laddie, I will drink it all if it's not your tipple, but you might need a drink after you hear my report," Henderson added enigmatically.

"You know me, Professor. I am not a man for suspense. Let's have the details."

Henderson perused the menu with a wry smile. He liked suspense, delaying the moment; and he was a traditionalist, attached to local North-East fare,

"Smoked haddock chowder? My Aunt Fanny! - I will have the '*Cullen Skink!*' then corn-fed chicken with the mustard mashed-potatoes," he barked precisely to the now quizzical-looking, confused, nodding waitress.

"That's *two* chowders and.....the turbot for me please," said Ross with a resigned smile, helping out the waitress.

Henderson listened with pleasure to the sound of the chilled, golden Italian wine chugging out of the bottle, filling his glass; no sooner had the waitress withdrawn the bottle than he lifted the glass to his nose, and with a look of appreciation, he gulped the glass dry.

"Very acceptable, very acceptable indeed..."

He refilled his glass immediately, filling Ross's, despite his co-diner's blatant protestations.

"Chemistry first then," said the Pathologist, "The bodies contained very high doses of plant-derived Scopalamine or Burundanga as it's known in Colombia. Does this ring any bells?"

"I am afraid it does, Professor. I got a briefing on it from the consultant attending Mark Stewart about an hour ago."

"Ah..!" Henderson was disappointed; his thunder had been stolen, but he had plenty more to say. "Did he tell you that Joseph Mengele experimented with Scopolamine as an interrogation drug in Nazi concentration camps? Did he also tell you that a gang of Bogota prostitutes preyed on men by smearing the drug on their breasts enticing their victims to take a lick? Losing all willpower, the men gave up their bank access codes. These nipple-temptresses held them hostage for a week, '*sucking*' their bank accounts dry. And, because the drug deactivates the memory processes, the men had no recollection of the ordeal, only empty bank accounts."

Henderson was a mine of information,

"There were also traces of Rohypnol, Ketamine and GHB in all the bodies. Doubtless, Mr. Mark Stewart will test positive for these unpleasant substances as well." Henderson watched Ross, waiting for the mists of uncertainly to clear.

"Date-rape drugs?" Ross suggested.

"Quite. You see the irony?"

"Perhaps, but I am not really in the mood for anything too cryptic today. What can you tell me I don't know already, Professor?"

"Trepan skulls." Henderson was happy to have the upper hand again.

Ross had the measure of him.

"Trepan skulls were used by the cult of the assassins. The skull of an enemy was pierced and the blood drunk through the hole in the skull prior to battle," Ross replied.

"Very good, Ross, but a skull could also be trepanned or pierced to allow evil spirits to leave the body of an individual possessed by demons and other evil spirits. Did you notice the small holes in the victim's heads?"

"Small calibre bullet wounds I assume?"

Delighted to finally have the drop on the policeman, Henderson put him right, while spooning a dollop of haddock chowder, aka Cullen Skink, into his mouth.

"No, Davie. Did you not notice that there was no powder or heat damage around the entry wound? Those skulls were drilled, probably with an electric, hand-drill. Usually a trepanned skull would have a large hole, but these were just large enough to be noticed. Presumably the hole was deliberately kept small to minimize blood loss, prolonging the horror of being mutilated, castrated and hung up to dry - partially aware of what is happening, but entirely incapable of preventing it..." Henderson delivered this last sentence like a ghost story: ghoulishly...

Ross spoke his mind.

"What I cannot work out Professor, is how they managed to organize it? How do you drug five people, two of whom are virtual strangers to the other three, and hang them from three separate bridges without anyone noticing? Admittedly, only one of the three bridges is accessible to the public so they could

operate without discovery on the other two, but it suggests tremendous organization, night vision and coordination verging on the military. It is certainly not the work of just one or two men. More like a company or brigade of clinical, committed, trained and equipped vigilantes or assassins."

"Byron's 'Band of Boys'?" suggested Henderson almost dismissively. He was now tucking into the chicken with a voracious enthusiasm, simultaneously wolfing down glasses of wine in single gulps. Ross wondered where Henderson had gathered his limitless knowledge of secret societies, witchcraft and legend.

"Band of Boys?" Ross said, sampling his turbot.

"It's all related you know, David, The Knights of the Temple of Solomon, Byron's freethinking rebels, the cult of the assassins. Hear, see and be silent."

"Are you telling me something, Professor?"

"I think all I can do is state the facts, Ross. Whoever did this had plenty of time to hang the three from the rail bridge. That bridge is high, at least twenty feet above the river. In the half-light, it's as good as invisible. Similarly the old suspension bridge is relatively secluded; closed to the public."

The pathologist continued,

"The audacious act was the Torry hanging, but again that could have been accomplished in ten minutes. Drive onto the bridge. Put up the '*bridge closed*' signs. Secure the body by hoisting the steel rope up and over the relatively short iron lamppost, throw the body over the side and *Hey Presto!*"

"It needed a crane to lift it." Ross reminded him.

"Two men could easily get the rope over the lamppost then lift the body over the side. Gravity was in their favour." Henderson grinned.

"Wonderful grasp of the criminal mind…"

"It's physics, not criminology, Ross - oh, and one last thing, take a look at this again?"

He handed the policeman the small metallic object removed from the throats of the bodies.

Ross studied it closely.

It resembled the skull from the pirate flag, the Jolly Roger, except it was a side elevation and flat, giving it an Art Deco appearance; ancient Armenian or Persian in style.

"Another skull?" Ross stated obviously, "What does this one signify?"

"It's an iconic representation of the Skull of Sidon, another symbol of the Knights Templar, widely associated with Masonic rituals and legend. The story is that an ancient Templar had sex with his dead mistress and nine months later she gave birth to a child from within the grave. The physical manifestation of the skeletal child was a small skull and crossed leg bones: the famed, skull and crossed bones, of pirate notoriety."

Henderson was enjoying his didactic discourse,

"The story has connotations of necrophilia and the black arts, but the point is the Templars and their modern disciples, the Freemasons, can call on great powers to guide and assist their good work."

The pathologist quaffed yet another glass of wine as if it was the last bottle in existence.

"I assume you are a Freemason, Professor?"

"Yes, I have been in the Lodge for thirty-five years."

"And you think your brother Masons killed these men? I do recall the Freemasons were alleged to have hung a financier from Towerbridge in London a few years back."

"No, Ross, I do not. The Freemasons are good people; conservative, pious and law-abiding."

"A set-up then? A false trail?"

"Looks very much like it, Superintendent. It makes the whole affair more attractive to the media, to the conspiracy theorists. And, of course, it sets you off on a wild-goose chase leaving the real culprits free to execute whomsoever they choose to make an example of next."

"You should be the detective, Professor. You have this all worked out."

"Pathology is scientific detection, Davie. It's just based on medical certainty rather than hunches." Henderson said smugly.

Ross ignored the jibe.

"So, who do you think did it, Professor?"

Henderson smiled and drained his glass, finishing the first bottle of wine.

"Well, Davie-boy, in the words of Inspector Morse: *'the last person to see the body alive was the killer'.*"

Ross eyed him thoughtfully.

"Indeed, Professor."

The Banks of the River Dee

Ross needed to think, a chance to contemplate the inexplicable recent eruption of violence and mayhem surrounding his world these last few days, engulfing him in its darkness. He had requested his transfer back from London because Aberdeen had almost zero serious crime, a fact no doubt linked to negative unemployment and great prosperity. He wanted to raise his children in peace and harmony and distance himself from the organised crime gangs and terrorist cells that could so easily have threatened or kidnapped any member of his family in London.

He had been a 'specialist resource' at the Met, recruited for his erudition and detailed knowledge of criminology, philosophy, psychology, anthropology and numerous other disciplines he seemed to naturally excel in. An intellectual, he could normally crack any criminal scheme using deductive reasoning; studying the nature and culture of the processes and individuals involved. He had helped solve complex money laundering scams, art theft and forgery, lottery scams, terrorist plots and numerous drug smuggling and people smuggling networks. His phenomenal success had seen him rise to the rank of Superintendent at the age of 29. The Metropolitan Police were sorry to see him go, hoping he would return after he got bored of solving all that sheep rustling (a Met joke) in Aberdeen.

In the last two weeks Aberdeen had proved to be a bloody, violent place. He needed solitude.

As a child, Ross had walked the banks of the River Dee regularly, and he was in the area buying some sun-block for a weekend of mountaineering he was planning with Diane.

Returning from Boots the Chemist, instead of getting back into his car, he decided to duck under some particularly fragrant, Cherry Blossom trees in full bloom. He stopped to appreciate the simple beauty of the line of perfect flowering *Arborae Floridae* before walking to the riverbank.

Beyond the row of beautiful trees was unkempt wet, overgrown coarse-grass: weeds, hemlock and nettles; about fifty yards of it to struggle through before he got to the public footpath that leads along the banks of the River Dee.

If he had remained familiar with the area, he would have known there was an adjoining path a few yards away, saving him the nettle stings and mud on his Prada boots. He was half way there, starting to regret this little unplanned diversion, when he noticed something odd.

To his left, between where he stood and the arches under the old Bridge of Dee, a man was digging. He was not a workman; he was a fat, bald, middle-aged man, dressed in casual clothes, digging. Ross stopped and studied him for a few minutes. The man, who was partially obscured by the flora, was engrossed in whatever he was doing.

A policeman, a real detective, is ever-curious so Ross deviated and approached the digger who was pale and sweating profusely. On sighting Ross, the full-moon face looked up, gathered its things and scampered off up the bank to the main road.

Ross crossed to the ground where the excavations had been taking place. A small, shallow hole about a foot deep, a foot wide and three feet long had been newly dug; a macabre scene, but perhaps innocent enough, a grave for a dead dog or a cat?

Ross trudged onwards, finally arriving at the relatively unused footpath that continued miles upstream. From his current position he couldn't see the fat man speeding away in a Red VW Golf.

There is nothing quite like walking to clear the mind and raise the spirits.

Arthur Schopenhauer, the brilliant German philosopher who once described humanity as *'at best a mistake, at worst a bad practical joke',* walked four miles every day of his adult life, no matter how inclement the weather. Ross admired Schopenhauer's genius, but avoided reading him because of the latter's proclivity towards cynicism and nihilism, but he did agree with him totally about the benefits of ambulation.

Ross's mood was immediately transformed as he walked along looking into the clear, gently flowing river that emanates in the Cairngorm Mountains. Ross had walked to the source of this river one summer's day, an awesome trek from the Lynn of Dee near Braemar, all the way up to the source of Dee wells on Braeriach, 4,000 feet above sea-level, a round trip of over twenty-five miles on foot. That had been a memorable day; the river's first few miles are an epic sight as it flows through the bare rock, and although ten to twenty feet deep, and flowing fast as it meanders and cuts through the light grey and yellow bedrock, the almost freezing water is crystal-clear. The bedrock below can be clearly seen for at least ten miles of the river's early passage. It's quite a sight to behold.

Today was beautiful by Scottish standards, warm and sunny with a gentle breeze; the path he was walking along, almost deserted.

Ross was not dressed for walking, wearing new clothes: distressed grey denim Prada jeans, soft black Prada boots, a light blue Paul Smith pullover and a tight-fitting dark brown leather jacket. Ross loved Prada; the Italian designer produced classic, practical clothes and footwear that fitted him perfectly. Despite the pretentious connotations, he had to confess, Prada and Gucci were experts in their field. It amused Ross that Aberdeen's Prada purveyor was named after his favourite writer and thinker, the sartorially elegant Czech genius, Kafka.

Inappropriately dressed or not, Ross was a spontaneous man and at this moment in time he wanted to walk along the river, drink in the scenery and relive happy memories from his adventurous childhood.

The River Dee is a wide, relatively shallow, slow-moving river as it passes through Aberdeen into the North Sea. Ross noticed little areas of golden sands along the riverbank having the appearance of mini-beaches he could not recall from his boyhood days, perhaps because he was now seeing things from a higher vantage point.

The river was awash with life. Beautiful dragonflies and damselflies darted around near the bank displaying a kaleidoscope of shimmering metallic blue, green and red. Ross admired these fabulous, fast-moving, flying torpedoes, partly because of their superb plumage and aerial genius, but also because they caught and consumed large numbers of pests, namely midges. Beautiful, brilliant and useful, just like his wonderful wife, he mused happily. Further from the riverbank, in the middle of the river, hundreds of swifts darted in close formation like squadrons of tiny, stealth-fighter jets.

He considered these marvellous birds; their ability to sleep 'on the wing'. How did they do that? He was constantly in awe of nature and by contrast he often despaired of its ostensibly 'highest' creation - man. He decided long ago *Homo Sapien* was not divine or even particularly noble. Man was just capable of destruction on a scale no other creature could match. Other animals managed to live long and healthy lives without any impact on the planet: eat, sleep, breathe and rear young, without any pollution or destruction of any kind, something man could take a great lesson from.

Ross was a few miles upriver when he made a serendipitous discovery. A wooden footbridge had been constructed on an elevated position about thirty feet up, overlooking a wide bend in the river. He stood on the hand-made platform, leaning forward, pressing his weight on the wooden handrail. A truly panoramic position, the river very broad here, he could see miles up-river.

Hypnotised by late afternoon sunlight flickering on the delicate ripples, he watched the birds flash silently to and fro on the surface of the water.

The vista from the footbridge resembled a John Constable painting, great trees on each side of the river framing the picture. The yellows and oranges of the sunlight were Turneresque.

Ross was captivated by the natural magnificence.

He had rarely felt so relaxed, so far from the madding crowd: so totally removed from the endless strife and conflict of the human race. He started to sing. When a man is truly happy, he sings. He received a text message. It was from his wife.

"Hello, big boy. Come and eat me! And have some dinner afterwards! ;) BC"

The text was a little reminder from his wife, aka Baby Cheeks, that it was five p.m., and she was missing him.

He took a long last look upriver before turning his back, starting his return journey downstream, singing as he went his happy way.

He gave way to fellow walkers, a young couple, coming the other way on the narrow footpath; they exchanged pleasantries as they passed by.

A couple of large dogs ran up behind him and the policeman noted they were Rottweilers. They were unleashed and un-muzzled. They sniffed around his feet, but Ross was not unduly bothered; imposing, but seemingly placid animals.

Two men followed fifty yards behind the dogs, walking quickly; with definite purpose.

"Get here!" One of the newcomers hollered. The dogs ignored his command. The owner walked across to Ross and grabbed each dog by the collar.

"Are these your evil dogs?" Ross enquired good-naturedly, masking his boyhood fear of dogs with the quip. It was an innocuous remark delivered with humour by a man in a relaxed and jovial mood. It was not received as such. Both men closed threateningly on Ross. He could see they were physically strong; dressed in jeans, short sleeve t-shirts and Dr Marten Airware boots. Their well-developed arm muscles suggested they were manual workers - bricklayers or labourers. Both were slim, late twenties, cropped hair, tattooed arms; gaunt, wasted features.

"What the fuck do you mean by evil?" the owner said menacingly, throwing the dogs to one side, coming within inches of Ross's face.

A situation was developing Ross could never have imagined a few minutes ago.

The other man stood a few feet behind and to the left of the first man. Ross was taken aback. He had expected a few friendly words; now he felt he was in danger.

The man was waiting for an answer and the response would determine whether this situation escalated or not.

Ross, a trained martial artist, was also a realist. These two were probably petty criminals, possibly soccer casuals. They were likely from a known trouble spot in the nearby council housing estate, using this path as a means of travelling incognito, safe from any passing police cars. It was also fair to assume from their aggressive reaction they were used to resolving disputes with a fist and a boot. It was probable they carried knives.

Ross considered telling them he was a senior police officer, but this was a risky manoeuvre; even increasing the inevitability of a violent attack.

The dogs watched-on placidly, their tongues hanging out as they panted indifferently. No doubt these could turn very nasty if violence erupted. The dogs were a real, potential threat.

The only way to deal with two assailants is to remove the first one with maximum force leaving a one-on-one situation against the remaining aggressor ensuring a correspondingly greater chance of escaping serious injury. Ross was wearing tight jeans; his boots offered little or no grip. His natural reaction was to remove the man nearest to him using a combination of Taekwondo kicks. He went through this in his mind.

Ultimately his jeans and footwear made this tactic impractical and if the second man was fast enough and he did have a knife, then Ross could lose his life.

It was one thing tackling thugs when he was in uniform, surrounded by trained and armed officers, but it was quite another matter when alone, relaxed and dressed inappropriately. Ross decided to try diplomacy to defuse the tension,

"It was a joke. I did not mean anything by it."

He watched both men for the first sign of movement. If the man nearest him closed any further he would be forced to smash his left fist into his face. It was not an easy decision. As a police officer the whole episode would be investigated in great detail; sure to make the newspapers and the local TV news.

The man looked at Ross; he was also considering his options. Ross could feel the 'fight or flight' adrenalin rush. He prayed this was not going to go against him. He thought about his wife and his two lovely children. What a waste and tragedy if his body was found dumped in the river without apparent reason or explanation.

The difference between life and death is often a very fine line. One thing was obvious. The man standing no more than six inches from Ross was a violent, aggressive individual. His eyes could best be described as 'dead'. Judging by his menacing, dark countenance he would prefer to give Ross a good kicking; the policeman hoped the man would not want to risk prison if Ross survived to tell the tale.

A middle-aged couple came across the footbridge heading towards Ross and the two aggressors. Ross stepped back and put a little distance between him and his potential foe.

The man facing up to him glanced at the older couple, turned his back, and without uttering a single word, walked away quickly with his accomplice and the two muscular dogs.

It was over as suddenly as it began. Ross noticed something strange. He was shaking and felt cold; tranquillity and happiness had been stolen from him. One moment, he had been an observer of beauty, all wrapped up in the warmth of his inner happiness; a few minutes later, he was facing mortal conflict.

Ross was surprised at his own fear, his feelings of vulnerability; shock that such a situation could arise out of nothing, in a place of seclusion and harmony. Ross was now a victim, feeling all the emotions of a victim of crime: the invasion of personal privacy, the theft of confidence and the violation of personal integrity. No actual physical blows had been dealt, but the threat was real and the threat was enough. It was the threat that invoked the fear and it was the threat that forced the victim to deal with the situation.

Ross had been threatened and it had caught him unawares. He would no longer be able to walk along the riverbank without looking over his shoulder or wondering if it was safe to make conversation with passers-by. From now on he would be on his guard. He even considered carrying a peace-maker or some similar device in the future. After all, he would be fighting as a husband and a father, not just to protect his own skin. He would no longer be able to be so objective in his discussions with Diane about criminology. No matter what caused these people to be so aggressive, so ready to attack other people, the consequences were unacceptable.

Ross started to sympathise with whoever had hung the five bodies from the nearby bridges!

Des Res

It was bad enough that Bobby Turnbull and Deborah Glennie's killer had so far evaded justice, but now there were four, probably five, more murders and no obvious suspects. The homes of the victims had to be searched post-haste. Ross investigated with Detective Sergeant Laura Mac.

Jason Jameson lived in Rubislaw Den, the finest address in the city centre. Ross's Dulmunzie was debatably more desirable, in the suburb of Cults and Milltimber, the 'stockbroker belt', but the Den is famous for its exclusivity.

Rubislaw Den, sarcastically known as '*Rubbishy Den*' by those who had moved out of town or were simply jealous, is a fantastic area complete with its own private, ornate park, 'The Den', running along the rear of the large Victorian granite mansions. Although near the city centre, 'The Den' is home to a variety of wildlife: owls, deer, badgers and foxes. The majority of the *Silver City's* residents have never seen this private oasis with its babbling brook and miniature natural waterfalls.

Jameson's house was far too big for a single man, but doubtless all that legal-aid had to be invested somewhere and Rubislaw Den is a *granite-solid* investment.

Inside the *Silver Fox's* former lair, the décor was dark and luxurious; navy, black, gold; scarlet silk-drapes and soft furnishings; classical paintings; white marble statues of the male nude in the drawing room, study and bedrooms.

Ross had seen too much marble recently, "Bloody white marble," he sighed.

"I think it's actually plaster," said Mac.

The young policewoman rocked the naked Greek Olympian 'white marble' discus thrower backwards to see what was beneath – nothing,

"Sure is gay!" she added with a smile.

"That seems to be the general consensus of opinion about Mr Jameson," Ross concurred.

Generally the place was immaculate. Jameson either spent little time at home, had a regular cleaner, or both. Things of interest in Jason Jameson's grand abode: a library full of homo-erotic literature and criminal law; a bedroom full of homosexual pornography, sex toys and criminal law; large amounts of cash and jewellery.

Laura Mac lifted a string of pearls and held them up to her neck, posing for her superior, fluttering her eyelashes, "Gifts from clients?" Mac was sardonic.

"No doubt," Ross replied, "You better put them down, you never know where they might have been," he smiled.

Mac frowned, "Oh yuck!" She grasped his meaning.

"This might be something?" She passed Ross a book on secret societies. A few pages were marked, 'Templars Park, Maryculter, Aberdeen' and 'Freemasons in Scotland'.

"He was probably a Mason," replied Ross.

Ross knew about Templars Park. Dating back to the thirteenth century, 1225, it was now just a graveyard in the grounds of Maryculter House Hotel.

"Well, this is definitely something," said Mac.

The young woman was engrossed, clearly admiring the images in her hand. She passed the Polaroid photographs of the teenage boy, circa 13 or 14, proudly holding his considerable erect penis to Ross.

Jameson may have taken the pictures.

"I think we have already established Mr Jameson is gay, possibly verging on paedophilia, but that's no child judging from the size of his member and I don't think he was killed for his sexual preferences."

"What about this?" Laura Mac handed Ross a letter lying on the walnut writing desk. Ross scanned it. No address, it was hand-delivered.

Dear Mr. Jameson,

As chairman of a group of concerned citizens, it has been brought to my attention that you are skilled and effective in your job defending the perpetrators of anti-social behaviour and violent crime. This letter is a request that you consider the victims of crime. We ask you to consider the best verdict for society. Perhaps there are times when a custodial sentence would better protect potential victims; times when a guilty plea, more appropriate. As an honourable man, I am sure you will consider this genuine request to make Aberdeen a safer, more pleasant place to live.

Yours sincerely
Hans Kool, Chairman, ACTION

"Well done, Sergeant. This looks relevant."

Laura Mac was pleased. She was tenacious, persistent and ambitious. Her aim was to be Grampian's first female Chief Constable. She was 27 and fancied Ross. She thought Ross was 'sexy and cool'. "Let's get over to Northfield and take a look at how the other half live," said her idol.

They got into Ross's Range Rover and pulled away. Mac was amused at the prospect of pulling up to the flats in Mansion Avenue in a new Range Rover.

179

She wondered if Ross had ever been to any of the city's more colourful areas. Chalk and cheese, black and white, definitely rich and poor, definitely *not* ying and yang; these expressions might compare Mansion Avenue with Rubislaw Den; a few miles apart they might as well be on different planets.

An area the size of Jameson's feu contained no less than 48 separate, flatted properties in Mansion Avenue; low-rise blocks of twelve; very small apartments, squeezed so close together as to be almost one. The ground floor properties were all boarded up. The first floor properties had heavy wire mesh over the windows. Only the top floors seemed safe from intruders.

Outside, old fridges, cookers, microwaves and television sets lay abandoned; tossed out of windows at invaders or during furious domestic disputes - broken, rusting. Ross shook his head,

"Why call this place Mansion Avenue?"

"Irony? optimism? delusions of grandeur?" Mac was a graduate recruit; fast-track, loquacious.

Ross gave his opinion,

"Scrap-yard Avenue is more appropriate."

He drove past the worst of it and parked behind a newsagent. He sensed his luxury SUV stood out like a bishop in a brothel.

698h Mansion Avenue was a top floor property. Ostensibly, the home address of Davie, Gegsy and Mark Stewart, the rent was paid from Davie Allen's benefit money so the other two probably had 'no fixed abode', the kiss of death when it came to getting a job or applying for any kind of loan - a poverty trap with no escape.

Ross and Mac were in uniform. There was nothing cordial about the reception they received.

Climbing the stairs, they encountered a gang of youths, boys and girls, aged between 8 to15,

"Fucking pigs, oink, oink, oink!"

"Fit's that stink of pig shite!"

"Blue-nosed bastards!"

"Here piggy, piggy, piggy…"

Mac smiled - she had seen it all before.

Ross was less amused. The unwashed gremlins reminded him of the dreadful Scottish *midgies*: tiny creatures with a ferocious sting; impossible to swat.

One of the foul-mouthed youths picked up a dehydrated dog stool and threw it at the two officers, narrowly missing them by inches.

Mac called for backup.

"Let's get a few burly constables up here to put the fright'ners on those wee bastards."

Ross found the place incredibly depressing.

Entering flat h, it was clear it had been turned over, either by the neighbours or the executioners.

Chairs, and what little furniture there was, had been overturned or smashed-up.

One thing was immediately obvious.

Sprayed across one wall was the none-too-subtle, but patently obvious graffiti legend:

JUSTICE FOR THE VICTIMS

R.I.P ASSHOLES!

The Dutchman

Ross had contacted **The Aberdeen Guardian** and asked them to search for all correspondence from a Hans Kool.

It transpired Kool was a frequent contributor and had submitted numerous pieces over the past twelve months; letters complaining about anti-social behaviour, boy-racers, litter louts, Muslim extremists, insufficient police on the streets, overly lenient sentencing by the criminal courts and other topical subjects. The paper printed more of these than normal because Kool was a leading oilman and chairman of a local residents campaigning group known as ACTION – Aberdeen Citizens Together in Opposition to Nuisance.

Ross discovered ACTION was well known to the Chief Constable who was constantly receiving letters and petitions from its various members to increase police numbers and patrol cars throughout the wealthier areas of the city where the residents feared for their property and personal safety.

Ross decided to pay Mr. Kool a personal visit and they agreed to meet at nine-thirty that evening.

Kool lived alone in a large detached house in Woodburn Road, a much sought after address in Aberdeen's exclusive AB15 postcode. The AB15 area boasted more millionaires per capita than any other city in Scotland and included the prestigious Rubislaw Den in its boundaries.

Ross pulled up outside the Dutchman's house and noticed the garden and grounds were immaculate.

Ornamental hedges were carefully sculpted into the shapes of animals; a squirrel, a stork and a bear.

The front was beautifully crafted into a Japanese ornamental garden with a fountain; water cascading across a large obelisk of pink granite, the kind of thing that might be encountered in the reception area of an investment bank in London or Wall Street. Ross climbed the five granite steps that led to the front door of the Victorian house. The property was built in the gothic style, crafted from the famous local granite, a cold but incredibly hard silver stone. The general appearance was of a small castle or stately home. The top half of the front door entrance was shaped like a Bishops Mitre; the door itself was constructed of ten solid pieces of dark oak held together with iron bolts.

The impression was of a veritable miniature fortress. Ross pressed the antique-effect, blackened iron-doorbell and waited for Hans Kool.

A giant of a man appeared before Ross. He filled the entire 'Bishop's hat'. He stood at no less than six feet six inches in height, but that was not the impressive thing about Kool; the impressive thing was his physique; enormous shoulders; biceps inflated with a pneumatic pump; this was not a man you wanted to be drawn against in an arm wresting contest. Kool's jaw-line and general facial features reminded Ross of Arnold Shwarzenegger, except Kool was bigger than *The Terminator*, much bigger.

He greeted Ross warmly with a massive hand that made the policeman feel like a small and very insignificant child.

"Good evening, Superintendent. I am delighted to meet you." Kool spoke with a heavy, sophisticated Dutch accent.

He led Ross through a perfectly preserved Victorian vestibule laid in antique ceramic tiles with the inscription *Via Crucis*[5] inscribed on the ornate mosaic tiling. The significance was not lost on David Ross. They continued into a dimly-lit drawing room where two red-leather, wing-backed chairs sat facing a roaring fire. The giant invited Ross to take a seat.

"Very extravagant in the middle of summer," said Ross looking at the conflagration.

"I have just returned from a few years in Oman and, to me, Scotland feels like the Artic in the evenings; even in the middle of summer. Would you like a drink or some tea, Superintendent?"

"Thanks. I will have a glass of red wine if you have any."

"I have an excellent Pinot Noir from New Zealand. Just let me get it for you."

While Hans Kool was looking out the wine, Ross had a look around the room.

It was a large room about twenty-five feet square with high, ten-foot ceilings decorated with original plaster cornicing and a spectacular ceiling rose surrounding an antique brass chandelier. A large bay window with floor-to-ceiling glazing displayed religious scenes in decorative, leaded stained-glass. The walls had pitch-pine paneling, rising to about a third of the way up. Around the room were paintings in the style of icons; modernist depictions of famous scenes from the bible. The icons were richly painted in deep reds, strong blues and bright yellows, individually illuminated by antique-brass picture-lights. The room combined an art gallery, a small church and a gentleman's study.

---

[5] **The Way of The Cross**

There was no sign of a female's touch - no superficial ornaments or pictures of children or family; no television or even a music system in evidence.

Kool returned with the bottle of wine and two very large cut-crystal goblets. He set them down on a small side table, poured two glasses and passed one carefully to Ross.

"Here we are. Now, how can I assist you?" asked the Dutchman politely.

"You have a lovely house. No white marble statues."

"I am sorry, Superintendent?"

"Simply an observation about your excellent taste, Mr.Kool; I want to ask you about ACTION. Could it be linked to the recent appalling incidents on the bridges? Do you have any militant members, fanatics?" Ross suggested.

"Well, I will say this, Superintendent. You do not mess about. Why don't you just ask me if I did it?"

"Did you do it, Mr. Kool?" Ross looked carefully at the other man eyes.

"Mr. Ross, I have been campaigning publicly for several years to rid society of the kind of anti-social pests hung from those bridges. It would be foolish of me to announce my intentions so obviously beforehand."

"You did not answer the question, Mr. Kool?" Ross repeated.

"I did not do it, Mr. Ross." Kool smiled slightly, unphased by the question.

If he was lying, he was a good liar; relaxed and confident.

"Did you play any part in the crime?"

"Yes," said Kool, "I hope so."

Ross did not react. He took a mouthful of the warm Pinot Noir from the chunky crystal glass. As anticipated, the wine was excellent; very fruity: raspberries, strawberries and blackcurrants. Hard to believe it was made solely from grapes. Ross was also drinking-in and evaluating Kool's character and personality. He already liked him. He had style: a thoughtful directness. He was obviously intelligent and successful. No white marble here. Kool spoke,

"I will tell you my story, Mr. Ross, because you will no doubt discover it soon enough…if you don't already know it?"

Ross shook his head slowly, indicating that he had not yet looked deeply into Hans Kool's background, as he surely would, in due course.

"About ten years ago, my daughter, who was just seven years old, was abducted while she was playing outside our house in Houston, Texas, where I was working at the time. We waited for what seemed like an eternity before we heard news of her. It's really impossible to describe how it feels when your defenceless baby, your entire reason for living, is taken by a stranger. Even now, I cannot begin to find the appropriate words…"

Kool fell silent. His eyes glazed over.

"Believe me, Hans, I can imagine exactly how it feels," said Ross, thinking of his own two darling, precious children and feeling the anger rise inside him at the thought of anyone so much as looking at them inappropriately.

Kool took a copious mouthful of wine and stared into the fire. Ross wondered if he would ever say another word.

Eventually, he did,

"I knew, almost immediately, we would never see her alive again. Two days later, her body was found in what the Americans call a dumpster. Her body was unrecognisable. I will not go into the details, but what happened to her was worse than anything you can imagine. So terrible, my wife took her own life a few months later. One selfish act, by one sick mother-fucker, destroyed my whole family and my whole world in a moment. The son-of-a-bitch was caught and sent to an institute for the mentally ill where he will rehabilitate in relative luxury until he is released. I tried to get five minutes alone with him, but it proved impossible. I would have killed him without a second's thought."

Kool lapsed into quiet meditation again.

Ross didn't know what to say. He was thinking about his wife's reaction if Jo or Tim were to be taken by a stranger. It would destroy them both.

For a moment, swayed by the pain Kool was clearly suffering and under the influence of the heady red wine, Ross wanted to lynch every rapist, murderer and child molester on the planet. Yes, and he wanted to torture them first.

He remembered the comment of a fellow officer after Thomas Hamilton murdered 16 children in 1996 in the nearby town of Dunblane: *"I wish we could bring the bastard back to life, so we could kill him again - as slowly and as painfully as possible."*

The officer had meant every word of it.

Ross was now a little embarrassed to be questioning a man so obviously robbed of family and love as Kool, but the law required a fair trial and vigilante behaviour was not acceptable in a civilised society. He took another mouthful of wine and waited for Kool to recover.

"I assume you are here because of my letters to the local newspaper and to your Chief Constable." Kool seemed relaxed and calm again, past caring.

"Yes, and your letter to Jason Jameson; and my wife noticed your letter just yesterday congratulating whoever killed the five men hung from the bridges. That one must have been written around the actual time of the incident: immediately after the bodies were discovered?"

Ross was choosing his words carefully as the two men played out a game of psychological chess.

"I know your wife, Superintendent, indeed she counseled me on a few occasions. She is a brilliant and charming woman, but she does not really understand suffering. She has not lost everything. Philosophy is one thing, but it's a luxury afforded to the fortunate. Nothing can repair your soul after the loss of your family. Time erases memories and God gives me hope, but my honest opinion is that those men got what they deserved."

Kool refilled his glass and topped up Ross.

"I did not, of course, actually congratulate anybody, Mr. Ross."

Ross produced a copy of the letter.

"May I read this, Hans?" asked Ross.

Kool nodded, raising his glass to his mouth.

Ross read out the Dutchman's letter from the press clipping,

ACTION

"Dear Sir,

While I regret any distress to innocent members of the public that must surely have been caused by the sight of the five mutilated bodies strung up from those bridges, I do think there is a degree of natural justice in what otherwise has the appearance of a barbaric act. Criminal law in our country favours the murderer, the child molester and the rapist. The sacrifice of those five unholy souls serves as a warning to evil-doers and a reminder to society of the suffering of the victims of violent crime.

Yours faithfully,
Hans Kool, PhD,
Chairman, ACTION"

"You do not pull any punches," Ross surmised.

"I am Dutch, Mr. Ross. We are a direct speaking people. Some would say blunt," Kool replied.

"But as a Dutchman you enjoy a liberal society. Surely you believe in human rights - the right to a fair trial?"

"Superintendent, I am in full support of human rights. I believe wholeheartedly in freedom of speech, freedom to have a family life, freedom to practice any religion, but the Human Rights Act is being abused by a section of the legal profession to focus sympathy on criminals and encourage clemency in the punishment of violent and anti-social crimes. When someone rapes and murders a child for amusement or to punish the child or to gain notoriety, then they should lose their rights. They should have a fair trial, but that trial

must be fair to the victim and the punishment *must* fit the crime. It is ludicrous that directors of companies manipulating share prices get greater jail sentences than a child molester. White collar crime is about fat cats stealing the cream from other fat cats. *Caveat emptor* - you buy shares, you take your chances, but I can walk out of here today and kick an old man to death and as long as I can prove I was depressed, on drugs or some other fatuous excuse, I will get five years - out in two years, with good behaviour. My position is this, Superintendent - if I kick an old man to death, then I should be prepared to be kicked to death as retribution. If rapists faced rape and brutal assailants faced brutal assault, crime levels would drop massively."

"I am not sure I can agree, Mr. Kool. I have studied criminology, there is no evidence whatsoever to suggest the death penalty prevents murder. I doubt moving towards an Islamic model of criminal justice would be beneficial or acceptable to the majority in this country."

"I know your background quite well, Mr. Ross and I expect you to be our new Chief Constable before long, that's why I am having this discussion with you now, but I am not talking about the death penalty. I am talking about *evil*. People who stamp on the head of another without the slightest concern are evil. People who burn a baby with a cigarette to hear it scream are evil. People who gang rape two teenage girls, then stab them to death are evil."

"Evil has always been hard to define," Ross interjected, watching Kool intently.

"Evil is easy to define, Superintendent. Evil is a total absence of empathy, sympathy or compassion for the victim. Evil is a positive desire to inflict pain

191

and suffering. When you confront evil you will have no problem recognising it, Superintendent."

Ross recollected the recent incident on the Banks of the River Dee. He recalled the look in the eyes of the man with the dogs; a look that said 'You mean nothing to me - I could kill you now and it would mean no more to me than if I stood on an ant'.

Ross remembered the fear such evil invoked. He could feel himself agreeing with Hans Kool; the Dutchman was highly persuasive.

"Evil does understand one thing, Mr. Ross. It understands greater evil. It understands fear and it understands pain. You will remember the school bully. How he enjoys beating and hurting the smaller boys, until one day, someone turns and gives the bully a taste of his own medicine. The bully starts to cry like a baby and loses all confidence. He can then be defeated by almost anyone. Evil can be defeated. It just needs to be terrified into submission."

Ross was unsure whether he was hearing a confession or a lecture in psychology.

"Are you saying we should return to the days of putting people in stocks - throw rotten fruit at them to shame and ridicule?" Ross pressed the Dutchman.

"Yes, if they have already done something similar to an innocent, helpless victim. What I am saying is this, Mr. Ross. Evil succeeds because it preys on the weak and the indifferent. It is like a dog bred to attack. If you do not run, if you do not turn the other cheek; if you lift a large stick and attack the dog with greater venom than it displays towards you, then it will think twice, turn and run. If it bites you, then break its leg. It will have learned that biting someone leads to excruciating pain in its leg and unless it has amnesia it will never do it again."

Kool concluded,

"What I am talking about, Superintendent is conquering evil using the only language evil understands: rational, proportional physical retaliation - Direct Action."

"And the police force, the courts, the law?" said Ross, introducing a little reality.

"The criminal legal system is not working. Criminals have no fear of the law. Prison is an occupational hazard. Somewhere to meet old friends and live rent free for a while. Community service is a chance to commit crime in a new geography, with the added bonus of state-sponsored free transport to the inevitable, new crime-scene. Evil in particular has nothing to fear from a collection of middle-aged, well-fed academics debating whether the accused should pay a fine or go to jail. If anything, evil is encouraged by the tacit approval it receives from its defence lawyers - the grandiose, erudite speeches explaining why *evil* was not really to blame for maiming, crippling, terrifying, torturing and killing an innocent. Ordinary crime can be managed by the current system, but evil is flourishing, Mr. Ross. It can only be stopped by special and extraordinary measures."

"Taking the law into one's own hands - a society of vigilantes?" Ross probed.

"No, Mr. Ross, that implies a degree of premeditation. I am talking about zero tolerance. Society decides now it will no longer tolerate evil. Evil will be countered at an individual level with proportionate and reasonable means."

Ross finished his glass of wine. It was truly wonderful. Kool noticed his visitor's appreciation and offered him a bottle to take home to Diane.

Ross accepted the gift with appreciation. If nothing else, he would have Kool's fingerprints for reference. The wine had a New Zealand label and a vintage Ross did not recognize.

"Surely we can tackle evil by prevention, Hans, by knowing where our children are at all times, taking care not to wander into dark alleys late at night, fitting alarm systems to our property."

"True, Superintendent, but evil is devious. It lurks within boy-scout leaders, school teachers and swimming-pool instructors: the very people we expect to protect our children. Evil is a master of disguise. Look at Peter Sutcliffe, he looks like an ordinary, inoffensive man, but is a brutal, sex attacker. Dr. Harold Shipman looks like an Old English Sheepdog, a kindly old man and yet he was a mass murderer. You cannot see evil coming. It does not wear a red costume and horns with a forked tail. You can only take care as you rightly say, and then, when evil shows its hand, cut it off!" concluded Hans Kool.

Ross found the giant Dutchman's arguments compelling. He looked forward to tackling Diane on the subject of Kool's thesis on evil and how to deal with it. But first, he had to ask the familiar question,

"Can I just ask you where you were last weekend, Mr. Kool?"

"I was in Amsterdam visiting my aged parents and my sister. Am I a suspect, Superintendent?"

The question was unemotional.

Kool seemed entirely unmoved by the possibility of arrest.

"Let's just say that I may yet need to ask you some more questions, to eliminate you from our enquiries. It has been a pleasure meeting you, and thank you for your hospitality."

"The pleasure was mine. I am glad to see the future of the police force is in such reasonable and capable hands. My best wishes to your good wife."

Kool shook Ross's hand warmly with his enormous mitt. Ross drove away in contemplative mood.

Kool was almost confessing to involvement, but at the same time he seemed detached; he was surely too relaxed to have recently committed murders involving such atrocities?

Ross drove home to *Rose Cottage* to discuss Kool and his theories on evil with his closest advisor, his wife.

Fear of Evil

Around eleven p.m., the black Lamborghini crunched over the granite *chuckies* that covered the long and sweeping driveway leading to the garage complex at the back of his house. Ross considered for the first time, the little granite stone chippings added protection, alerting them as to when a car was coming up to the house. Already he was looking for evil, anticipating its presence everywhere. Kool had got through to Ross's subconscious very effectively.

Rose Cottage was eerily silent. After his conversation with Kool, Ross needed the reassurance of seeing and holding his family. Admittedly, it was late, but he had hoped to see Diane sitting in the kitchen reading the newspapers, as she was apt to do at that time of night.

He was about to shout *'Is there anyone at home?'* when he checked himself. If the kids were asleep, his wife would not thank him for waking them up. He decided just to look in on them.

He carefully started to climb the stairs, but stopped when one old wooden floorboard creaked and groaned under his feet. He took off his soft leather boots and walked the rest of the way to the landing in his socks. At the top of the stairs he put his boots back on.

To the left was the master bedroom where his wife would be sleeping and to the right were three bedrooms; the remaining two bedrooms were in the attic. He headed to the right where in the first of the bedrooms his children would be fast asleep dreaming sweet, innocent childish dreams.

The children slept together, in the same room, because little Jo was scared of the dark and Tim, despite his occasional, acerbic comments to the contrary, was very protective of his little sister.

Ross opened the door carefully and bent down to kiss Jo's cherubic rosy cheeks when panic hit.

His blood turned to ice. She was not there! He put on the light. Tim's bed was also empty! Running to his bedroom, shouting his wife's name, he burst into their room. She was not there. Their bed had not been slept in. Ross was dizzy. His breathing became erratic and the asthma that had not affected him since childhood threatened to return as he gasped for breath; there must be an explanation - stay cool...

He ran down the stairs through to the kitchen.

Empty!

From there, he ran through the snug and into the conservatory. The fire was burning in the snug, but the door from the conservatory, out onto the patio, down to the river, was open! Panic! Through the conservatory, out onto the patio, about to run down the little path under the flyover to the river's edge when he heard a shout,

"BOO!"

It was a woman's voice. It was his wife.

"What......!" screamed Ross, petrified.

"Hello, Big Boy," purred Diane Ross. She was wearing a black, fishnet, see-through body-stocking and black ankle-boots with aluminium stiletto heels. She looked like a stylish, designer prostitute; an expert in, *'how to dress to keep your marriage healthy and interesting'.*

"For fuck's sake!" Ross was panting, close to collapse: in shock.

"Is this your idea of a joke? Where are Jo and Tim? I am having a heart-attack."

"Oh, baby, don't you remember they are staying over at their Aunt Eleanor's tonight. It's their cousin Tristan's 5th birthday tomorrow and they are having a big party. It was to be our night together, but you didn't come home at nine and I decided to surprise you. I have been out here drinking champagne under the stars, all alone, showing my little shaven-haven to the owls and the badgers." She put her arms around him and hugged him close.

Her incredible smell revived him and he began to feel like the strong man he normally was. Despite this, he started to cry.

"Oh baby, what's wrong? It was just a little surprise. What did you think had happened?" She stroked his hair and licked the tears carefully off his cheeks.

"I thought someone had taken the children. I thought they had taken you all. I could not live without you and the kids." He choked.

He sat down on a garden chair.

She sat on his knee and covered him with warm and tender kisses.

The Succubus

Diane Ross peeled off her body-stocking in a slow and seductive lap-dance routine. She unbuttoned her husband's trousers and sat on his lap, her back facing him. She spread her legs taking him inside her, moving up and down on his erection, looking at him straight in the eye over her shoulder. They made love with enormous intensity.

Slowly and deliberately, she moved her gorgeous backside, massaging his shaft with her internal muscles, staring unflinchingly. He gasped with excitement, tears rolling down his face. She leant back and wiped the tears from his cheeks with her cheeks. They became one. Their souls united as he burst inside her, exploding upwards - time and again.

At that moment, he knew their third child had been conceived. So, it seemed, did his wife.

She leant back, adoringly, whispering,

"What shall we call her darling?"

"Her?" said Ross, spooked by her telepathy.

"Oh yes. It's a girl. I know these things."

"What about Succubus? Like her mother."

"Suki?" pondered Diane Ross, "Agreed." She nodded, curving her spine, pressing her hips deep into her husband's still raging erection, her orgasm sucking up every last sperm into her cervix.

"Mmmmmmmm….lovely…" she purred, her arms wrapped around his neck in what amounted to a double-jointed yoga position. She was still sitting on his lap with her back to him.

Not for the first time, Ross looked at his wife in awe; he was the luckiest man alive.

An hour later, they were in each other's arms, on the four-poster bed Diane had designed herself.

A beautiful night; warm by North-East standards at around 15C, the sky was dark navy-blue, never getting black like other latitudes. The bedroom had French doors, opened to let in the gentle breeze; there was a balcony, created for watching sunsets and sunrises. An owl hooted somewhere nearby.

The two lovers kissed and cuddled, pausing to reflect on their mutual days.

"I went to see Hans Kool this evening. That's why I was late," Ross said softly.

"Why didn't you tell me?" she replied.

"I assumed you would object; client confidentiality and all that."

"Did you breach any confidences?"

"No."

"Then you held out on me under false pretences."

As usual, she was running rings around him. He smiled at her adoringly.

"You considered being a courtroom lawyer?"

"Too many unsavoury characters."

"Someone has to represent the accused."

"I was talking about the lawyers not the criminals," she chuckled.

He kissed her and gave her a squeeze.

"Anyway," she said, "I would have objected on other grounds."

"Such as?" Ross probed her.

"There is something about Kool. Something menacing," she opined.

"He was your patient."

"Client, not patient. I counsel and provide guidance based on philosophy and psychology as you well know, I am not a medical expert."

"Ok. He was your *client*."

"Yes and I had to terminate the sessions."

"Why?"

"Well, that is confidential. It might prejudice your view of Mr. Kool."

"I could request a court decree ordering you to tell me, if it's relevant," he teased.

"I will tell you, but on two conditions."

"Ok. What are your terms?"

"One, you go down there and use your tongue on me because I think I will come again in about ten seconds; thinking about my new daughter has made me incredibly horny."

"I think I can manage that," he said, leaping at the opportunity to practise his favourite duty as a husband. He poured a little honey from a tiny jar she kept in the bedside cabinet onto her *mons veneris*,

"What's the second condition?" asked Ross, moving his tongue carefully and slowly around her honey-covered outer labia.

"You do not use what I tell you in evidence against Hans Kool," gasped Diane Ross, her orgasm building rapidly inside her.

"Mmmm......ok" said Ross moving his tongue in and out of his wife's pulsating warmth, flicking her clitoris rapidly with his well-practised tongue.

"Oh my God... OH MYYY GOOOOOOD!!!!!!"

She exploded, jack-knifing in spasms of ecstasy.

Ross could feel her internal muscles grasping his tongue. It reminded him of the way a baby automatically clenches its little mitt when you put your finger into the palm of its open hand: spontaneous, innocent; it warmed his heart.

He licked his lips. "Ok, you horny bitch - confess!"

Her breathing erratic, she paused for a few moments before gasping her reply.

"Hans Kool has an absolute belief in the power of revenge. He believes criminals should be tortured. No matter how I reasoned with him, he was immovable. In the end, he started to persuade me *'an eye for an eye and a tooth for a tooth'*, was the only tenable solution to the problem of truly evil criminals."

"He had a similar effect on me, but that's no reason to give up on him. Not at two hundred pounds an hour," laughed Ross.

His wife looked at him, a school mistress disciplining an errant child. She did not like her hourly rate being questioned.

"That's not why I terminated Hans Kool."

"Then do tell" demanded Ross.

She hesitated, considering the best way to convey her secret about Hans Kool,

"Beneath the 'cool' exterior is a coiled spring, a loaded weapon. Hans Kool is lethal."

"And has this ever manifested itself in real violence or is it just a hunch?"

"It's far from a hunch, honey. He is a killer."

Ross sat up in bed, the police officer on full alert.

"Down boy - you can't use this in evidence and anyway he was never charged," Diane cautioned.

"Do proceed, Pandora."

"He was living in Dubai at the time, around two years ago. One night, asleep in bed, he was awoken by an intruder breaking into his flat. I suspect it was the opportunity Kool had been waiting for; in that sense you could say it was premeditated. Stark-naked, he confronted the interloper and discovered a local Arab tradesman, down on his luck, looking for something valuable to steal. It transpired later the trespasser had been dismissed from his job over a false allegation and had taken to burglary to pay for

an urgent medical operation for his infant daughter. It was to be his first and last job as a burglar."

Ross was silent, listening carefully to his wife, soaking up every detail. She continued,

"The intruder took one look at Kool, the naked, furious behemoth and made a beeline for the French doors through which he had made his entry in the first place. Kool grabbed him by the neck and was in the process of breaking it when the Arab pulled out a carpenter's knife and plunged it deep into Kool's thigh. Unflinchingly, Kool threw the man onto the floor and with the knife still deep in his leg he took hold of the Arab's wrist and brought his foot down on the prostrate ex-carpenter's arm, snapping it in half."

Diane Ross looked at her husband for signs of a reaction. Ross did not react. He was thinking,

"Go on…" he said.

"Well, this is where it gets disturbing. Kool sat himself down on an armchair and watched the hapless Arab writhe in agony. He asked the intruder what he would have done if he had discovered a defenceless woman or an innocent child in the house. The Arab did not speak much English. He did not fully understand the question; he just screamed, 'Please, sir', 'Please, sir', 'Hospital'."

Ross thought he knew what was coming: it was not a happy ending.

"Kool pulled the knife out of his own thigh, walked across to the unfortunate tradesman and cut his throat - with his own knife."

Diane Ross went quiet.

Recounting Kool's confession was disturbing; as disturbing as when she first heard it,

"He was never charged. The local police assumed it was self-defence; Kool was working for a major multi-national oil company; the Arab was a penniless, unemployed tradesman. Ridden with guilt, Kool made enquiries about the victim the next day. On discovering the dead man had a young, sick daughter, he was distraught. He paid the girl's medical bills and set up a financial arrangement for her. She is a beneficiary of his estate after his death. Kool was convinced evil possessed him that evening. He said he was entered by evil and evil passed through him as he killed the intruding Arab. While he remains convinced that evil must be defeated by superior force he was appalled by the consequences of his own application of that superior force. I just could not make any progress with Hans Kool. He is a deeply troubled man. His eyes are pools of the deepest despair. He reminds me of Richard Burton in that movie of yours."

"The Medusa Touch." said Ross.

"Yes. That's it, *The Medusa Touch*."

"Except, Burton's character causes disasters through projected mental energy and he despises God. By all accounts, Kool appears pious and even collects religious icons." Ross pointed out.

"Yes. An iconoclastic collector of icons," replied his wife cleverly. "Did you know he religiously attends every meeting conducted by the preacher who discovered those bridge bodies, Big Jack McKay? They are personal friends. Big Jack was coaching Kool on biblical interpretations of revenge and justice."

"Is there anything you don't know about Kool?" asked Ross.

"I know he is not gay." said Diane coyly.

"Really?" said Ross anxiously.

"Yes. The first time we met in my office he demonstrated his party trick - guessing someone's exact weight by lifting them up. He swept me up off my feet and guessed correctly I was 55 kg."

"And that means he is not gay?" said Ross, rather tetchily.

"Well, as he was lowering me, I was almost impaled."

"Right - you are for it now, you lying wench!"

Ross turned his wife over and put her across his knee, spanking her until her bare buttocks were glowing red and his own right hand was stinging.

When he'd finished, there was a tear in her eye, but a smile on her face.

She dived on top of him and within minutes the mock-fight turned into a furious, lustful love-making session until they collapsed happily in one another's arms, falling into a deep, blissful sleep.

Silver Darlings Restaurant

Silver Darlings is named after the humble Herring; the small, oily fish that was smoked, salted and pickled, providing the people of North East Scotland with plentiful, cheap nutrition for hundreds of years. Times have moved on and it's lost its appeal, replaced by more exotic seafood.

The eponymous restaurant excels in serving an aquatic cornucopia offering contemporary favourites: Tuna, Sea Bass, Rock Turbot, Halibut, Monkfish, Scallops and Lobster. The poor Herring is not even on the menu.

Although Jack McKay had been living no more than fifty yards from the restaurant since its opening twenty years ago, he had never eaten there. It was 'too fancy' and 'awfy expensive'. Tonight was to be his first experience sampling its delights, at the invitation of Diane and David Ross.

Mary and Jack McKay were nervous. They had dressed formally, in clothes last worn at a wedding. She wore a scarlet silk dress tied at the waist with a bow and Jack wore a three-piece black evening suit with a white shirt and black tie.

Despite the fact their style was from the 1950's, they were a handsome couple; healthy, happy, comfortable together.

The Ross's were seated near a window with a view of the beach when the McKay's arrived.

The restaurant is elevated, offering a splendid view, far out to sea. It's a lovely spot and Ross felt it would be interesting to meet the man Hans Kool considered his mentor in spiritual matters; the man who had discovered Mark Stewart hanging upside-down, crucified from the bridge at nearby Torry.

The four were immediately at ease. Jack oozed human kindness, warmth and generosity of spirit. Within minutes, Ross felt uplifted, laughing at Jack's stories about fishing, preaching and Aberdeen. Big Jack had a massive personality. The only hiccup came when Jack and Mary perused the menu.

Ross calmed their fears,

"Order whatever you fancy. It's our treat."

"I cannae expect you to pay these prices, Mr. Ross."

"Mr. McKay, I am a lucky man. I am delighted to share my good fortune with you and your wife."

"That's awfy good of yae, Mr. Ross. Mary will be delighted to cook for you and Mrs. Ross to return this great honour."

Mary nodded with a huge, genuine smile. Ross wondered why everyone couldn't be like these delightful people.

"Would you care to order some wine, Jack?"

It was strange to use Big Jack's first name. A real throwback; he was polite, manly and genteel. It was easy to see why he was revered. In a different time or place he might have been a great statesman, except he had no desire to be placed above anyone. He was happy to be modest; a pious, humble man.

"Oh aye, Mr. Ross, David, I would love a dram."

Mary gave Jack a look that signified caution and restraint,

"Just you be careful wae yer drink, Jack McKay. Ye ken yer blood pressure is no so good these days."

"We'll just hae a couple o' glasses of red wine, darling. If it was good enough for The Lord, then it's nae gan to kill us."

He laughed, opening his heart and soul as he did so. Diane burst into laughter. She wasn't even sure why. Big Jack's effervescence was highly contagious. Diane looked forward to spending the evening with this charismatic character. She suspected Big Jack was a rascal. Ross still had a job to do and he needed information from the former skipper. He needed to know more about Kool. Was it a coincidence the preacher found the body or was Kool exorcising his demons; confessing his sins to his religious leader in some bizarre visual symbolism?

'Via Crucis'

Despite Jack's love of red wine, they settled on a white burgundy, Corton-Charlemagne, a Grand Cru at sixty pounds a bottle. They toasted and said grace.

"Thank you, Lord, for our good fortune and bless this wine with your spirit," Big Jack proclaimed.

Diane smiled at the pun. McKay was a hoot.

They all gulped a mouthful of the aromatic, flavoursome wine. Ross decided to use the wine-tasting to disguise his gently probing questions.

"I had some fabulous wine just last week, a Pinot Noir. In fact it was Hans Kool who gave me a bottle, you remember, darling?" Ross directed the question to his wife, who nodded.

"From New Zealand," she replied.

The preacher nodded,

"Aye, Mr. Kool is a wealthy man, his own vineyard. He could do onything he fancied; engineering, wine...music."

"Music?" said Ross, surprised at the revelation.

"Yes, Mr. Ross, he was a classical guitarist. He gave wonderful concerts to hundreds of people. It all stopped after his tragedy. He never played again."

The food arrived, Big Jack was gracious,

"It's a bountiful harvest, Mr. Ross. We could never afford to eat scallops or monkfish when I was at sea, too valuable."

"I hope you have recovered from your shock of a few days ago?" Ross was sympathetic.

"The De'il is always trying to defeat Our Lord. It's our solemn duty nae to let him succeed, Mr. Ross, David."

Diane talked to Mary while Ross prized information from Big Jack. She was a little aggrieved her husband was talking shop.

"I have always wondered about the Old and New Testament, Jack; how God changed from a vengeful God: *'an eye for an eye'*, to a forgiving God: *'turn the other cheek'*. I am not sure if this is the place to discuss it, but I understand you are expert in these questions."

"Come now, darling, Mr. McKay doesn't want to discuss such weighty matters over dinner," Diane squeezed his hand, trying to lighten his aura.

"Mrs. Ross, I am happy to discuss the *Good Book* at any time." The preacher smiled and continued,

"The Lord made man in his own image, Mr. Ross, and I believe Our Lord is learning as he experiences his own power and his own creation. Initially he expected total obedience, but later he realized true love was not about obedience; it is about free choice. If you love someone you must set them free and you can only hope they will return your love. Our Lord gave us a great gift when he set us free from sin, by sending His Son among us. He sent us His love through Jesus Christ, Our Saviour. Jesus saved us by absorbing and cleansing our immortal souls of sin. After that, it was up to each of us to choose - love and salvation or evil and damnation."

"*Amen!*" A woman sitting at the table behind them made the sign of the cross on her chest and bowed her head. Such was the power of the Holy Spirit in the fisherman's words.

"You do not believe that man should ever resort to evil in order to overcome evil? Kill to prevent a killing?"

"*Revenge is the Lord's,* Mr. Ross, but it's a fair complex question. If someone attacked my children or my wife, then I would stop them, nae doubt: lethal if needed, but if the terrible deed had already been done then I'd hae tae forgive them - *forgiveness is divine*, Mr. Ross."

McKay was a gentle man and unless Ross was wrong, the preacher clearly had no part in any violent retribution.

After another blessing, they ate a hearty meal. The conversation lightened and they had a splendid evening.

Mary and Jack left early, skipping dessert to relieve their babysitter; Tim and Jo Ross were sleeping over at friends so the Ross's ordered lemon and orange parfait with a dusting of real chocolate.

"Let's have some champagne to celebrate selling the Ferrari to Harry, honey." Diane was tipsy - very happy.

"Baby, I'm driving and I've already had two glasses of wine. We'll open a bottle at home."

"What lovely people. Let's go and hear him talk on Sunday. He's really sexy in a pedagogic, ecumenical sort of way. He has lovely strong hands and such a deep voice." She replied, her voice soft and sensual.

Ross decided he must keep a closer eye on his wife. Her appreciation of men knew no bounds.

The black Lamborghini eventually rumbled away from Silver Darlings and Footdee.

Ross drank a small bottle of Evian to keep his alcohol count down.

He decided to drive home through town.

A decision he would live to regret.

The centre of Aberdeen on a Friday and Saturday night can best be compared to the Wild West - Dodge City. It's mayhem: Bedlam - Sodom and Gomorrah

As Ross attempted to negotiate his way safely through the town at around eleven p.m., some youths 'mooned' him, someone threw a chip supper at the black super-car and endless cries of *"wanker"* were directed at the Lamborghini.

This kind of thing didn't happen in Kensington or Chelsea, where Ross was more used to dining.

Suburb-dweller, lover of the countryside, Ross was reasonably unfamiliar with the city-centre at the best of times; he'd never actually been there recently, late at night.

To reduce the attention the car was getting he took a left turn at Bon Accord Street intending to take the back streets out of town. He ended up in Langstane Place and Justice Mill Lane, the busiest thoroughfare for drunks on a night out.

He cursed his luck.

Diane squeezed his hand to comfort him, sensing he was getting tense and irate.

A red light indicated that they had to stop at a pedestrian crossing separating one horde of binge-drinking drunks from another.

They sat watching the revellers stream across in front of the car.

Ross was uneasy.

A hand came down hard on the bonnet of the Gallardo,

'Bang!'

Tattoos on the forearms, shaven-head and two baseball-cap wearing accomplices, the belligerent pair of eyes staring at Ross indicated his worst nightmare had just materialised.

The lights were still at red. No escape.

"Where did ye nick this fucker? Wank-heed!"

The words were spat at the windscreen, covering it in phlegm laced with pure alcohol-spirit.

"Gie us a shot o yer car and yer ho!?"

One drunk moved to Diane's door, putting his hand on the lever to open it. Ross pressed the security button, locking the doors from the inside.

"Ye sneaky fuck!" They started to rock the car.

The assailant took a swing at the front bumper with his foot, missing it, falling over. Ross wanted to run the bastard over. He sat there furious, his heart thumping. Diane held his arm, petrified.

The lights changed. The three just stood in front of the car. Not a uniformed policeman in sight.

Ross reversed his car as fast as he could through the crowds, pursued by the malevolent drunks. He managed to reach the junction he'd taken earlier and was confronted by another red light.

The three closed on the Lamborghini, throwing bottles, one hitting the rear of the car; a thousand pounds of damage for sure.

Ross had two options; reverse straight back into them, an idea he favoured, or run the red light.

He took his chances with the red light and was almost hit full-on by a bus. The bus driver gesticulated wildly as Ross waved his apologies from the wheel-spinning Lambo.

The trio of frustrated hoodlums shouted and screamed abuse at the vanishing sports car.

"You did the right thing, honey. There was nothing else you could have done."

Diane was right. What else could he do? He was caught unawares again. He was furious, so angry he couldn't reply. He wanted to kill them. Stringing them up and cutting off their balls was too good for them.

Diane turned on the CD player; Pink Floyd's *Shine On You Crazy Diamond*, calmed him.

"What the hell is it with these people? What is it with this town?" It was rhetorical, but his wife replied.

"It's not just this town. It's every town. There is an epidemic of anti-social behaviour. The causes are boredom, alcohol abuse and a total lack of respect for other people or any acceptance of personal responsibility.

It probably emanates from the breakdown of family life in our culture. These people are lost; stray dogs, hunting in packs; kicking and punching at strangers because they have no-one to love and no purpose in life. They are arrogant, useless, ignorant and dangerous. The question is - what is the solution?"

As usual, she was right,

What was the solution?

Justice Mill Lane

The three car attackers: would-be hijackers, walked back towards the bars in Langstane Place and Justice Mill Lane, bumping and barging; ready for a fight.

"Fucking wank in his fuckin pimp mobeel!"

"I'd've fucked his tart!"

"Aye, a right dirty bitch - cock-sucking ho!"

Bumping into two girls, they lifted the girls' skirts.

"Hey, nice camel-toe, sweet tits!"

"Come here and feel my cock, you wee slut!"

The two seventeen year-old schoolgirls, managed to break free, diving into a nearby bar.

"A need a piss afore a piss ma pants!"

"Aye, me too!"

All three of them stood on the pavement and urinated straight into the road. Throngs of people walked past exclaiming disgust. The reprobates responded viciously,

"Piss off or I'll piss o'er yer heed, yee fuckers!"

As they relieved the pressure on their beer-bloated bladders, a vehicle pulled alongside. One of them urinated over the kerbside passenger door. He couldn't be bothered not to. The driver of the vehicle shouted at them,

"Yer a bunch of fucking shit-stabbers!"

He gave them the finger and drove away slowly.

They went berserk, chasing after him.

He drove into Silver Square, then down a lane off Bon Accord Crescent, where he parked-up in an office car-park. The first yob arrived in the dark lane, filled with bile and bloodlust.

He received a baseball bat full in the face. He hit the deck and didn't move again.

The other two arrived together. They saw their comrade lying, apparently dead, in a pool of black blood.

One man held a bottle; the other took out a kitchen knife.

"Ah'right fucker, say yer fuckin prayers!"

"What are you two fucking pussies going to do?"

The loner's confidence made them hesitate. To make things more insulting, he dropped down on his knees and taunted them.

"Look. I am giving you pussies a chance!"

They closed on the kneeling brave-heart. The bottle-yielder swung at the loner's head. He missed and got a knuckleduster in his testicles. He fell to the ground.

The loner stood up and produced a set of Nunchukas - two hardwood rods held together with a 3-link, speed chain.

Before the remaining, knife-wielding thug could even make a move, the free-moving, eleven-inch solid rod caught him on the temple, stunning him. He stepped back, reeling, seeing stars as the second blow hit his fibula, bringing him crashing to his knees.

Too easy!

Pete got back in his Isuzu Rodeo truck and went in search of more challenging adversaries.

Before he did, he rubbed liquid Anadrol cream into his forearms, biceps and neck and swallowed five 50mg tablets of Oxydrol, 'stacking' his anabolic steroids. His muscles bulged, rock hard. The veins on his neck stood out. He was horny, very horny.

He drove off in search of more anti-social, would-be combatants - to beat the shit out of...

"Right, which of you fucking assholes is next?"

214

Pete

Pete spotted his next target. Two teenage boys, in a Union Street shop doorway, viciously kicking an old wino, but before he could reach them he was thwarted by the police; one of the rare occasions when the police actually managed to prevent a violent assault.

He was hungry, but not for food. He needed a woman. The drugs had quadrupled his testosterone production. He needed oestrogen and he needed it fast. There was no point in trying a bar or a nightclub, success was too haphazard, a fight with a drunk inevitable. He had an idea.

The Slippery Pole was being run by a caretaker-manager until the business could be sold to a new proprietor. Pete had never been in a strip-club, but it was just what he fancied. He parked his truck outside, on a double yellow line, and entered the establishment. The doorman put his hand on Pete's chest, barring his progress.

"That'll be five pounds, mate."

"Take you hand off – now!" Pete replied.

The doorman did as he was told.

"It's still five pounds, mate."

Pete turned to the desk and paid the receptionist. The doorman watched him cautiously.

"He's a bit touchy," the receptionist whispered. The doorman shrugged his shoulders.

Pete headed for the bar.

"Southern Comfort on the rocks"

He was ignored.

"A fucking Southern Comfort – NOW!!!"

The barman shuddered then looked at the doorman.

The doorman nodded, indicating he should get Pete a drink.

"Ok. Just a minute, pal."

Pete's expression said it all.

"I'm not your pal; get a fucking move on."

Pete drained his whisky and ordered another.

He felt unstoppable. A tall black girl with enormous breasts introduced herself.

"Hi honey, I am Precious. Fancy a dance?"

She wasn't Pete's type, "Nope."

"Charming," She moved to the next guy at the bar, asking him exactly the same question.

Pete swallowed his second whisky liqueur.

A Hungarian blonde bombshell wearing a black PVC thong-bikini approached him.

"Hi handsome, where did you get those muscles?" She felt his biceps, "Ooh sexy! Fancy a dance?"

She was more his type, but her delivery was mechanical. Her eyes were cold. No warmth.

"No thanks."

She walked away without saying a single word.

"Barman!" Pete was forceful, dominant.

"Yes, sir?" The answer was immediate, "Another Southern Comfort, sir?"

Pete nodded. Funny how aggression and physical presence can get you respect. Carrying his drink, he decided to explore the delights of the place.

Decorated in the usual brothelesque colour scheme, scarlet velvet, the club featured two large public areas; each area had a bar. Between the bars, a hall of sorts led open-plan to another room with private dancing booths where, behind a curtain, the girl of your choice would expose her body for twenty pounds, less if you haggled.

The club was obviously busy because all ten booths were occupied.

Pete wandered around, breathing in the heady, cocktail: perfume and female sweat produced by thirty, athletic, hardworking strippers. Airborne pheromones and whisky relaxed him. He sat down in the quieter of the two bars, feeling very much at home. This bar was the furthest from the entrance, only two or three lap dancers walked about trying to get his attention. He ignored them.

Two youths stood at the bar wearing the usual garb: Baseball caps, Quicksilver jackets, Burberry jeans. A fabulous blonde walked across and joined the two, spotty plebs. She bought her own drink.

Pete's interest was aroused for two reasons.

First, the young woman was indescribably perfect.

Second, the two youths looked familiar.

Pete decided to investigate.

One spotty youth made the stunning blonde an offer,

"We'll gie ye a fiver, but we'll hae to feel your tits."

The girl looked sad and totally out of place taking abuse from these two wretches.

"Are these two winding you up?" Pete directed this at the two youths. They recognized Pete, but couldn't place him.

"No. Is okay, is my last night. I am a leaving tomorrow." She was sincere; polite, but frightened.

"That's a pity." Pete stared into her soul.

"Hey, fuckface, fa asked you tae butt in?"

Pete looked at the venomous youth.

He recognized the voice. The last time he'd heard it, Pete had a bloody nose, about to pass out to, *'Happy fucking slapping!'*

He played it cool.

"I'm just going to the Gents. You two better be gone when I get back." There was no anger - cool, relaxed. He knew what was about to happen.

"Aye, away and wank, yae fuckwit – cunt!"

Pete looked at them: calm, collected, patient - he walked slowly to the toilets.

"Am nae takin that fae a fuckin cunt, let's happy-slap the fucker!"

They followed him to the toilets, menacingly.

They moved fast; once in the gents, they would attack Pete before he knew what had hit him.

They were about to be disappointed,

"Far the fuck's the fucking homo?"

Pete walked in. He had been waiting, watching. Now he had the element of surprise, the upper hand. Two against one, they didn't stand a chance. Like two feral cats they were upon him in an instant, but he was way too fast. He caught the first one by the throat, lifting him off the ground, strangling him in mid-air, positioning the dangling body between himself and the other reprobate.

Crunch! Pete head-butted the elevated thug, square on the nose, casting him into a toilet cubicle: *out with the garbage!*

"Now you know how it feels, you little shit!"

The second youth drew his blade. Two knives in one night; Aberdeen was catching up with Glasgow. Pete needed a weapon. With one mighty pull, he wrenched the automatic hand-drier off the wall, smashing it straight into the face of the other happy-slapper.

It was all over in less than a minute. Both were unconscious. They might be dead. Pete didn't care. It was self-defence. There were no witnesses.

He returned to the bar and the stunning blonde.

He made her an offer,

"How do you fancy leaving with me right now?"

"But I must work my last night," she replied.

"I will pay you for your time. You can trust me, what do you say?"

"Well, okay, but you take me to a bar, not your house, ok?"

"Ok."

The doorman was not about to let any stripper leave the club, not until she'd paid her fifty pounds for the use of the premises that night. He stood in front of Pete, joined by a second, mean-looking, associate.

"Oh, I do not have enough to pay yet," she said.

"How much?" Pete asked the doormen.

"Fifty."

Pete paid him. They didn't move.

"I am not going to ask you again" Pete stated, staring at the doormen. His blood was up: he was ready for action. They moved aside.

Pete held the door open for his amazing companion. He wasn't going to let her out of his sight. She needed looking after and he was going to make sure she never needed to work in such a place or worry again.

"What is your name?" she asked. Her English was broken, but she had a sweet voice.

"Pete. And yours?" Pete smiled. He hadn't felt like smiling for a long time.

"I am being called Mirka," she replied.

"Well, Mirka, how do you fancy getting out of Aberdeen and heading to a beach in Mexico?"

She looked at him like she had just won the lottery, "I am a fancying that very much a lot."

Pete smiled a second time. He drove away with his new friend to pack his bags.

News

Weeks had passed since the bridge murders, over a month since Bobby Turnbull and Debby Glennie had been executed. Nothing new had been unearthed.

There had been no disclosure of the alleged confessions.

No new evidence.

No progress.

The phone rang. Ross picked it up.

It was Jimmy Turnbull.

"Speak to me, Ross!"

"I have nothing to report, Jimmy. It's a total mystery."

"Listen, Ross, I can't just do nothing. If you guys don't get the bastard in the next seven days I am suing Grampian Police for negligence. You guys are fucking hopeless!"

"I understand how you feel, Jimmy. These things take time."

"You don't understand, Ross. No-one understands."

The oil magnate put the phone down sadly. He was devastated. He could make anything happen, buy anything or anyone, but he couldn't bring back his son. Death can't be fixed.

Jimmy was looking into the void: money and power were no substitute for his child.

Ross had visited Des Glennie at his estate near Monymusk, beneath Bennachie, the 'Mither Tap,' with its *Mons Graupius* where the people of Grampian held out against Roman invaders thousands of years ago. The small, but prominent mountain resembles a large,

lonely rocky nipple surrounded by multi-coloured, patchwork farmland where ancient Pictish standing-stones stoically face the bitter cold of North-East winters with steely resolve.

Des had been unable to talk about the car crash, blaming himself for getting drunk, for not protecting his beautiful precious child. His wife, Teresa, seemed more upset that the wedding and union with the Turnbull Empire would remain unfulfilled. Ross had heard nothing from the Glennies since his melancholy visit. It appeared that Debbie would be mourned forever by her father, but no motive had been uncovered - no crazy ex-boyfriends or bitter business rivals.

Morven Hancock was fairly sure the alien silver paint on Bobby Turnbull's car was from a Land Rover model, probably a Range Rover, but Aberdeen was full of these; Ross owned one and Range Rover drivers were forever scraping the bodywork of the automotive leviathan on some hard surface. It was time-consuming work, chasing-up all the silver Range Rovers repaired across the country in the last few months. It was unlikely the killers would be foolish enough to take it to an approved dealer for repairs; the car concerned might not even still be in the country. One car, stolen in Leeds, had been found burnt-out near Dundee. It was a silver 'Supercharged' Range Rover. It was burnt to a crisp, only identifiable by the vehicle ID on the engine-bay: not a trace of evidence.

Vigilante retaliation was now rife.

Numerous individuals were fighting back, if robbed, attacked or even threatened. Several hitherto law-abiding citizens were under police surveillance, suspected of assault.

The city, however, was being reclaimed from the anti-social element; but there was a real danger the *bridge-bodies murderer* would become an adopted vigilante patron-saint of law and order.

As a disciple of Hume and Bentham, Ross couldn't let that happen. The rule of law, ultimately, was the only foundation for lasting stability and harmony in a civilized society.

Ross got a call on his mobile. It was the hospital. Mark Stewart had made a statement. Ross dropped everything and made a beeline for the Infirmary. He got there just fifteen minutes after the call. He was too late. Mark Stewart died as Superintendent Ross entered the hospital reception.

Ross questioned the consultant in charge about the statement and was astonished when he heard the man who had hung onto life so precariously, after such an ordeal, had managed to actually write something down. The consultant handed Ross the note. As he read Mark Stewart's final words, Ross welled up. It was heartbreaking.

After all his suffering, *'The Thug'* had simply written:

Sorry Ma
Mark

Ross had to solve this case.

Tim

Tim Ross had a new mountain bike. He'd pestered his father for weeks about it. At just seven years old, even junior mountain bikes need a degree of proficiency associated with a child of at least 11+, but Tim was persuasive and persistent; eventually his father conceded, buying him a pristine, junior mountain bike. Tim was not happy when stabilizers were fitted because he just did not have the strength yet to control his bike. He considered the added assistance, childish, more appropriate for his baby sister. Even with the extra set of mini-wheels to help him stay upright he struggled to control his oversized and far too heavy-duty, personal transport. He spent fifty per cent of his time falling over and dusting off. His knees and elbows were a tapestry of cuts and bruises, but this could not dissuade Tim from conquering the challenge.

Today, he'd almost managed to negotiate his way down Dalmunzie Drive to the main North Deeside Road, but the last 50 yards were steep; he was hanging on, squeezing the brakes to control his speed as he approached the pavement, separating the busy main road, from the almost deserted private road where he lived. His short life flashed by as he lost control, grabbing the brakes with all his might. He catapulted over the handlebars, crashing down on the pavement with an ignominious thump.

The shock of the impact made Tim weep.

As usual, the backs of his legs and his inner forearms were grazed and bleeding.

The cuts stung badly; he felt helpless and frustrated. The bike was overturned; the seat twisted by 180 degrees. The front wheel spun freely in the air.

Tim sat near his bike on the pavement, dazed and confused, feeling dejected.

He was rubbing his left knee, carefully extracting a few small stones from the bleeding flesh, when a small red car pulled up and stopped in the bicycle lane, next to the pavement, about ten yards along the road.

The red car's door began to open, but before the driver could emerge, a second car, a silver Range Rover, pulled up directly alongside Tim and his prostrate mountain bike.

The driver of the large, luxury SUV pressed the button to wind down his nearside window and called out to the boy.

"Are you okay?"

"I fell off my bike," Tim croaked, managing not to cry.

"Ah well, it happens. Do you live near here?"

"Yes. Just up the road." An unwelcome tear started rolling down his cheek.

"Put your bike in the back; we'll get you home."

Tim had been told a thousand times never to accept lifts or talk to strangers, but he felt so helpless: it's not falling off your bike that hurts - it's having no-one there to help you get back on.

The stranger seemed trustable; a big, strong, honest-looking man. He loaded Tim's bike into the SUV and looked attentively at Tim's injuries.

He ruffled the boy's hair; Tim managed a smile.

"Come on. You'll be ok. You look like a fighter to me."

'*I am a fighter*,' thought Tim. He felt happy to get the approval of this giant of a man. He got in the driver's door and crawled across into the passenger's seat and put on his seatbelt.

The small red car indicated it was pulling away and drove off slowly with reluctance: usurped.

Tim was surprised by the speed at which the Range Rover sped off after the red car.

"I thought you were taking me home?" Tim said apprehensively.

The SUV driver said nothing. He pressed the throttle to the floor and was at once within a few yards from the rear of the red VW Golf. With another accelerated flourish, the big SUV was past the Golf. The red car veered to the left almost leaving the road, as the giant stared menacingly at his counterpart in his rear view mirror. Tim was frightened,

"Can we go home?"

The Range Rover driver appeared to snap out of a trance. He looked at the boy, "I am sorry. That man behind us, in the red car, is a very bad man."

Tim looked back to see the other car take a rapid left turn and disappear down a quiet country road. The Range Rover made a u-turn and headed back towards Dalmunzie Drive.

Tim relaxed, looking at his knee again.

"You better get that washed when you get home."

"It really stings," Tim replied.

"I think that bike is too big for you."

Tim smiled. The big man was right. He would wait a few months before he tried the bike again.

Diane Ross saw the car pull up. She assumed it was her husband. The Ross's had two Range Rovers and one was silver. It was not her husband - but this man was no stranger to her.

"Mr. Kool, I did not expect to see you here?"

Hans Kool opened his passenger's door and lifted Tim and his bike out of the car. He carried Tim under one arm, like a baby, to his mother.

"I believe this one is yours?" He said.

"Oh Tim, what a mess, that looks really sore?" said his mother.

Tim started to cry. He couldn't help it.

Hans Kool got back into his car and looked out at Diane Ross.

"Mrs. Ross, he is a brave boy, but do not let him near that main road on his own. There are many dangers out there. Dangers you do not want to know about. Heed my words."

With that ominous warning, he took off at speed, back to the main road.

Diane Ross was trembling - breathless and fearful.

Hans Kool always made her nervous - now she felt she'd failed as a mother. And what exactly did he mean?

She focused her mental energy on her son.

"Ice cream?" she said, looking at Tim's big blue watery eyes.

"Yes please," said her son.

With that, they headed indoors, back to the security and comfort of *Rose Cottage*.

Oak Tree Avenue

Graeme Twinkle looked out his window.

He was watching the children walking home from Oak Lane Primary School near Hazlehead, a leafy suburb of Aberdeen.

Twinkle had been lucky, or maybe not.

The city council had purchased a block of flats directly opposite the school and offered him an apartment at a very reasonable, subsidised rental. He needed a place to live. Five years is a long time to spend in jail with real criminals. Twinkle's only crime had been to love. He loved children. He now loved one child in particular. Her name was Carole and he had met her a few weeks ago when he was walking on a secluded path, near the school.

He liked that walk because it was enclosed by an avenue of trees and hedges and even at midday, it was dark and secluded. Twinkle liked privacy. He always walked there at certain times of the day; just before nine in the morning, when he could watch the children skipping and walking to school, and he returned at around three p.m., when they were walking home again.

He would pretend to stumble and they would help him up. He would brush against them and smell the soap and toothpaste still fresh on their tender, young bodies and warm breath.

It was how he met Carole.

He had noted she always walked alone.

She was seven years old with platinum blonde hair and big, wide, baby-blue eyes.

She was a little doll in her green cardigan, white blouse, short grey skirt, little white socks and black shoes.

She was always late for school because her father had left home for good and her mother was struggling to cope, usually sleeping off the effects of alcohol or hiding some man she had taken home the night before. Sometimes Carole's tie was tied wrong or her knickers were inside out. She even put her right shoe on her left foot and vice versa, in a hurry to get to school on time one morning.

Carole missed her father; he had recently relocated to Australia. Her father was a good man, driven off by her mother's moods, tantrums and unreasonable attention-seeking behaviour. Her mother was beautiful, which may have explained her impossible, uncompromising nature. Carole had her mother's stunning blonde good looks and her father's, caring, understanding temperament.

Twinkle had seen Carole many times and he wanted her badly. A few days earlier, he had pretended to fall down and Carole helped him up. As she squatted down, to ask after his well-being, he took the opportunity to look up her skirt at her white panties. With her help, he arose slowly, taking time to feel the warmth of her little hand and to breathe in her girlish aroma. He had allowed his other hand to brush up her leg as far as he dared. He thanked her by patting her head; his hand lingered, stroking her blonde hair. Luckily for Twinkle, Carole was very late for school; all the other children and adults were safely inside the school gates, or suspicions would have been raised. He'd asked Carole a few questions about herself, ascertaining that her favourite beverage was a peculiarly Scottish soft drink called *Irn Bru* (Iron Brew). The manufacturer of *Irn Bru's* slogan was:

‘Made in Scotland from Girders’

Carole imagined the sugary, fizzy drink would make her strong and invincible. Twinkle had also discovered that she dreamed of owning a 'spotty' dog.

Wee Willie Winkie

Twinkle's apartment was opposite the front of the school. It was one of a small, modern block of four flats, in a development of four blocks, built in the 1960's and refurbished in the last twelve months.

Originally these apartments had been built to house single, old people; the flats featured faux balconies, once decorated with beautiful displays of hanging baskets, resplendent with colourful flowers: red and yellow poppies. Now, things had changed.

The flats had been allocated as safe-havens for rehabilitated sex-offenders. The hanging baskets had gone. The balconies were bare and bereft of colour and life, the curtains remained drawn in the windows as the new inhabitants put a veil of privacy and protection between themselves and the hundreds of furious, local residents incensed by the council's decision to house 'perverts' opposite a primary school. Inside No.4 Oak Tree Avenue, Graeme Twinkle was rehabilitating in his own happy way. He had been a council employee for most of his adult life: an assistant school janitor and an instructor at a public swimming pool. In his spare time he'd been involved with the Boy's Brigade and the Boy Scouts, mainly the junior divisions, the Cubs and the Beavers. He had loved his work which gave him ample opportunity to furtively fondle and surreptitiously photograph both young boys and girls until just after his 40th birthday, one of the recipients of his 'affections', blew the whistle.

The whistle-blower, a brave eighteen year-old young man, encouraged by a television programme called 'Child-Watch', contacted the BBC and eventually the police were summoned. After that, it was a house of cards. Twinkle had taken advantage of his position as a swimming instructor to touch the genitals and masturbate dozens of children, boys and girls, aged between six and ten years old. Usually the children were unaware, thrashing about, trying to learn to swim, but Twinkle had one hand under their bellies, supporting the young swimmer, while his other ventured beneath their swimming costumes. Many children were distressed, but the prevailing social climate was against confronting authority so many of the children just avoided him after the initial molestation.

A few little girls, whom Twinkle had penetrated with his fat fingers, cried when they were alone, without knowing why; several had terrifying nightmares about a bald man with a hair-lip touching their 'front-bottoms'.

No sooner had Twinkle served his first sentence when the police charged him with other offences. He'd recently been released from his second term; ten years, reduced to five for good behaviour and significant signs he would never again be a danger to children. There was a chance he would have been free of his demons forever had they not offered him a flat overlooking a primary school.

This was the result of an error by the council.

They thought they were housing the offenders near Oakbank, an institution for wayward youths, but by an oversight they housed the former jailbirds in Oak Tree Avenue.

By the time the mistake was realized, the flats were occupied and the new residents were disinclined to be relocated. A legal battle was being slowly processed, but in the meantime, the dubious, controversial tenants were *in situ* by the law of occupancy: ***'possession is nine tenths of the law'.***

Twinkle stood naked in front of the bathroom mirror. He realised how revolting his body must look to another human being. If Brad Pitt was ultra-violet then he was infra-red. He was the antithesis of a healthy, athletic, adult male. His belly was swollen like a pregnant pig and his snow-white skin was covered with an unsightly red rash: psoriasis caused by a poor diet and zero exposure to sunlight. Twinkle preferred to avoid the light of day, but it was not good for his health. He suffered from alopecia; his body was entirely hairless apart from a few tufts above his ears. He looked like a big fat baby. All he needed was a pair of diapers and he'd be looking at a large, swollen, ugly baby with an all over nappy-rash.

He looked at his penis. It was inordinately small.

In prison he had been given the nicknames 'Wee Willy Winkie' and 'Tiny Tinkle' - cruel names, perfectly reflecting his miniscule manhood. Even thinking of little Carole's white panties his fully erect penis was no more than two or three inches long. It resembled a swollen thumb caught by an errant hammer blow.

Twinkle was deeply ashamed of his diminutive dick. In prison he had seen monster phalluses. Some were three to four times bigger than his pathetic little thing. Several prisoners had taken joy in swinging their enormous cocks in his face to wind him up; but he knew a way to solve his problem, a way to overcome his misfortune.

Twinkle had managed to sneak a laptop computer into his flat and using a dial-up connection (he was not allowed to subscribe to broadband) he'd been able to visit various illegal websites. He'd been shown in jail how to disguise his IP address, in case the authorities were monitoring his online activities.

Horrific internet sites, showed pictures of adult penises, in close proximity to infants; the result was the deviant erection looked enormous.

Graeme Twinkle was going to have sex with little Carole Anderson and record the experience on a digital camera. He would sell the pictures over the internet and become famous with his paedophile fraternity. He would also, for the first time in his life, have a penis that at least looked like a big dick.

Of course, he would need to get the child into his 'care' and in order to do that he would need to entice her away to a private place. With this in mind, he had that day, purchased a beautiful Dalmatian puppy. He knew it was little Carole's dream to have a 'spotty' dog.

Twinkle had already practised taking pictures of his penis a few feet above the pup's head and he could see the desired effect. His stunted erection appeared much bigger.

It made him excited about his plan.

He got so worked up he ejaculated all over the little dog's head, causing the innocent baby canine to lick it up and eat it. That made Twinkle smile.

It gave a new meaning to being a 'dog-lover'.

He concocted a potent cocktail, dissolving GHB and Benzodiazepine into four small screw-top bottles of *Irn Bru*. He put them in his fridge to chill. The cold would disguise any taste of the drugs. The cool drink would appeal to Carole on these hot, summer days.

He just had to choose his moment carefully and make his move.

The weather forecast was for hot and sunny days all week; he had high hopes.

A Trusting Child

It was a hot morning.

Graeme Twinkle parked his old red VW Golf near the tree-enveloped pathway that was his regular haunt just before nine o'clock in the morning. He watched the children and the adults walk past - relieved to see Carole was not among them.

At just two minutes before nine, a lonely little figure could be seen running towards the path. Her hair was perfect blonde; her school tie was pulled in a tight knot. She was disheveled and tardy, but a beautiful little girl.

Twinkle let out the puppy; it was kind enough to bumble along towards the sprinting child.

Carole could not help but stop and stroke the cuddly little Dalmatian pup. He was just what she had always dreamed about.

Twinkle followed nonchalantly behind the little dog, giving the appearance of a fat man in no hurry at all. In fact, his heart was racing - up around one hundred and fifty beats a minute. He was almost afraid someone might hear it.

"Hello, Carole," he said, "I see you found Spotty for me. Would you carry him to the car? He seems to like you."

Carole knew she was in a hurry, but she could not resist lifting up the adorable pup. The pup started licking her face as she carried him behind Twinkle.

"I better go now because I am so late," she said with a slight lisp.

"I know what. Why don't you let Spotty and me drive you to school? Then you can be on time," said Twinkle convincingly.

Carole knew it was wrong to accept a lift, but the puppy was so cute and the fat man seemed very helpful. He reminded her a bit of the cartoon movie character, Shrek. It would also be the first time she had ever been on time.

"Ok dokay," she replied, climbing into his car.

"Gosh! It's hot today," said Twinkle, who had turned up the car heater, on this already hot summer morning, to maximum, "I know. Would you like a nice cold drink?"

Carole had just brushed her teeth, but when she saw it was *Irn Bru* she accepted and took a big gulp, then motioned towards Twinkle for him to have some.

"No thanks. It's all for you, my dear," he said generously.

Carole took another gulp and started feeding the puppy some. Twinkle considered this and decided the sleeping puppy would make a useful prop for his photos.

"Oh yes. That will make you big and strong. Finish the bottle and you can have another."

The comment was wasted on Carole. Her blood was pumping fast from running to school and Twinkle had put enough sleeping draught in the bottle to put a horse to sleep. Within a few minutes she was out cold. Twinkle was absolutely delighted; the puppy was sleeping on her lap.

Twinkle had a powerful two-inch erection.

He was headed for Countesswells Woods, a few miles from town and no more than five minutes from where he had abducted Carole Anderson.

In the boot of his car were a large PVC gardening sack, a travel rug, a digital camera, a spade/shovel, a jar of petroleum jelly and a large, sturdy canvas tent bag. Many years as a Cub leader had taught Graeme Twinkle to:

'Be prepared'

Countesswells Woods

Countesswells Woods cover a large area of the fast diminishing greenbelt to the west of Aberdeen, split into numerous, wooded areas. They are used by a diverse range of individuals. One area between Kingswells and Cults is an alleged 'dogging' site where couples arrive late at night to have sex in cars, while others stand around outside the car; watching, masturbating; fondling aroused partners. It is said that sometimes, the female in the car will offer herself to all the assembled watching males; a 'gang-bang' ensues, where the woman, watched by her husband or partner, is fucked by up to a dozen strangers.

Such behaviour was anathema to Graeme Twinkle. He found post-pubescent women revolting. He disliked the large motherly breasts, the body hair and the sickly stench of an adult pussy. He abhorred the lustful, voracious sexual appetite of adult women. He wanted a powerless, virgin child; smooth-skinned, hairless, smelling of soap; submissive, terrified, sexless. In his darker moments, he fantasised about raping a child. As it cried out, calling for its mother, its tears and cries made him feel powerful, dominant: a real man.

He looked at Carole sucking her thumb as she slept. His hard, little, fat cock felt like it was about to explode. He wiped copious sweat from his upper lip with the sleeve of his anorak.

At nine-fifteen on a Tuesday morning there were no *'doggers'* about, but there were always a few people walking dogs. They tended to follow a few well-established, clearly marked paths which included depositories for canine excrement. Twinkle had rehearsed his route several times in order to avoid dogs and dog owners.

Countesswells was one of several areas of Aberdeen he had visited with infant abduction and sexual gratification in mind. His first choice had been the *Archways* under the Old Bridge of Dee: dark and secluded caves resembling dungeons; but he was disturbed while experimenting digging a practice grave: *'too many busybodies by the river,'* so he settled on the forest instead.

He parked his car close to the start of a path that led quickly into dense forest and thereafter offered the opportunity to deviate into the silent depths of the uncharted blanket of pine needles that was the forest floor.

He put the shovel inside the PVC sack and placed it lengthwise at the bottom of the tent bag. He put the traveling rug on top of the PVC sack, laid the sleeping puppy on top of the rug and zipped up the large canvas bag. He put the digital camera and the petroleum jelly in the pocket of his brown, quilted anorak.

He put on a pair of prescription-free, black, thick-rimmed spectacles and a Burberry baseball cap as a disguise, before picking up the sleeping Carole and putting her over his shoulder.

She was fast asleep, still sucking her thumb.

At this point, his plan revealed a significant flaw. Carole weighed a lot more than he had imagined.

He had envisaged casually carrying the sleeping child over his shoulder as if she was his daughter having a peaceful nap on their way to a picnic and carrying the large bag in his other hand. This was proving impossible.

Carrying a limp, lifeless little girl and dragging an enormous bag was virtually advertising to the world that he was a child molester. He therefore decided to make two trips. He put Carole Anderson in the boot of the car and made off to the scene of his intended crime with the canvas bag and its assorted contents, including *Spotty*.

He met no-one on his first excursion, selecting a very private spot, deep in the forest, about one hundred yards from any path, surrounded by fallen trees and a dry-stone dyke. It was well-hidden: invisible to any passer-by, a perfect spot for the conclusion of his evil deeds. He emptied the contents of the bag behind the wall and covered them with branches. *Spotty* was sleeping peacefully.

He was startled to find another car parked next to his on his return to the parking area. It was a silver Range Rover. He looked around, but could see or hear no-one.

He considered calling it off, but he was aroused; his ardour full-on; he was determined to have Carole as his sexual partner in the next twenty minutes.

Twinkle opened the boot of his old VW Golf and lifted the sleeping blonde child into the canvas bag, wrapping her in the rug. This was not to keep her warm, but to hide her should he be stopped and challenged.

The purple swollen glans comprising at least half its total size, the normal silky velvet skin of his cockhead was covered in little blisters, symptoms of herpes contracted from his one engagement with a prostitute. The experience had disgusted him and left him with a painful, incurable viral infection.

Graeme Twinkle's penis was an organ no woman would wish to encounter and putting it inside a child was a criminal act worse than any brutal murder.

The flash went off again as he stood above the sleeping child, his bizarre erection several feet above her genitalia, creating the effect he so desired - making his penis look enormous.

Finally, it was time to put his hideous, herpes-infected, hard-on inside the velvety virginal vagina of little Carole Anderson. He reached inside his pocket and took out the jar of petroleum jelly lubrication, smearing a little on his fat fingers.

Flash!

Twinkle froze.

His camera was in his pocket!

Had it gone off of its own accord?

He stood up, standing on a twig, snapping it with his weight.

In the silence of the forest the snap of the twig was the only sound to be heard. It had a distant, muffled quality to its sound.

Twinkle couldn't move.

Someone had set off a flash and it wasn't him.

He instinctively reached for the shovel, only to be lifted off the ground by a massive pressure around his neck.

It was over in a flash.

There was another eerie 'crack' as Twinkle's neck was broken by one mighty contraction of the huge forearm surrounding his soft, fat, blubbery, sweaty neck.

His body hit the forest floor like a sack of *tatties*[6].

Thud!

He was dead before he hit the ground. His revolting penis filled up with blood from the instantaneous heart attack.

In the throws of death he was granted his wish: a reasonably normal erection; a horrible, pathetic sight.

His executioner, however, had not finished with him. The termination of this predatory pervert needed to serve as a warning to others considering abducting and abusing children. The newcomer lifted the shovel and with a single blow let the sharp leading edge down on Twinkle's winkle severing it from his body. Blood gushed out from the lacerated pubis; the penis lay in a pool of dark scarlet blood; a pork chipolata served on a bed of cranberry sauce, only considerably less appetizing.

The killer considered smashing Twinkle's face to a pulp with the shovel, but his concentration was disturbed by a groan from the little girl lying on the rug. The sight of this beautiful creature, exposed to the selfish savagery of the mutilated menace at his feet, made him raise the shovel again to remove Twinkle's grinning death-mask from his fat face; but again she murmured something, so he decided it best to remove her from the unpleasant scene.

He dropped the shovel onto Twinkle's head, closed the child's legs and pulled up her underwear.

---

[6] Potatoes

He put her over his shoulder and lifted the puppy up by the scruff of the neck.

He hesitated again by Twinkle's body, fighting the temptation to kick him repeatedly in the face, but the little girl's murmuring was getting louder so he started back to his car.

On his way back to his car he met a woman walking an Irish Wolf-hound. The enormous dog bounded up to him, but he shot it a glance that made it think twice and it returned to the business of chasing imaginary rabbits.

The owner was a woman in her late sixties who carried herself with an air of considerable self-importance. She was clearly about to confront him with a comment along the lines of

'What are you doing with that child?'

But she was pre-empted by the man carrying the child and the small spotted dog;

"Hello," he said, walking straight past her.

Here was a man with justice on his side, a man with a clear conscience, a man of action.

The woman stood aside, eventually getting as far as saying,

"Well, really!"

By that time he was out of the woods and back by his car.

The Giant and the Castle

Carole woke up about an hour later. Still drowsy, she sat up and saw she was lying, fully-clothed, on a large four-poster bed with soft white cotton sheets. The enormous room was entirely white except for the old, ornate, mahogany bed she was lying on and a few pieces of antique furniture. She could see out of a window across a large, beautiful garden. The sleeping mixture and GHB still swimming in her bloodstream removed any anxiousness she might normally have felt about the unfamiliar surroundings.

She smiled when she saw the spotted puppy sleeping at the end of the bed. On a bedside cabinet, next to her, was a rock-cake, a glass of milk and a bottle of sparking mineral water. She took a bite of the rock-cake. It tasted of currants, apples and cinnamon. It was lovely. She had two mouthfuls of milk and put her head back down on the pillow.

"I must be in a castle in heaven," she said groggily, thinking about the Shrek movie and went back to sleep.

Downstairs her guardian angel was looking at several sheets of printed paper: a complete dossier on the new residents of Oak Tree Avenue. He crossed out the name of Graeme Twinkle and moved his large finger down to the next sex offender on his list.

At 2 p.m., Carole was awoken by a massive hand stroking her gently on the cheek. She wasn't afraid. She knew this must be the Giant who lived in the castle. He was enormous (a word she struggled to pronounce), but he seemed gentle and very sad. She smiled at him.

He told her to get up and come downstairs, so she slowly started getting out of bed.

There was a bathroom in the bedroom so she went there to use the toilet, to wash her face and brush her teeth. She had to stand on a chair to see her face in the bathroom mirror. She thought she looked very pretty. Then, she drank a big glass of fizzy water because she was very thirsty.

Her dog was still asleep; she stroked him a few times. He was very warm. He was so cute. She was very happy to have him. She hoped the fat man would not ask her to give him back.

She walked carefully down the very grand staircase placing her unsteady feet deliberately. She felt dizzy, hazy - in a dream.

It was like a palace, she thought. There was carved wood everywhere and lots of paintings.

She ran her hand down the smooth wooden banister and thought it would be great fun to slide down, but the Giant might think she was silly if she did that. At the bottom of the stairs, she was a little lost, so she called out for the Giant.

"Hello?" she shouted, "Mr. Giant?"

In a flash, the Giant appeared in the doorway of a huge room. Carole had never seen such a beautiful room. It had a big fireplace and lots of lovely colourful pictures of Jesus on the walls.

The Giant asked her where she lived, and if she knew her phone number. She put her hand in her satchel and gave him her mobile phone. The Giant smiled.

"Have you called your mother or father yet?" he asked

"No," said Carole, "I did not want to disturb her."

The Giant's heart was almost bursting. That someone might want to hurt this innocent, charming child made him want to sob. He checked himself,

"I think we need to get you home," he said, smiling affectionately.

"I am happy here. I can stay here with you and Spotty in your castle," she suggested.

"That would be very nice," said the Giant, "but your parents will miss you."

"They will not miss me," she said forlornly.

"Well. We will see. Let's go now."

Craigiebuckler

Melinda Anderson was sitting in her kitchen, nursing yet another hangover. There were several messages on the answering machine telling her Carole had not arrived at school that day, asking her to confirm her daughter's absence, but she had not checked the machine. She was thinking about the man she had taken home last night and then thrown out when he became too presumptuous. He seemed so nice, but then his hands were all over her. She had to get a grip. She had to be strong.

Just as she was lecturing herself about the need to be a better person, a better mother, she heard the doorbell. She ignored it. She was in no fit-state to talk to anyone. Her mobile phone rang; she ignored that as well. Her mobile phone buzzed, indicating a text message, so she walked over and looked at it.

The call was from Carole. She immediately sobered up. Then she saw the text.

At the front door with a friend. Please let me in.

She felt dizzy with panic.

Carole had a key for the house, but she thought it best to warn her mother that she was not alone. She knew what her mother was like.

Melinda Anderson was flustered. It was only two-thirty in the afternoon. Carole wasn't due home for another hour. Had she been sent home early? Who was this friend?

She was tempted to call Carole, but,

'Carole was at the front door!'

She looked in the mirror and decided that she looked okay. She was only wearing her knickers and a t-shirt, but Carole's friend would be another little girl, so that was alright.

She ran to the front door; astonished at what she encountered.

Carole was standing on the doorstep with the biggest man her mother had ever seen. He was at least six feet six inches tall and he looked like a movie-star, a very muscular and very serious-looking movie star. Rather more disturbingly, he was holding her daughter's hand and carrying a black and white puppy.

Melinda Anderson thought this might be a hallucination of some sort. The result of too much alcohol and too little sleep, but it seemed too real to be a dream. Her trance was broken by the muscular, movie-star,

"Mrs. Anderson. My name is Hans Kool. Carole got lost on her way to school today. I am returning her to you."

Melinda blushed furiously. She could feel her face on fire. She was standing in the doorway in a tight fitting t-shirt and a thong. Her daughter and a giant stranger were looking at her as if everything was normal.

Her maternal instincts came to the fore,

"Lost?" she said, "What do you mean lost?"

"Perhaps if I could come in, I will explain," said Hans Kool.

Carole was holding his hand and jumping up and down clearly delighted that he was coming into her house. She wanted to show him her room and her toys.

"Well, I suppose so," said Melinda Anderson, backing up against the wall, behind the door, trying to hide her virtually bare backside.

As Hans Kool made his way to the lounge, Carole dropped back a little and whispered to her mother.

"He's a Giant and he lives in a beautiful castle."

Her mother just watched him with awe as he dipped a little in order to prevent his head catching on the doorframe as he walked into the room.

Hans Kool sat in an armchair. It became a baby-chair the moment he settled in it.

Carole sat near him on the floor, stroking the puppy. The puppy was still sleeping. Melinda decided she could not address Hans Kool in her underwear so she excused herself and went to put on a pair of jeans; she returned in a pair of denim hipsters, still in her bare feet.

Hans Kool looked at her.

She reminded him of someone; someone very beautiful and very special.

She reminded him of his wife.

The Lord of the Flies

Graeme Twinkle's body was discovered by the Irish Wolf-hound shortly after his abrupt termination.

The hound had been all over the forest; chasing squirrels, rabbits, deer and various ground birds; generally being a total nuisance, until it finally picked up Twinkle's, no doubt, highly unpleasant and pungent aroma.

When her dog refused to come to heel, the hound's owner, Ms. Dorothy Still, trampled and trudged her way to the remote spot.

The former headmistress of St. Margaret's High School for Girls in Aberdeen (the only school in town not to consider admitting boys) was an old fashioned pedagogue. She expected her instructions to be obeyed. She was furious her dog was ignoring her commands,

"Spartacus! Spartacus!" she shrieked at the absent animal.

Spartacus, meantime, was barking enthusiastically in the distance. He was in a secluded nearby spot, behind a wall and a fallen tree. Something was making him very excited. Eventually Dorothy Still caught up with her dog and proceeded to chastise him severely,

"Spartacus. You have been a very naughty boy……" Her voice tailed off.

It was a hideous sight.

Twinkle's body had swollen to an even larger size than usual. The face was ashen; the tongue protruded repulsively and of course there was the small matter of the lacerated, separated genitals.

The bloody penis was covered in flies.

Dorothy Still was hysterical.

"Beelzebub!" she screamed.

It was all she could think of,

'Beelzebub, Lord of all the flies!'

Spartacus barked at the swarm of repulsive, blood-filled horseflies and bluebottles. They ignored him and continued to feast on the fat, meaty, little blood-stained phallus, the testes and the mutilated pelvis of the ex-paedophile.

She grabbed Spartacus by the neck and ran through the forest in a directionless panic, stumbling and falling as she went. All she could think about was millions of black flies, buzzing loudly, sucking every last drop of blood out of Twinkle's body and his *'thing'*.

She thought about her own mortality and the horror of having a heart attack and dying in the forest.

What if Beelzebub should find her body there and send in the flies?

She ran and ran from the black flies.

Dorothy Still was a true luddite. She did not approve of mobile phones. She thought, not unreasonably, they were an invasion of privacy. The last thing she wanted during a walk in the countryside was a phone call from some annoying relative.

It, therefore, took her a long time to report the body to the police.

Bluebottles

Ross got the call around 3 p.m., to say a body had been found by a hysterical woman in Countesswells Woods.

The mutilated body strongly suggested a connection to the 'bridge murders'. Ross was given the deeply unpleasant task of visiting the crime scene before the body was removed.

At 4 p.m., the whole area was packed with police cars. There must have been at least two dozen vehicles illuminating the forest with silent, flashing, ice-blue light.

Ross wondered if it required quite so many officers. He knew it was to prevent a claim against the police for negligence. If a member of the public found the body and was upset by this, then the police could be found to be negligent and liable to pay compensation if they had not taken due care to prevent the discovery. Until the body was removed they had to cordon off every possible route. Another waste of police resources created by the legal profession supposed to be protecting us from criminals.

Ross walked through the forest following the police tape, saying 'hello' to a few officers along the route to the body.

He noted how tranquil the forest seemed. The canopy of trees gave the whole area a blanket of serenity. The air was filled with the aromatic scent of pine needles and cones.

He breathed deeply, filling his lungs with nature's sweet perfume, his mind momentarily a million miles from the world of crime and murder.

He could have happily walked through this forest all day, but a surreal vision interrupted his reflections.

Spacemen!?

Two small people dressed in what appeared to be biological warfare protection suits beckoned him - *an Anthrax attack?*

A booming voice indicated that one of these spacemen was pathologist, Johnny Henderson.

"Ah, Ross! Here at last! Better late than never!"

He sounded more like a Drill Sergeant than ever.

"Put this on!"

Henderson handed Ross germ-warfare head protection.

Bewildered, Ross pulled the plastic balaclava over his head. The clear Perspex viewing-window steamed-up as he breathed claustrophobically inside the synthetic head-cover.

Ross was apprehensive to say the least.

"What's all this about?"

"The flies, Ross - swarms of the bastards!"

They walked across to the corpse where the other biological suit was examining a travel-rug. From the perfect curves this had to be Hancock. She waved to Ross.

Ross checked his impulses – too happy to see her.

Driving, heavy rain bounced violently off his protective visor: torrential sleet.

Except...it wasn't raining.

Millions upon millions of flies swarmed, viciously attacking anything within ten yards of the body.

It was obscene.

Reaching the body, Ross was shocked; waves and waves of buzzing, swarming black bloodsuckers engulfed him - positively appalling - intimidating.

Ross was short with Henderson,

"You might have warned me!"

Henderson was resilient as usual,

"Not too pleasant is it? The warm, wet weather causes these bloody flies to breed in plagues. I have never seen so many."

Ross, the nature-lover, hated very few creatures, but those he did detest all had wings, made unpleasant noises and could attack; wasps, seagulls, flies, midges. He especially hated the buzzing, aggressive flies and the midges – the silent vicious Scottish assassins. The pathologist interrupted the policeman's thoughts, barking his words,

"We'll get it in a bag in a few minutes, Ross. I just wanted you to get a look at it *in situ,* before we take it away." Henderson made his observations, "You'll notice the resemblance in *modus operandi* to the bodies hanging from the bridges - the obvious malevolence towards the male genitalia."

Ross could barely see anything through the clouds of bluebottles,

"Thanks for pointing that out. How long has he been here?"

Henderson's body language suggested disdain and contempt for the simplicity of the question.

"Approximately," added Ross.

"Six to eight hours maybe," said Henderson.

"Cause of death?"

"You want it all today, don't you, Davie-boy?"

Henderson shouted through the endless drone of the buzzing.

They retreated twenty paces followed by a wave of menacing insects.

Ross could finally hear Henderson clearly,

"His neck has been snapped. The C3, C4 and C5 vertebra have been latterly displaced, or to be more accurate, crushed and obliterated, causing the spinal chord to be severed. Death would be instantaneous due to spinal shock. Come on, I will show you."

They walked back to the body.

Henderson sprayed Twinkle's head with liquid chemical insect-repellant - killing and dispensing thousands of upturned flies; their tiny, blood-stained legs kicked frantically and defiantly in the final throes of death. The pathologist lifted Twinkle's head in his hands and let it play from side to side. It was as limp as a dead daffodil.

"Any idea how it was done?" asked Ross.

Ross was pushing his luck. Henderson looked at him through his visor with piercing pale blue eyes. Ross waited for a reply through the incessant drone of the buzzing swarms.

"Well, Ross, this wasn't done by your frail, old granny, that's for sure."

"Meaning?"

"The killer was as strong as an Ox!" shouted Henderson.

"Thanks, Professor. You can wrap it up now."

"Gift-wrapped or just plain-paper-wrapped, Ross?" quipped *Rubber Johnny*, spraying the entire body with a foot pump connected to a canister of chemicals.

Ross feigned a smile and walked across to Morven Hancock for forensics.

"Well, Doctor Hancock. What can you tell me?"

Hancock was an unusual sight. She looked like a sexy bee-keeper.

Ross strained to hear her muffled, shouted report,

"There are a few long blonde hairs on the rug. I will give you the rest later. I can't do a bloody thing for these flies."

She retreated, gathering her things, waving her hands to fight them off.

"Do we know who he is?" shouted Ross, following her.

"Yes, one of the officers arrested him previously; a Graeme Twinkle, convicted paedophile; rehabilitated, but the officer reckons they should have locked him up for life."

"Okay, let's get the hell out of this nightmare."

The body was zipped up.

Chased by a googol of buzzing bastards, the threesome made a hasty exit.

Ross got a call from Hancock a few hours later,

"The hairs on the rug are probably from a child: good condition, no split ends, no heat damage from a hair drier. There were a couple of very large fingerprints on the shovel, not the victim's, but the victim's fingerprints were in evidence elsewhere on the shovel. I checked the larger fingerprint against those on the bottle of red wine from Hans Kool you supplied: a perfect match; the blood on the blade of the shovel is the victim's and it looks like the leading edge was used to remove the testes and penis. Professor Henderson tells me there were traces of semen on his legs, matching his own DNA."

"Thanks, Doc. That's pretty much what I expected"

Dorothy Still had seen a huge man carrying a little blonde girl and a puppy through the forest around the time of the killing, the pathologist had corroborated the killing was the work of a powerful man and forensics had confirmed that Twinkle had a blonde-haired child on the rug. Conclusively, Kool's prints were all over the instrument of mutilation.

It didn't need a brilliant criminologist to work this one out. Ross had another appointment with Hans Kool and this time it was official. Kool had killed Twinkle. There was no reasonable doubt about that simple fact.

Hans Kool was telling Melinda Anderson the whole story.

Carole had gone upstairs to play with the waking puppy and Kool chose his words carefully. The girl's mother would be upset, but it might be the bitter medicine she needed to get her life in order. Within minutes she was sobbing.

Kool had Twinkle's camera containing the perverted photos in his pocket, but he did not reveal these to the distraught mother.

He would hand the camera over to the police, after he had copied its incriminating contents - contents that would ensure no jury would convict him of Twinkle's murder.

The Aberdeen Guardian

Crime Collapses in North East
Vigilantes Crush Criminals
Aberdeen is now the safest city in the UK!

"Latest figures show violent crime in the Granite City has fallen dramatically in recent months. Ever since several brave, law-abiding members of the public decided to stand up and defend themselves from the terror of victimization, criminals have had second thoughts about attacking innocent people."

"The much publicised 'bodies on the bridges' executions epitomise the public's stance on violent crime.
Attacks on innocent people are being met with zero tolerance."

Stop Press: *"Late last night, police arrested well-known oil executive, Mr. Hans Kool, for the murder of convicted child molester and paedophile, Graeme Twinkle."*

The Aberdeen Guardian *in no way advocates vigilante activity.*

Editorial comment and your views - pages 9 and 10

Kool in Court

Crowds gathered outside Aberdeen Sheriff Court. There had not been a celebrity trial like it in years. The national press was there in abundance. Pressure groups with banners and placards amassed.

On one side, local agents of the Human Rights organization *Liberty* protested with placards declaring, '**No Vigilante!**' and, '**A Fair Trial by Jury**'.

On the other side of a police line, ACTION supporters displayed equally emotive slogans including, '**An Eye for an Eye**' and, '**Make the Punishment fit the Crime**'.

Dozens of police officers in riot gear ensured order was maintained as the witnesses and the jury arrived for the trial.

Lord Simpson, the High Court of Judiciary's foremost exponent in conducting murder trials, had been given the dubious honour and privilege of presiding over proceedings. He had family connections in Aberdeen and kept an apartment in town. He was preparing for an unconventional tribunal.

A packed courtroom included Superintendent David Ross, his wife Diane, Chief Constable Stuart Rennie and Preacher Jack McKay. Professor Johnny Henderson and Dr. Morven Hancock were there as expert witnesses. Ms. Dorothy Still was to be called as a witness for the prosecution.

The jury of fifteen had already been heavily influenced by the press who had unanimously lauded Hans Kool for ridding society of a menace it could well do without.

Lord Simpson addressed the defence and the prosecution.

"Mr. Kool, I understand you intend to represent yourself. You have also tendered a special defence of self-defence; you intimate necessity. You do not deny killing the deceased. Is this correct?"

"That is correct, My Lord." Kool was relaxed as usual.

"Mr. Reid, you represent the Crown in this matter. I understand you have accepted Mr. Kool's plea of self-defence?"

"Yes, Your Lordship", replied Charlie Reid.

Charlie Reid, Her Majesty's Advocate, was not at all satisfied with the plea of a special defence of self-defence, but in the circumstances, pressure from the media and the Scottish Executive, he had accepted the plea in defence, in the genuine hope and expectation that Kool, as a novice, would be easy to expose in court. After all, Kool had killed Twinkle; that was accepted; all that was needed to convict him was an admission of excessive force, proof that his actions were entirely out of proportion to the threat, either to the accused himself or the little girl.

Reid just had to prevent the jury getting too emotionally involved. This trial was, after all, about the law, not about moral crusades.

The Defence of Self-Defence

Lord Simpson instructed the jury.

"Ladies and gentlemen, the accused has entered a special defence of self defence. This is a total defence, and if you honestly believe that the accused killed the deceased in order to save his own life or the life of the child then you must find him not guilty.

I must advise you about the nature of self-defence. It must be considered within narrow constraints. There must be an imminent threat to life. There must be no other possible response and the force used must be proportionate.

In other words, if you believe that Mr. Kool's life was not in imminent danger or that the little girl's life was not in imminent danger, then there can be no defence of self-defence. If, however, you genuinely believe there was no other course available to the accused to prevent murder, then you must find in favour of self-defence and find the defendant not guilty. Much of the evidence is circumstantial; it is up to you to decide what you honestly believe occurred on the day in question.

*I would ask you to disregard personal prejudices, press and media comment. Please concentrate on the facts as presented **only** in this court of law."*

Charlie Reid was in the unique situation of questioning both the accused and the defence counsel, who in this case were one and the same.

"Mr. Kool, I think we can get to the heart of this matter very quickly. You admit killing the deceased, Mr. Graeme Twinkle. You are obviously a physically powerful man. That much is self-evident. How can you possibly expect us to believe that Mr. Twinkle, a small

fat man, was a threat to your life or that you could not have prevented the deceased from harming the child by applying physical force, short of, indeed, well short of, lethal force? Is it not therefore the case, Mr. Kool that you simply killed Graeme Twinkle because you believed he deserved to die? There was no imminent threat to life and there was, therefore, no self-defence! You simply executed him!"

Charlie Reid was closer to the truth than he imagined.

Hans Kool resisted the temptation to agree. It was important, if he was to continue protecting children from the likes of Twinkle, he remain at liberty. No doubt, he could remove a few child-killers in prison, if he was incarcerated, but he could not protect the potential victims. He had to do both: protect the victim and remove the evil - protecting the victim was *the* priority. At the time, he had not been there to save his own daughter, but he was going to save as many children as he could, and the best way to save them was to track the evil that intended to harm them.

He therefore replied using answers that would allow him to remain at liberty; to continue his important work.

"No, Mr. Reid. That is not true. I acted initially through necessity to save the child. When the pervert grabbed hold of the shovel I was convinced he intended to kill her. Given that he had stripped off her underwear, opened her legs, exposed her vagina and was masturbating over her, I do not think that I was wrong in my assumptions. He then grabbed the shovel and raised it above his head. At that moment, I managed to duck, get behind him and grab him by the neck. I am sure he intended to kill me and the child."

It was a convincing reply. Charlie Reid would have to expose Kool more indirectly, using the circumstances of the killing and Kool's own black and white view of justice to ensnare him.

Establishing a premeditated intent to kill would be a good start,

"Mr. Kool, you followed Twinkle that day into Countesswells Woods. You waited for an appropriate opportunity; you approached him from behind and strangled him. Are we agreed on this?"

"Not exactly, Mr. Reid. I was watching all the occupants of a block of flats in Oak Tree Avenue. I was watching them because I intended to intervene if any of them threatened the safety of any child. I could only do this by following them. On the day in question I happened to follow the man who was killed. I followed him into the woods and then I lost him. I found him again when I noticed bright flashes of light from within the forest. It later transpired these flashes were from a camera he was using to record a set of indecent photographs he was making of the child; the child he had drugged and then abducted."

Kool played his trump card,

"You will see from exhibit A - the paedophile's photographs of the child – he was at an advanced stage of his murderous, perverted plan."

The jury nodded. They had been suitably traumatized by the images taken by Twinkle. Kool capitalized on their shock and sympathy,

"I happened to have my own camera with me; I distracted the pervert by firing the flashlight into his vision; then I approached him to stop the crime. He grabbed the shovel and raised it as if to strike. I genuinely believed he intended to kill me and then kill the little girl."

Reid was less persuaded. He continued to press the accused,

"Mr. Kool, do you believe in the rule of law? Do you believe that individuals cannot be allowed to take the law into their own hands?"

Kool remained calm, impossible to provoke,

"I believe in the rule of law, Mr. Reid, but the law does not currently reach far enough. It should and must protect the victim before the crime is committed. A child molester or child killer may or may not be brought to justice <u>after</u> they have committed a heinous crime, but the law should surely intervene before the victim is harmed. As you say in this country, 'there is no point in closing the stable door after the horse has bolted!' Children and society must be protected before abuse and before the pain of crime against the person. It is of no value to a victim if the crime has already left its indelible scar for life. If this pervert had raped or killed the child, then it would be of little comfort to the child or her mother, whether the paedophile was convicted or not; because the evil act will have inevitably ruined the lives of the victims forever."

Several members of the jury nodded in agreement; there were utterances of 'Hear, Hear!' from the press and the public galleries. Charlie Reid felt that sinking feeling in his stomach.

Lord Simpson intervened,

"Mr. Kool, I am allowing you a degree of latitude because you have chosen to handle your own defence, but this is not a forum for moral or political speeches. Please try and keep your answers to Her Majesty's Advocate relevant and to the point."

Lord Simpson addressed the jury,

"You will not be swayed by any emotive truisms or moralising from the defendant. We are here to establish the facts and apply these to the law as it stands. We are not here to change the law. That is a job for Parliament not a court of law."

The jury looked suitably chastened by this statement. Charlie Reid continued,

"Thank you, Your Lordship. Mr. Kool, do you believe in the sanctity of human life and do you accept that killing a man is an act of evil and as such, should be punished?"

Hans Kool gave a measured, calm reply,

"I believe in the sanctity of all life. To me it is of huge regret that mankind does not make it a capital offence to kill any primate: the silverback gorilla, the orang-utan, any intelligent mammal; whales, dolphins, all of these should be protected equally with humans. I do not believe that mankind is in any way superior to these other high animals. We all deserve the utmost reverence and protection."

Lord Simpson frowned, "Mr. Kool, if you could just limit your reply to the question..."

Kool, however, continued with his theme,

"If killing a man is evil, then every army, and by implication, every government in the world is evil, because every army kills innocent men, women and children. Any bomb dropped or shell fired into any area where civilian non-combatants are located is then an act of premeditated evil. I believe that killing an _innocent_ human-being is evil. I live my life by the ten commandments, Your Lordship: **'Thou Shalt not Kill'** is fundamental to God's Word, but killing a monster to protect an innocent child is _not_ an act of evil, it is an act of necessity, an act of mercy and an essential act of protection of the good."

"It is defence of an innocent self."
"It is self-defence!"

There were further murmurs of approval from the public galleries; most of the jurors had to try very hard indeed not to nod enthusiastically.

Charlie Reid, not for the first time in his career as a prosecutor, was wondering if this was the time to push for a seat on the bench rather than suffer the futility of trying to enforce the law any longer. It would be so much easier just to direct the jury and leave them and others to get the ulcers; to let them worry about the outcome. To be honest he couldn't disagree with a word Kool had said.

The jury was instructed to bring in a proper verdict based 'only' on the facts.

Due process followed.

The jury took just twenty minutes to reach a unanimous verdict.

Hans Kool was found not guilty by virtue of a successful plea of self-defence.

Several members of the public cheered in court, much to the apparent displeasure of Lord Simpson.

As Kool left court, a beautiful blonde woman in her early thirties threw her arms around him, covering him in kisses.

Together with her angelic daughter and a Dalmatian puppy, they got into his silver Range Rover and headed for his castle.

Grampian Police HQ, Queen Street

Chief Constable Stuart Rennie was a mild-mannered man. He was fair, reasonable and diplomatic; he was excellent with the press and admired by everyone on the force. If he had one failing it was a tendency to get too involved, to take things personally.

At 50 years old, he was nearing the end of his career and his ability to manage criticism and pressure was being eroded with the years.

A copy of a memorandum from the Secretary of State for Scotland sat on his desk. He had read it several times since it had arrived by fax, twenty minutes ago.

Dear Stuart,
Strictly Confidential
Bridge Murders, Aberdeen
Turnbull/Glennie Murders, Aberdeen
Make arrests today. Justice must be seen to be done. Let the courts decide.
Yours sincerely
John Carlyle, MP
Secretary of State for Scotland

So that was that. It had been taken out of his hands. Clearly the boyish Secretary of State was not party to the deadly secrets kept by the Prime Minister and others.

He felt like a man bound at the wrists and stretched between two rampant stallions running in opposite directions. His position was untenable.

He'd put the best officer in the country on these cases and, of course, it was futile.

Only one man was a viable, credible suspect and he was innocent. The truth was unfathomable and unknowable, but orders were orders, so they might as well arrest the only suspect; just to satisfy the press, the public and the Executive.

No doubt, the one man who could be tried for the crimes would be acquitted - there was only weak circumstantial evidence, but that was no longer his problem. Early retirement looked compelling. It was a dirty business and no place for an honourable man.

He picked up the phone,

"Ross. It's Rennie. Arrest Hans Kool for the Bobby Turnbull and Deborah Glennie murders; hold him on suspicion of killing the five men hung from the Bridges of Dee. Yes, I know, but my hands are tied. Thanks, Ross, I will explain later."

So an innocent man would be arrested, tried and, most likely, acquitted, simply because one government minister was not party to a macabre secret.

Rennie could not help but recite the familiar Masonic motto: *AVDI, VIDE, TACE*.

It could have been created just for this predicament:

Hear, See, Be Silent.

He left the office and headed home; home to a double whisky and an understanding wife.

Dunnottar Castle

Ross had received one call at 2 p.m., from his Chief Constable, telling him to arrest Hans Kool; then, minutes later, a second call telling him to, *'hold the arrest: be at Dunnottar Castle at nine p.m.'*

The Chief had not said much. It seemed there was new, vitally important, information about the 'Bridge Murders'. He wanted Ross to meet a third party on the grounds of the castle. Ross had tried to ascertain exactly what this information was? Who was this third party? But the Chief had told him just to be there at 9 p.m.

Ross had a thousand questions and thoughts racing through his mind as he pointed the black Lamborghini down the narrow exit from the motorway to the seaside town of Stonehaven, 15 miles south of Aberdeen.

He was late and screamed down the narrow one-way road, slamming on the brakes as he arrived at the sleepy, picturesque town famous for its outdoor swimming pool and gourmet seafood restaurants.

The Lamborghini attracted numerous curious, envious looks from the various youths hanging around the town square.

Leaving Stonehaven, he raced up the steep, zigzagging country road, finally reaching the old coast road where he turned left towards Inverbervie and Montrose, and before these towns, his destination, Dunnottar Castle.

He was now on the old, main highway south from Aberdeen. This road was now virtually abandoned since the dual carriageway had been built.

Ross decided to open up the black beast, tearing up the tarmac as he flew towards the castle at over 150 mph. It was his last chance. This car had now also been sold. Aberdeen was not the place for exotic, attention-grabbing status symbols. Focusing on racing the super-car took his mind off what might lie ahead at the ancient ruins.

Almost immediately, he arrived at the castle car park.

He slid the car to a halt, just in time to prevent a nasty collision with the old dry-stone dyke that enclosed the parking area. The Chief's white Range Rover was already there, together with a Jaguar XJ6 and a BMW 5 Series Touring.

Night was falling at Dunnottar; hundreds of tiny Pipistrelle bats swooped past Ross's face, investigating the newcomer with an aerial, acrobatic display that would shame any other flying creature on the planet as they consumed thousands of insects 'on the wing'.

Ross was un-phased by these darting, flying fur-balls; he was a great admirer of these animals. He recalled reading they weighed no more than a twenty pence coin and of course they detected their prey and navigated using sonar. It was remarkable to think that, right now, they were buzzing around him using what we consider to be high technology to echo-locate his precise position and his every movement.

His awe was interrupted by a text message.

The bats scattered as the electromagnetic waves from the cell-phone disrupted their sensitive navigation systems.

"ARRIVED AHEAD OF YOU, ROSS, MEET ME INSIDE THE CASTLE, RENNIE."

Ross looked ahead at the eerie silhouette of the distant castle, standing isolated, about a mile away.

Dunnottar is perched on a giant rock reached by a narrow pathway that descends steeply down to the seashore before rising dramatically giving access to the ancient strong-hold via a steep, narrow, stone-stairwell, cut out of the base-rock. The North Sea pummels away at the giant bedrock and, over millions of years, caves have been eroded into the rock beneath the castle. Over the centuries, bands of smugglers have used these caves to import contraband - brandy, rum, gunpowder.

A walk of about a mile from the car park, along and down an at times precarious path, across the cliffs, takes the visitor to the point of ascendancy - up into the gloomy ancient fortress.

The castle would normally be locked fast by eight p.m., in summer; it was now almost nine o'clock. Irregular, but Ross had total faith in his Chief Constable; no doubt everything would be in order.

He sent his wife a text,

"HI BABY CHEEKS. MEETING THE CHIEF, HOME IN AN HOUR, X."

He walked boldly along the path.

Halfway, he stopped to look over the wooden fence that protects the tourist from a one hundred foot drop, over cliffs, to certain death on the rocks below. Now this was a perfect spot for a murder, if ever there was one, he thought grimly.

He turned left and carefully started the hundred or so steps, down the wooden gantry, to the seashore below.

As the light started to fade, care was needed to avoid a potentially nasty fall.

The ground at the seashore was muddy. Ross was glad he was wearing heavy police boots rather than his usual designer attire.

Despite this, he slipped and fell covering his uniform in wet, sticky mud. He cursed his luck. He rarely wore uniform and now, within hours, it was caked in mud. It would amuse his wife, but not the Chief Constable who was a stickler for pristine clothing and perfect conduct.

The waves lapped up onto the shore strewn with pebbles as Ross looked up at the ominous dark edifice high above him in the half-light.

He clambered up the muddy path to the beginning of the rocky steps and plodded onwards into and up the dark corridors of black rock to the entrance gate: '*four pounds for adults, two pounds for children*'.

He felt claustrophobic. Even during daylight this was a place for a spelunker or a troglodyte.

No marauding army could have successfully attacked this castle, single-file, through this narrow entrance, little more than a long cave rising steeply to about sixty feet above sea-level. The only way to have taken this fortress would have been to lay siege and wait months, perhaps years, to starve out the defending militia.

There was still no sign of Superintendent Stuart Rennie, MBE.

The heavy, iron-gated entrance was not locked so Ross pushed on under the rocky archway, up the never-ending spiral stairway cut out of the wet, black rock.

Panting, he moved forward in the dark until he was able to breathe the fresh sea air.

He had finally reached the elevated, open grassy grounds of the ancient settlement above.

The ground on top of the rock is fertile, covered with manicured lawns separating diverse buildings: a thirteenth century ruined Chapel, a sparsely furnished seventeenth century Hall, the largest of its kind in Scotland at thirty-five metres in length. Set wide apart, adjoining buildings since perished, the sprawling sandstone ruins were once home to peoples of myriad status and function: the garrison and animals kept remote from the Lord and gentry - a miniature allegory of modern Aberdeen with its wealthy west-end and its deprived east-end.

A self-contained fortress like Dunnottar had been a tiny town with its own bakery, farmyard, freshwater-well, blacksmiths and carpenters; anyone or anything that was needed to ensure self-sufficiency.

Tonight, the old buildings were mere silhouettes and shadows as dusk covered the rock.

A sea haar had started to roll in from the North Sea. On the furthermost battlement, a lonely figure looked out over the waves. Ross correctly assumed it was his superior officer. He walked over to join him.

Chief Constable Rennie was a serious man. He often appeared to be carrying the weight of the world on his shoulders. He did not have Professor Johhny Henderson's apparent resilience and ability to laugh off dead bodies and terrible crimes. Rennie took it personally. Every victim, every unsolved crime, every criticism of the police, it all hurt; he felt responsible, the buck stopped fairly and squarely with him. Ross watched him look out over the choppy seas at the approaching haar. Rennie did not acknowledge Ross. A tear rolled down his face. Ross could see his Chief Constable was deeply troubled. He decided to coax him away from the cliff edge, distracting him from his morose meditations.

"Good evening, sir. It's a bracing night."

"Ah, Ross," the Chief replied, as if Ross had just stepped into his office. "Thanks for popping out here; if you could just come with me to the Great Hall."

Ross was baffled. The Chief offered no explanations. Ross would, at least, have expected some conversation given that they were in a castle closed to the public at nightfall. At the very least, the Chief might have asked after Ross's family.

Stuart Rennie just looked ahead, leading Ross in the direction of the largest building, the Great Hall. Ross saw a faint light glowing tentatively from one of the hall's windows on the upper floor.

The Chief arrived at the building first and showed Ross in; the head of Grampian Police looked about as if they might be being observed.

Ross entered.

Together they climbed the ancient stone staircase to the hall above.

The Great Hall was a vast empty space, typical of seventeenth century architecture; wooden beams and a high ceiling; it resembled a church hall without the pews or stain-glass windows. Apart from a few colourful decorative inscriptions, hand-painted on the splendid carved wooden ceiling, it was austere. One could imagine rugged fighting men hastily treading the boards with vital messages in hand having ridden all night with news of victories or defeats in crucial battles. Great feasts would have been held here; ale and wine flowing, wild boar consumed straight from the spit; legs of chicken tossed to hunting hounds. Duals would have been fought and blood spilled during heated arguments over allegiances to Kings, Queens and the Church.

Despite the dark and the vastness, Ross felt strangely calm. The place had a spiritual quality. It was tranquil. At the far end, about thirty yards away, two men were seated at one end of the wooden replica medieval banqueting table. Several candles illuminated the area where they sat. They did not speak. As Ross got nearer, it became clear that these men were known to him, but in a different environment. He knew these men from another world of power and grandeur, another place of huge halls, officials, heated debates and matters of life and death.

He knew these men from the law courts.

Seated at the head of the table was Lord Simpson, Scotland's foremost criminal trial judge and on his right, with his back to the wall and the giant, open, unlit fireplace, Charlie Reid, Her Majesty's Advocate, Scotland's Chief Prosecutor of the criminal law.

"Ah, Superintendent Ross, I don't think we have been formally introduced. I am Harry Simpson or more officially, Lord Simpson of Argyll."

The judge shook Ross's hand warmly and looked at Charlie Reid.

"And I think you know Mr. Reid here."

"Hello, Ross," Charlie Reid nodded with a wry smile.

"Hello, Lord Simpson. Hello, Charlie." Ross returned the prosecutor's nod.

He sat down opposite Lord Simpson.

The Chief Constable stood nearby looking wistfully out of the adjacent window even though by now it was almost entirely dark.

"I am sure you would like to know what this is all about, but could I firstly just ask you to take off your jacket please, Mr. Ross?"

Ross took off his jacket and put it on the table. The Chief walked across and unbuttoned Ross's shirt. For a moment, Ross feared that he may have been lured into some homo-erotic, jurisprudential cult.

Simpson watched as the Chief indicated to him that Ross was not wearing any electronic surveillance or recording equipment.

"We cannot take the slightest of chances," said Simpson.

The Chief shook his head with resigned stoicism, resuming his position, looking out of the window. He was a solemn individual, but Ross had never seen his superior officer this preoccupied; so plain, downright miserable.

Lord Simpson collected his thoughts, looking as if he was about to deliver a verdict - to sentence a guilty man. Sensing Ross's increasing unease, he smiled before he started to talk.

"The Chief Constable informs me you are about to arrest Mr. Kool for the so-called, *bodies on the bridges'* killings, Superintendent. He also tells me the decision is based on circumstantial evidence?"

Ross looked at the Chief Constable. The Chief Constable looked mournfully at Ross and nodded his head slowly. With reluctance, Ross replied,

"Yes. He seems to be conducting a one-man vigilante killing campaign. As you know, he admitted killing the paedophile Twinkle and we are close to charging him with the death of young Bobby Turnbull and Deborah Glennie. There could be sufficient evidence to link and charge him with all these execution-style killings."

Simpson was clearly unconvinced,

"How could one man locate, entrap, drug, torture, mutilate and hang five individuals from three separate bridges in just a few hours, Superintendent?"

"Kool is a powerful man; he may have had assistance."

"You have proof of these accomplices, Mr. Ross?"

Was Simpson fishing or cross-examining?

Ross continued his case for an arrest,

"The bodies contained evidence of ritualistic killings, symbols of assassins, Knights Templar and Freemasonry. It's possible he had help from a Masonic or other society or this ACTION organisation. It is obvious from the mutilations, truth serums, date rape drugs and lethal injections that these killings were designed to strike terror into the hearts of violent criminals and other anti-social menaces. They all appear to be vigilante-style killings."

"Dear me, Superintendent, that's a very weak case. Twinkle was not a ritualistic killing, Mr. Ross. Kool just followed him and killed him. His aim was to prevent a crime and protect a victim. That seems to me to be a quite different *modus operandi* from the bridge killings. Would you not agree?"

Ross was hard pressed to disagree. Kool was just the only suspect; no witnesses, no material evidence, no fingerprints, no DNA; Kool just stood out as the obvious perpetrator - the only credible, identifiable suspect, "It can only be Kool or some mysterious group of vigilante assassins. The latter is ridiculous. Law-abiding citizens do not commit murder except in self-defence or in retribution for the killing of a loved one. Anne Daley and Rupert Byron do not have relatives capable of committing those brutal acts. It has been checked out. The Bobby Turnbull murder is

even more puzzling. In many ways, that is easier to explain as an accident or a hit."

Lord Simpson looked at Charlie Reid; the Prosecutor returned his gaze. It was a glance between two men who shared a secret; for better or worse, it had been decided to share this secret with Ross.

"AVDI, VIDE, TACE," said Lord Simpson.

Ross said nothing as requested. He feared this was, after all, a Freemason affair. Bodies hanging from bridges had been linked to that brotherhood in the past.

Ross was surprised to be asked a question by Scotland's senior High Court judge.

"Do you know how many people are in prison in the United Kingdom, Mr. Ross?"

Ross knew the answer,

"About 90,000, I believe, for the U.K., as a whole."

"And the minimum cost of keeping one prisoner per annum?"

Ross was well aware of the costs,

"According to your colleague, Lord McCluskey, about £30,000.00 a year," he replied.

Simpson summarized the predicament.

"Precisely, a total cost of £2,700 million a year or £2.7 billion if you prefer a smaller number."

Ross was surprised Lord Simpson chose such a time to make a joke.

Simpson continued his *Ratio Decidendi*,

"This means society is paying a high financial cost to protect itself from crime *after* it has been a victim of crime. It is a bit like being forced to buy an insurance policy *after* you have been robbed. It adds insult to injury. To exacerbate this tragic irony, the insurance policy is not working. The prison system is falling

276

apart at the seams. Many prisons already contain twice as many prisoners as they were built to accommodate. This overcrowding causes angst and is not conducive to rehabilitation; 70% of prisoners re-offend and are sent back to prison. The system cannot be sustained for much longer. The irony is, Mr. Ross, Hans Kool killed one of a group least likely to re-offend. I suspect that if the authorities had not accidentally housed Twinkle overlooking a primary school he may well have been a very low risk indeed. The high risk re-offenders are the thieves, yobs and anti-social types like the three miscreants who killed that boy in the toilets and raped the old lady."

Simpson was warming up.

Ross hoped he would get to the point.

"My point is this, Superintendent. Twinkle was not hanging from the bridge. He was killed to protect a child from imminent danger. That was a killing of 'protection': of self-defence. The bodies on the bridges were a display: a warning. A warning to violent evil individuals, intent on harming others."

"Jason Jameson and Danny Thompson were not violent or evil," Ross pointed out.

"Jameson was responsible for more criminals walking free from court than anyone else in the country. He was a menace. A silvery tongued serpent, an agent of the Devil. He was a predatory homosexual with a penchant for teenage boys."

Clearly Simpson had not been a fan of the *Silver Fox*,

"Danny Thompson was a vicious rapist and blackmailer. The only reason he could not be brought to trial was that a good man would have been ruined in the revelations bound to follow."

"I do not hear much about the right to a fair trial; innocent till proven guilty or the rule of law?" Ross felt he needed to remind these men they were bound by a code of professional conduct.

"These men were all guilty, Mr. Ross, but the system failed the victims and failed society. Three of them got a fair trial, but it was not fair to the victims. They all confessed to their crimes under mild sedation and the influence of moderate doses of truth serum." Simpson rested his case.

Ross was nervous. He did not like the sound of that last sentence one bit. Charlie Reid sat silently, looking down at the table, while Chief Constable Stuart Rennie looked out the window, into the dark night, as if in a trance.

"Don't worry, Superintendent, you are not in danger. We three are subordinate in this matter, our part is simple – AVDI, VIDE, TACE."

"If you are so keen on silence then why are you telling me?" Ross was direct as ever.

"We do not want another trial with Mr. Kool. He is already a celebrity vigilante. He is inspiring others to adopt zero tolerance to anti-social behaviour. Crime is falling in this town, partly as a result of his lethal example and acquittal, but if he is found 'not guilty' of killing five men then anarchy will surely follow. If found guilty then an innocent man will face five life-sentences for a crime he did not commit." Simpson was eloquent, logical and precise.

The detective closed in on the truth.

"How can you be so sure he is innocent?"

Lord Simpson looked at Charlie Reid and then at the Chief Constable.

"At this point, I feel we must tell you the whole truth, Superintendent. The truth is a burden - hard to bear. You will be party to a great secret, perhaps the greatest secret of the age. You can never breathe a word of this to anyone, even to your wife - *especially* not to your wife."

Ross wanted nothing to do with it.

"I'd rather not know." He frowned: determined.

"That is no longer an option I am afraid, Superintendent. This goes way above my head."

"Is that a threat?" Ross was pushing for closure.

"Any party to this truth will be silenced if it is suspected there is the slightest danger they might disclose the details to any third party."

"Silenced?" said Ross.

"Killed," said Lord Simpson sternly, exuding gravitas.

Ross stood up and looked at his Chief Constable who refused to return his stare. The Chief shook his head, looking at the ground. He was a defeated man.

Ross sat down again.

A deafening silence flooded the great hall.

It was ended by the Law Lord,

"Did you know William Wallace burnt this place to the ground in 1297, over seven hundred years ago, Mr. Ross?" Lord Simpson tried to lighten the mood; not an easy task; he cited local, ancient verse:

"Therefore a fire was brought speedily,
Which burnt the church and the Southern boys,
Out o'er the rock the rest rush'd great noise
Some hung on craigs, and loath were to die
Some lap, some fell, some flutter'd in the sea
And perish'd all, not one remain'd alive"

"Wallace knew how to set an example. His enemies were terrified of him: no survivors and no mercy," Simpson said proudly.

"Yes and look at what happened to him?" Ross stated rebelliously.

"Wallace laid the way for Robert the Bruce to unite the country, making Scotland free: independent," Simpson replied.

Lord Simpson nodded to Charlie Reid.

Scotland's senior prosecutor, Her Majesty's Advocate spoke,

"David, the killing of the five men hung from the bridges was carried out by Her Majesty's Special Forces. The operation was sanctioned by the Prime Minister and instigated by a substation of MI6 and SIS. This station will carry out sporadic executions across the UK as a display of retribution with the intention of causing fear and terror in the hearts of violent criminals. Its aim is psychological. It will give the public confidence and the criminal fraternity will never feel safe again. Violent criminals know they can easily psychologically defeat law-abiding citizens, but they have no chance, whatsoever, against the ultimate lethal force of trained, heavily-armed, state-backed assassins."

Ross felt dazed, dizzy.

Crime was normally chaotic: easy to defeat; state-backed executions by crack troops, unthinkable!

Ross was incredulous – becoming scared.

"Are you seriously telling me that the Prime Minister of this country has authorised death squads?"

The prosecutor replied,

"Only one death squad comprising a few men from the SAS and SBS regiments: known as SAIS. Initially set up to assassinate terrorists in advance of atrocities, hence the name, Special Anti-Insurgent Service, like many terrorist initiatives they are finding roles in novel areas. Violent, antisocial criminals are terrorists. They induce terror. The only difference is that, unlike terrorists, they are not indoctrinated with political or religious dogmas. In many ways, they are worse than terrorists. They believe in nothing. In recent past, wars ensured millions of these young men died. Now these aggressive animals fight their battles on our streets," Reid pontificated.

"A Scot's Law Lord controlling an elite unit of Special Force's assassins?"

Ross didn't believe it.

Reid replied,

"We were obeying instructions. Our part, Lord Simpson's and my own, was to inform the Lord Chancellor of any obvious cases where the accused or non-accused persons like Jameson were guilty of perpetrating or enabling an appalling crime to evade conviction on a technical defence or legal loophole. The Seaton Park murder and Tillydrone rape case were an exact fit. We assumed the Lord Chancellor was collating information on miscarriages of justice in conjunction with the Crown Prosecution Service. We were told twenty-four hours before the killings what was to occur and that we should inform only the Chief Constable and the senior investigating officer when, and if, absolutely necessary."

Reid seemed convinced this was reasonable.

"When did you decide to include Danny Thompson?" Ross was no fool. Thompson was unconnected; the reason for his death was a total mystery.

Lord Simpson interjected, flattering Ross.

"I can see why the Chief Constable has nominated you to succeed him, Mr. Ross. You have an uncanny knack of persevering to get to all the facts. It's commendable. Danny Thompson was blackmailing a senior public official and under interrogation admitted an appalling rape and assault on a helpless young woman. He had a black heart, enjoying wicked and evil behaviour without any remorse."

Ross wondered how Charlie Reid QC and Lord Simpson had such in-depth knowledge of a man who had never even been in court, but he decided he had pushed hard enough. He was going to have to tread carefully. Experience of secret government directives and Special Forces' activities from his time at the Met meant he had no desire to cross these people. They were every bit as dangerous as the terrorists they tracked and just as committed.

Ross sought the truth,

"I started this investigation to ascertain the reasons for the death of Bobby Turnbull and Deborah Glennie. I intend to bring the perpetrators of that crime to justice. I want to know what happened to those two young people and I suspect all three of you know how and why they died?"

All four men were silent. The great hall was heavy with suspense. No-one spoke.

It was unclear whether any of the men knew what was about to happen next.

Lord Simpson, Charlie Reid, Stuart Rennie and David Ross simultaneously exclaimed a variation of the statement:

"What the devil....???!!!!!"

Heavy footsteps emerged from the shadows at the other end of the great hall.

All four watched, petrified, as two heavily-armed men marched menacingly towards the assembled company.

Both newcomers were dressed from head to foot in black commando uniform - military webbing, full-face balaclavas, Kevlar body armour, small submachine guns, side-arms and knives. If ever two men looked like assassins, it was these two. Ross felt sick. All four men now knew a deadly secret; it looked as if they were about to die for it.

One assassin stepped forward, staring at Ross through the small eye-holes in his black head-gear.

It was a look Ross recalled, the same look he had seen in the eyes of the man on the riverbank; except this time there was no rage; these eyes were calm and collected; this man was a professional - a cold-blooded killer.

Ross was now certain he was about to die.

The assassin put his hand on his machine gun. Ross had seen this model before, the Micro Uzi - a small, lightweight, lethal weapon, capable of up to 1700 hundred rounds per minute; it could tear a human target apart in seconds.

Ross prepared to make a move. He felt sure he could remove the first man. Again, it was the second man who was the greater threat, but this time he had no option; there was no time for diplomacy.

Fists clenched, he slowly moved closer to the black-clad assassin. The man nearest Ross reached for his belt. A large commando knife and the machine gun were just a few of his options.

Ross did not hesitate.

He flexed, squatted, bending his knees, instantly flying through the air; spinning, rotating his head, shoulders, hips; his right leg leading the accelerating right heel smashing into the head of the nearest assassin. His target dropped to the floor with an ominous thud.

Ross landed from his highly effective assault, springing immediately at the second man; launching a flying side-kick, aimed directly at the second assassin's throat.

Inches from taking him out, Ross felt a crushing blow to his chest; a sledge-hammer; a burning hot sledge-hammer: pain - shocking pain!

Stunned, lying on the wooden floor, twitching with involuntary muscle spasms, Ross struggled to remain conscious: his system shocked; assaulted; electrocuted by 15,000 volts at point blank range.

The commando was an expert marksman.

Ross had taken two *TASER* darts straight to his heart. The policeman collapsed - falling deep into a sea of darkness.

The Sea of Darkness

Water, cold-water; a terrible scream, a creature from hell!

Darkness - cold, wet, darkness; another sickening screech......a sharp, painful bite; the flapping of......feathers?

'Where the hell am I?'

Ross tried to make some sense of the numerous, unpleasant sensations. His eyes started to adjust to the blue-black surroundings.

Crash! A painful blow to the head; concussion, stars: dazed, dizzy. He remained conscious.

His head was soaking wet; he appeared to be looking at black rock. His feet and hands were numb; his head felt like it was about to burst! The scream and the dreadful harsh, prickly feathers, followed by a tearing at his cheek, almost invoked a heart attack.

Stay calm.

'If this is a torture technique, don't let them destroy you. Work it out! Get a grip!'

Dangling upside-down from the ramparts of Dunnottar Castle, some sixty feet above him, it was not easy to remain calm. Half-submerged in an icy-cold rock pool, the salty North Sea waves lashed against his head. Several gulls were attempting to remove his face.

Almost pitch-black, he could just make out he was facing the bedrock. Every time a wave hit, he was thrown forward, his head bouncing off the hard rock in front of him.

Horrendous memories of the bridge slaughter flooded his mind.

'*He could not die like this! Alone! Helpless, in the cold, wet darkness!*'

"You fuckers! You fuckers! You fuckers!"

He focused his anger, increasing his heartbeat, warming his freezing frame.

He started to swing the rope, using his hips and shoulders to increase his momentum. Swinging wildly was not just his only hope; it was the only possible thing to do. His feet were bound together with nylon rope, his hands tied tight behind his back.

Helpless, exposed, and dead if he couldn't find a way out of the freezing darkness he moved his shoulders and hips, swinging the rope sideways in a wider and wider pendulum motion. If he caused enough movement, eventually, it might give way; then it was all down to luck - whether he fell into the sea or crashed, head-first onto the rocks – a horrific, Hobson's choice!

At least the swinging rope made it harder for the gulls to penetrate his flesh, but the harsh bristles of the feathered wings and the hideous cries could still be heard every few seconds against the beating of the waves on the rocks.

Ross prayed the tide was not marching inwards or he would drown in the next hour for sure.

He continued to swing using his body's motion.

It was exhausting, but it stopped the panic.

His efforts were frustrated as he moved too close to the main rock, smacking his head hard against the solid black mass. Dazed and disconsolate, he gathered his thoughts: shouting, screaming,

"Fuckers, Fuckers, Fuckers!"

The profanity helped. Soon he was making progress, wider and wider, faster and faster. Then it happened.

Bewilderment!

His swinging started to slow down as....the rope was being pulled up!

Was it a dream? A bad dream: a nightmare?

Was this a rescue? Was he imagining it?

The pulling stopped.

He stopped moving upwards. He was now about twenty feet up from the rocks below.

'Oh no, don't let them drop me!'

'Please God, don't let them drop me!'

His prayers seemed to be answered. The pulling started again. The gulls swooped past, fast and furious. If he ever got out of this he was going to shoot a flock of these flying fuckers. Dread gripped his heart at the thought he was being raised higher and higher simply to be dropped freefall on his head, smashing like an egg on the jagged rocks below. The pulling continued. He must be forty feet up by now. A fall from here was certain death. More pulling; he jackknifed his body, looking upwards at the ramparts. No sign of anything, just the rock dead-ahead; all the time the sound of the waves below; the swooping gulls, the blue-blackness of the night.

He looked up again and saw four small white beads, not beads, but...eyes!

"Please keep pulling!"

So near to living, so near to life.

"Let me see my family again! Please....life!"

The pulling stopped.

Rapidly, roughly, he was grabbed at the waist and thrown in the air. He landed on the solid ground: hard, cold stone.

'Thank God, please let this be the end of it.'

Freezing, soaking and bleeding, he was lifted up, floated on the shoulders of his saviours, dragged through the Whigs Vault, scene of historic barbarity, back into the dimly-lit Great Hall.

Dropped onto the large table, face-down, like a slaughtered animal: a slab of meat, he was restrained by one man as the other cut free his feet. Blood rushed back into his legs causing immense circulatory discomfort: *pins and needles.*

He was allowed to stand, falling at the first attempt, dragged back up onto his feet by his heavy-handed attendant.

He was pushed back onto a chair, his hands still bound tight behind his back.

Simpson, Reid and Rennie sat at the table looking terrified. Ross's captor spoke,

"Now, Superintendent Ross, I trust that has cooled you down? The next time my Sergeant reaches for his radio, I don't expect you to try and kill us both. Quite frankly, if I hadn't received a call ordering your release, I'd have happily left you there for the gulls. Kindly behave yourself or next time, there will be no next time for you."

Ross shook his head, trying to compose himself.

He failed. Coughing out water, shaken, spluttering, he exhaled his only thought,

"Who, the fuck, are *you*?"

The man doing the talking took off his black balaclava and looked at Ross - late thirties, cropped dark hair, rugged, fit, surprisingly pleasing on the eye, confident; he was almost smiling.

He was introduced by Lord Simpson,

"Gentlemen, this is Commander Harrington, formerly SBS; now SAIS."

Ross shook his head bemused, disbelieving,

"When did British Special Forces start carrying Uzis?" asked Ross regaining his confidence, but still freezing and shivering,

"What happened to the H&K MP5?"

Harrington smiled, impressed by Ross's perception in the face of adversity,

"Climbing rock-faces requires lighter equipment, Superintendent,"

"And bridges?" Ross was trying his best.

No answer. Harrington spoke,

"We had hoped Lord Simpson would satisfy you without the Bobby Turnbull episode being resurrected. You do have a likely explanation after all – the Russian Mafia hit. You could have saved yourself that demonstration of our seriousness."

"You know about the Russian oil deal?"

"We know everything, Ross. We know that *you* drive at highly illegal, dangerous speeds and we know what *your* wife keeps in her bedside cabinet."

Ross was filled with dread.

"My wife? You have been in my house?"

Harrington said nothing.

Lord Simpson spoke,

"Commander, now you have terrified, and almost murdered the Superintendent, do you think you might tell us what happened to the Turnbull boy and Deborah Glennie? I am quite sure no-one at this table has the slightest inclination to disclose anything you tell us. We are, none-of-us, keen to be thrown over the walls of this castle."

Harrington smiled - just another day's work,

"I expect I can tell you with impunity; disclosure of those facts will not compromise our objective. It was a mistake: an operational error. They were in the wrong place at the wrong time: Collateral Damage as the US military is so fond of saying. Our sources reported boy-racers causing havoc in Aberdeen. One individual killed a four year-old boy, escaping conviction on a lack of evidence: no eye-witnesses. We got hold of his associate, in the car with him at the time of the incident; under questioning, he told us the whole story."

Ross was cold, wet, in pain. He shivered, wondering what 'under questioning' meant as Harrington continued his disclosure,

"The individual, Russell McLeod, had been racing through a busy housing estate after consuming several bottles of alcohol. He hit a child, killing it. His associate told the police he had not seen McLeod that day. We discovered otherwise. McLeod therefore became our preliminary target."

"Let me guess. You got a tip off that McLeod was approaching Anderson Drive and you got Bobby Turnbull in error," Ross surmised.

"They were driving the same model and colour of car, silver Honda Civic Type R with all the usual trimmings. Turnbull was travelling at seventy miles an hour in a residential area. By the time our driver was informed that a second Type R was coming up Queens Road, at twice the speed limit, it was too late. The event was over."

Ross noted the euphemistic term, 'event'.

"Did you have to kill them?"

Ross was pissed off. Turnbull was no criminal, just young and foolhardy.

"Discovery was not an option, Superintendent; an instant decision had to be made. The boy and his partner had to be silenced; the event had to look like ritualistic execution. Sadly, there are times when a few innocents must die to protect the majority." Harrington was utterly certain of his own words.

Ross coughed out more questions,

"Why the hocus pocus over the bridge killings? - the lethal injections, talismans of assassins, Masonic red herrings, date rape drugs, truth serums?"

Harrington eyed him, measuring his reply,

"It is crucial the public draws its own conclusions and decides there are forces standing up against lawlessness. Obviously they cannot discover that the Crown has sanctioned these missions, so they need to believe the conspiracy theories. The usual people will be credited; Opus Dei, Illuminati, Knights Templar and the poor old Freemasons who get blamed for almost everything that is not obviously, terrorist or gangland related."

"And Hans Kool?" asked Ross

"Ah yes. Meneer Kool, a veritable one-man army. In fact, if he was a little younger and from a less morally corrupt homeland, we would be interested in recruiting him."

Harrington addressed this 'joke' to his comrade who acknowledged his superior officer by the slightest of nods. SAIS Sergeant Fury was less than happy with Ross for almost breaking his jaw. His head still hurt from the force of Ross's highly effective, spinning kick.

Harrington continued,

"Kool had no part in our activities, but he was a useful distraction. He also made short work of the kiddy-fiddler, that asshole, Twinkle. I wish I had got hold of *him* myself. We do not want Kool charged or convicted, Mr. Ross. As long as he is free, then every criminal in this city will be shitting in their, no doubt, already, filthy pants. It is important that our work looks like unsolved, mysterious vigilante retribution. That was our instruction; as far as I am concerned, our mission has been a total success."

"And the police look like incompetent idiots?"

Harrington's balaclava-wearing sergeant freed Ross's hands with an enormous combat knife.

'Jesus, these guys are killers,' Ross shuddered.

"You can't win them all, Ross, and if you read your local rag you will see that crime figures are falling fast. The police will soon be heroes in our new law-abiding society. At least it will offset your current, abysmal 35% clear-up rate.

Charlie Reid spoke up with unusual boldness,

"Can we hear the confessions?"

He would love to hear the truth from the three reprobates and his former nemesis, Jason Jameson.

"I am afraid not, Mr. Reid. All I can tell you is they were guilty beyond a shadow of doubt. The evidence is now out of my hands."

Ross couldn't help asking the question.

"Who the hell gives you people your orders?"

"I have two directives, Ross. The first is to follow orders. The second is silence: *AVDI, VIDE, TACE.*"

Thunder erupted outside the Great Hall; the entire edifice started to shake.

Charlie Reid ducked under the banqueting table.

Harrington smiled and rose to his feet,

"That's our chopper. I am sure I do not have to remind you all about the need for silence. Any disclosure will sadly lead to your immediate termination, not just your own, but those near to you will suffer the same fate."

Harrington smiled warmly as he started his exit.

Chief Constable Rennie's head fell to his hands.

Ross stood up, steadying himself. He grimaced; spasms of shocking pain coupled with the terrible bruising to his chest where the two TASER darts had hit him with enough force to knock him off his feet caused him to buckle at the knees.

The pain was crippling.

He bent forward, breathing deeply and deliberately.

"Don't worry, Ross. In a few days you will be as right as rain," Harrington said cheerfully - a tough guy - zero empathy: no sympathy.

Ross would get even with this bastard one day, but not while his family were at risk.

Stumbling, Ross followed the two assassins.

Outside, Ross shouted to Harrington.

"Harrington! Why Danny Thompson?"

"Who?" Harrington replied, through the booming helicopter blades.

"The fifth man, he was never accused or wrongly acquitted of any crime!" shouted Ross, "He had no connection with the others - why kill him?"

"Ask your Chief Constable, Ross!"

With that, SAIS Commander Harrington and his silent aide-de-camp disappeared into the blackness of the night.

Epilogue

You are probably a peaceable, respectful individual. You probably do not visit bars, clubs or strip joints and you probably don't experience the animosity of aggressive hooligans, but I can tell you this. This book is fiction, a novel, but it's based on fact.

A friend of a friend was punched on the face walking home one night by 'happy-slapping' low-life. His nose was badly fractured and he needed several operations to allow him to breathe comfortably again. He was minding his own business. They were 'having a laugh'.

I was attacked while sitting in my car one evening, at a set of traffic lights, driving home from a restaurant. My girlfriend, sitting next to me, was terrified for her life.

Hardly a day goes by without increasing anti-social behaviour; rudeness, road-rage, boy-racers and a never-ending increase in violence against the person.

It's time we looked to the heart of the matter. Human beings need love, affection and a sense of purpose. In a meritocracy, there are winners, but there are many more losers. Take a little time to say hello to your neighbour; be polite, considerate and be nice to one another.

Jesus said unto him:
Put up again thy sword into his place: for all they
that take the sword shall perish with the sword.
(Matthew 26:52)

The Wellington Suspension Bridge

The Rail Bridge over the River Dee

The Whigs' Vault, Dunnottar Castle

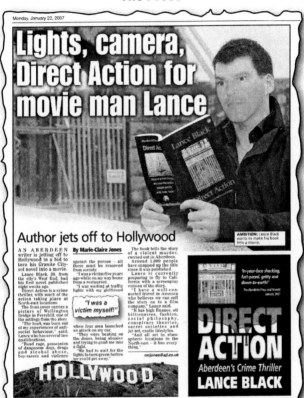

Monday, January 22, 2007

Lights, camera, Direct Action for movie man Lance

AMBITION: Lance Black wants to make his book into a movie.

Author jets off to Hollywood

By Marie-Claire Jones

AN ABERDEEN writer is jetting off to Hollywood in a bid to turn his Granite City-set novel into a movie.

Lance Black, 38, from the city's West End, had his first novel published eight weeks ago.

Direct Action is a crime thriller, with much of the action taking place at North-east locations.

The front cover carries a picture of Wellington bridge in Ferryhill, one of the settings from the story.

"The book was born out of my experiences of anti-social behaviour", said. Lance who has several law qualifications.

"Road rage, possession of dangerous dogs, drugs and alcohol abuse, boy-racers and violence

against the person – all these must be removed from society.

"I was a victim five years ago while on my way home from a restaurant.

"I was waiting at traffic lights with my girlfriend

"I was a victim myself!"

when four men launched an attack on my car.

"They were beating on the doors, being abusive and trying to goad me into a fight.

"We had to wait for the lights to turn green before we could get away."

The book tells the story of a violent murder, carried out in Aberdeen.

Around 1,000 people have snapped up the title since it was published.

Lance is currently preparing to fly to California with a screenplay version of the story.

"I have a well-connected friend in America who believes we can sell the story on to a film company," Lance said.

"It has high finance, oil billionaires, fashion, social philosophy, conspiracy theories, secret societies and jet set, exotic lifestyles.

"And all set in atmospheric locations in the North-east – it has every thing."

mcjones@ajl.co.uk

"In-your-face shocking, fast-paced, gritty and down-to-earth!"
The Aberdeen Press and Journal January 2007

DIRECT ACTION
Aberdeen's Crime Thriller
LANCE BLACK

"The centre of Aberdeen is now Scotland's crime capital. In 2006, 8,276 crimes were committed on the Union Street police beat alone. One third of these crimes were the offences of anti-social behaviour, assaults and breaches of the peace. Union Street is turning into a war zone!"

The Sunday Times, March 18, 2007

Lance Black

"Direct Action is a book written for people who might not normally read a book! It's fast-paced, easy to read and covers many topics: crime, law, sex, philosophy, finance, fashion, materialism, social and criminal justice - to name just a few. Direct Action is set in Aberdeen, but the story is widely applicable. It could be set anywhere. Hopefully, it will interest anyone with a social conscience and an interest in the criminal law"

I am a passionate supporter of the Direct Action causes pursued by Greenpeace; particularly, opposition to the barbaric murder of whales and dolphins by the Japanese and Danes. Therefore a proportion of any profits from this book will go to Greenpeace and the following worthy causes:

<u>www.greenpeace.org</u>
<u>www.smiletrain.org</u>
<u>www.wspa.org.uk</u>

The author is deeply distressed at the destruction of Aberdeen's precious green-belt and is campaigning against anti-social behaviour: boy-racers, speeding motorcyclists, aggressive drivers, litter-louts and noisy violent drunks.

And what is it like to write a novel?

"I spent most of the day putting in a comma and the rest of the day taking it out,"
Oscar Wilde